I0719133

Square Zero

A novel by
Dave Richards

**KITSAP
PUBLISHING**

Square Zero
By Dave Richards

www.daverichardsbooks.com

Copyright © 2020, Dave Richards

First Edition, published 2020

Cover pboto by Tyler-van-der-Hoeven–Unsplash
Author photo by Joel Sackett

Softcover: ISBN-13: 978-1-942661-66-5

Published by Kitsap Publishing
P.O. Box 572
Poulsbo, WA 98370
www.KitsapPublishing.com

Printed in the United States of America

For Marigene, with all my love.

Acknowledgments

Many thanks to Alan Corner for your great input and friendship. Also, a special thanks to Max Weber for your (at the time) adolescent viewpoint of the world.

Also by Dave Richards

The Drive-In Miracle

As the former marketing director for a tobacco corporation, Hank Sloan certainly knows how to generate buzz. So when he learns that his sister's diner is failing, he comes up with a money-making plan to fleece the faithful by arranging to have a so-called 'divine apparition' appear on an old drive-in movie screen across the street from the restaurant.

The faithful do indeed show up and the bucks roll in. But then, in a cosmic twist, rumors begin spreading about real miracles occurring around town.

When Hank suddenly finds himself in desperate need of a miracle of his own, his scheme backfires in a way he never could have imagined...

If I Could Give You A Day

Complacent, self-made millionaire Scott Northwood wakes up one morning to discover he's been given the ability to extend the lives of people who are about to die just when they are on the verge of achieving something important. But there's a catch—he must shorten his own lifespan by an equivalent amount of time. Scott plunges into a moral and emotional maelstrom as his desire to live out his own comfortable life collides with a growing sense of obligation to transfer time to others who are clearly more deserving. Complicating matters, he falls deeply in love.

Back in BEFORE, a writer named Arthur C. Clark once said, "Two possibilities exist: Either we are alone in the universe or we are not. Both are equally terrifying."

It's an interesting observation.

And cleverly phrased.

Except that the reality turned out to be a whole lot different.

I'm talking about the 'equally terrifying' part.

Mr. Clark couldn't have got it more wrong...

{The Zachary Stone Chronicles}

PROLOGUE

A boy named Zachary Stone sits in a rough-hewn wooden chair staring into the lens of a small video camera placed on the table in front of him. He's only 17 but seems aged far beyond his years. His longish dark hair falls unevenly over his forehead and ears, as if it's been cut by a drunken barber wielding dull scissors. A scruffy adolescent beard sprouts from his cheeks. He wears a crudely-made leather vest.

Numerous, freshly-healed cuts and bruises cover his face, hands and much of his body. Many will leave permanent scars. He looks like he came in dead last in a boxing tournament. Chilling to see this in someone so young.

But it's the eyes that hold us. His pupils burn black with inner pain and remembrance.

He speaks to the camera:

No one saw it coming.

No one was prepared for the day the world changed forever.

September 7th, 2026.

The day when all human history was rewritten.

It made "B.C." and "A.D." meaningless. Everything that happened up till then became known simply as BEFORE. Everything that followed was AFTER.

End of story.

I shouldn't say that.

Because it's just the beginning of the story.

For the life of me, I don't know why I'm still around to tell what happened. Some might call it blind luck.

But that would depend on your definition of luck.

Because I think I've been anything but lucky.

After you hear my story, I think you'll agree.

September 7th, 2026.

It happened on a Monday.

Labor Day, in fact.

It's strange to look back at the way things were in BEFORE. To know that those times actually existed.

Because now it seems like it was all just a beautiful, hazy dream.

But I have to remember.

We all have to remember.

So we can keep alive in our minds, in our hearts, in our souls, what was taken from us...

I remember very clearly the last day of BEFORE.

Sunday. September 6.

Southern California. The weather was perfect. Not too warm. A light breeze coming off the ocean. People going about their lives, enjoying the late-summer holiday weekend. Playing. Laughing. Loving. Living.

It was a day like any other.

My dad was a Project Manager for an international construction company. They did these massive jobs all over the world. His specialty was designing and building underground structures, everything from tunnels to mine shafts to bomb shelters. These projects were almost always in another country. Which meant he was usually away for weeks, if not months, at a time.

But his latest job was gearing up in Mexico City. Which was relatively close to Los Angeles, where we lived. Which meant he'd be able get home most weekends.

That made my mom really happy. So happy, in fact, that she decided the family was going to celebrate in style. We would have steak and lobster for dinner. Which was fine with me and my little brother, Jeffrey.

I was 14 at the time, a boy like any other boy. There was nothing special about me. Nothing that made me different from anyone else--except maybe for the fact I liked school. I liked learning. Sure, there were kids who were a lot smarter than me. But I will say I knew my way around a computer. I guess I'm confessing to being a geek. A dork. A nerd. Whatever you want to call it. I know I sure looked the part. Tall for my age. Skinny. Glasses. Braces. No clue about girls.

As you can see, I'm not like that now.

Not by a long shot.

Anyway.

The next day was Labor Day. And then the day after that, Tuesday, I'd be starting high school. Which I was totally nervous about, but still looking forward to.

I didn't know it yet, but my formal education had come to an end.

No one had a clue Sunday would be the last day of normalcy for the world.

The day before the alien spacecraft arrived...

{The Zachary Stone Chronicles}

PART ONE

THE PROBE

SHOPPING MALL

LOS ANGELES

SUNDAY AFTERNOON

14-year-old Zachary Stone and his 10–year-old brother Jeffrey stand at the seafood counter of a high-end grocery store peering into a glass tank teeming with live lobsters. The creatures have to crawl over one another just to move around. Their claws are rubber-banded closed. A couple of the shellfish stare back at the boys with eyes that are small black beads.

Jeffrey's fascinated by the giant crustaceans.

"Why are their claws tied up like that?" he says to his older brother.

"So they don't mangle each other," Zack says, adjusting his glasses.

"Why would they want to hurt each other?" Jeffrey's expressive blue eyes are set in a face that looks like it's been carved from innocence.

"They're not used to being all jammed together like that. Besides, if they mangled each other, they'd be damaged goods and the store wouldn't be able to sell them."

"Still. That doesn't seem like a very nice way to treat them. They could let each of them have their own tank."

Zachary shakes his head at his brother's naiveté. "That would take up half the store."

His nose an inch from the glass, Jeffrey stares into their black bead eyes. "Can they see us?"

"If we can see them, they can prob'ly see us."

"I wonder what they're thinking."

"They're thinking, 'Who's that ugly kid staring at us?'"

"Shut up."

Zack shrugs and grins at his brother. A metallic gleam of braces flashes. "You asked my opinion."

"They look mad."

"You'd be mad, too, if someone came along and tied you up and threw you in a box with fifty other people."

"Do you think they know we're going to eat them?"

"No."

"How do you know?"

"Lobsters don't have the ability of rational thought."

"I bet they know something's up. I bet they're scared."

"Lobsters don't have feelings."

"How do you know?"

"They're cold-blooded. They don't have emotions."

"But how do you *know*?"

Zack sighs in exasperation. "Fine, Jeffrey. You win. I hereby pronounce you Official Lobster Whisperer of California."

The boys' mom arrives pushing a cart filled with groceries. Nudging 40, Lydia Stone has brown hair, brown eyes, and brown freckles. She's fighting a winning battle to keep her figure. She points to a thick package wrapped in butcher paper and says, "Your dad picked out some beautiful filet mignons."

"I thought we were having steak," Jeffrey says, disappointed.

Zack rolls his eyes. "Filet mignon *is* steak, dip-thong. The best kind, actually."

Their dad appears with a bottle of red wine in each hand. "That's right," says Eric Stone with a grin. He's a large, strong-looking man in his early 40s. His thick black hair is going silver in places. Placing the bottles in the basket, he says, "Nothing but the best for my family." He looks at the glass tank. "Have you boys picked out the lobsters?"

"I changed my mind," Jeffrey says. "I don't want one."

"You don't want one?" says his father in surprise. "Why not?"

Says Zachary, "Jeffrey's afraid it'll hurt the lobster's feelings if he eats it."

Jeffrey points at the tank. "They're looking right at me."

Lydia says, "So don't look back at them."

"But they seem so helpless."

Zack nods at the butcher package and says, "You're going to eat steak, aren't you?"

Jeffrey responds warily, sensing a trap. "Yeah. So?"

"Steaks don't grow on trees." Zack speaks condescendingly as only a big brother can do. "They were part of a cow once. A cow that was as alive as these lobsters. In fact, I'll bet that cow had a lot more feelings. Imagine her standing out in a field with big, sad brown eyes, quietly chewing her cud, the poor thing minding her own business, when suddenly she's loaded onto a truck and taken to a slaughterhouse where they—"

"Zachary, shut up!" Jeffrey covers his ears. He's near tears. "Mom, make him stop!"

"Zack, stop teasing your brother."

Eric kneels down so he's eye to eye with his son. "I'll tell you what," he says. "You don't have to decide right now. We'll pick out four and take them home. If you still don't want one, I'll drive him back to the store and put him back in the tank, alive. I'm sure the fish monger will let me do that. What do you say?"

Jeffrey considers a moment. Decides the offer is a fair one. "Okay."

Eric gives his wife a wink as he says, "But you have to promise me you won't ask to keep him as a pet."

This gets a laugh out of the young family as they head to the checkout counter.

I've tried really hard to learn exactly what happened. And more importantly— why.

So it won't ever happen again.

It was only later, after combing through The Record, that I was able to piece a lot of it together.

On the day my family went shopping for our celebration dinner, things were happening in other parts of the world that were totally unrelated, but ended up being pieces of the puzzle.

One piece was a conference that took place every September in New York. It was held by something called the Paleoanthropological Society. The purpose of this year's conference was to try and make sense out of two discoveries that had totally baffled scientists around the world. It was a pretty big deal at the time. I even remember reading about it online.

They called it The Mystery of the Two Caves.

The First Cave was found in Kenya in 2021. It contained bone fragments and crude tools dating back something like 60,000 years. Tests showed that these cave people were some of man's earliest ancestors.

It also contained the earliest known cave art. Crude drawings of humans and animals. Hand stencils. Stuff like that.

But one drawing was different from the rest.

So different, in fact, that scientists were having fights about it.

I mean actual fist fights.

The drawing had been crudely sketched in a cartoon style, like it'd been drawn by a very young person. It showed dozens of blue balloons floating down from the sky to where a group of stick-figure people were standing around smiling 'happy-face' smiles.

But the craziest thing was that in the background was what looked like a modern village, with buildings and doors and windows.

Which was totally impossible. Right? Cause we're talking 60,000 years ago.

There was another twist to the mystery. The drawing had been made purposely blurry, as if everything on the ground was being hit by a dust storm.

Even though the illustration was in a cave, thousands of years of exposure to stuff like wood smoke and humidity had caused it to deteriorate quite a bit. But the images remained clear enough.

So far as the experts could tell, this was the earliest known painting in human history.

But all the geniuses were stumped. No one could explain what it meant.

And then someone came up with a theory that was totally off the grid: 'What if—the collection of structures in the background really was a village?'

'What if—there was a whole prehistory to man that we knew nothing about?'

'And what if—that entire backstory had been wiped out by some world-wide catastrophe?'

Practically every scientist in the world rejected this theory outright. They argued that, even if there was some mysterious precivilization to ancient man, with actual towns, villages, and roads, where was the evidence of it? Because if there had been some horrible event that wiped it out, remains would still exist in the form of crumbling foundations. Or pottery shards. Or garbage pits.

There would be something.

And, they reasoned further, if it really was a village, why in the world would people abandon it to go live in a cave?

These were all good arguments. But, though no one would admit it, the main reason the theory had been so quickly shot down was because of the guy who came up with it.

Professor Conroy Hamilton was this really smart young anthropologist with a promising career in front of him who, while studying a remote tribe in the Amazon rain forest, 'went native'. He left his position at Columbia University to go live full time with the Indians. He even married one. Her name was Una. She was an exotic-looking woman in her 20's with hair that cascaded down her back like black flames .

Anyway, whether it was true or not, word spread that Conroy's brain was fried from taking too many hallucinogens during tribal rituals. Which could explain why he'd show up at the annual conference with crazy theories on everything from the nature of time to the existence of parallel universes. The wild, swirling purple tattoos that covered his neck and hands—another tribal ritual—didn't help his cause. His former peers were convinced that Hamilton's belt no longer went through all the loops.

Shortly after his theory was rejected, Hamilton prepared to return to South

America and disappear back into the rain forest until the next conference.

But before leaving, he needed a food fix. After living and working in New York for a number of years, he'd developed a weakness for the food. The upper Amazon River was a long way from a piled-high Reuben or a double pepperoni pizza. So while on his annual trek to the conference, he would dip into grant money and use it to hole up in a nice hotel for a few days and eat his fill.

Una became as addicted as him.

Still, after Conroy's departure, no one could come up with an explanation for the drawing in the cave.

There the mystery simmered until 2024, when the discovery of another cave rocked the scientific world. The reason for the uproar was its location.

It wasn't in Kenya.

It wasn't in Africa.

It wasn't even in the Eastern Hemisphere.

The cave was unearthed when it was it was ripped open by a backhoe clearing land for a shopping mall.

In California, of all places.

In a town called Placerville located in the foothills of the Sierra Nevada Mountains.

After seeing what he'd done, the backhoe operator called his foreman over, telling him to bring a flashlight. Together, they peered inside the spacious cavern.

Old skulls and bones were in plain sight.

They could also see cave art on the walls.

A Stop Work Order was issued until a team of scientists from Stanford could do a cursory inspection to see if anything of importance had been uncovered. They took some photos and ran some tests.

They were floored by what they found.

The site was immediately put off limits to anyone but official personnel until a formal, in-depth study of the cave could be completed.

This quickly led to lawsuits and counter-suits by the owner of the land where the cave was discovered; the developer under contract to build the mall; the National Park Service; the California Department of Parks and Recreation; the Placerville City Historical Society; the Sierra Nevada Native American Coalition; and so on, and so on.

While the courts tried to sort things out, the initial discoveries of the Stanford scientists made waves.

For starters, this new cave had big similarities to the Kenyan Cave:

It, too, contained bones and primitive tools dating back 60,000 years.

And—although the painting style was very different—it, too, had crude drawings of blue balloons floating down to happy-face stick-figures. It, too, contained what appeared to be a small town consisting of buildings and windows and roads. Also, like in the first painting, much of it was blurred out as if by a dust storm.

But there the similarities ended.

Because instead of just a few bone shards, the Second Cave contained dozens of perfectly preserved skeletons. The scientists theorized that the entrance had collapsed during an earthquake while the inhabitants were asleep, sealing them into an airtight container.

Another big difference: the DNA of the skeletons was not linked to modern man.

The conference organizers naturally expected Professor Conroy Hamilton to show up. But this time, instead of Una being his lone supporter, he was accompanied by a small but dedicated band of graduate students motivated by the man's passion for anthropology and his groundbreaking, if unorthodox, methods of research.

The debate over the Mystery of the Two Caves raged nonstop through that Labor Day Weekend.

{The Zachary Stone Chronicles}

PALEOANTHROPOLOGICAL CONFERENCE
NEW YORK CITY
LATE AFTERNOON

Smiling in a way that looks as if he's just tasted something unpleasant but has to pretend it's delicious, the Program Director speaks into the microphone on the podium.

"...And now, for the final presentation of the day, I give you Doctor Conroy Hamilton, who has taken time away from his 'work' in South America to join us." One can hear—if not see—the air quotation marks. "I'm sure we all can't wait to hear his insights into the discovery of the Second Cave. 'Doctor?'"

Hamilton strides across the stage. The Program Director walks away, not bothering to shake his hand. A couple of people in the audience clap loudly and slowly, mocking the rogue scientist.

Conroy takes his place behind the podium. Tall and wiry, he wears a 20-year-old blue sport coat with frayed cuffs. Long black hair falls half-way down his back. His skin is deeply bronzed from the tropical sun. Purple tattoos peek from his wrists and neck.

The 35-year-old, scruffy yet weirdly handsome scientist smiles defiantly at his stone-faced colleagues packing the auditorium. He grabs the microphone off the lectern and cries cheerfully into it, "Good afternoon!"

A thundering silence.

Conroy ignores the frosty reception. Continues to smile at the sea of crossed-arms and set jaws.

"Okay! Let's get right to it then, shall we?"

Conroy runs both hands through his shaggy mane, rolls his shoulders and bobs his head from side to side like a boxer prepping for a match, then begins his presentation.

"As everyone here is very much aware, all anyone's had to work with so far with are the photographs taken by the team from Stanford. To be sure, they're top notch pictures. But if we're going to come up with a viable theory about what this ancient cave art is trying to tell us, we need more evidence than just photos. Unfortunately, access to the Second Cave has been categorically denied by 'The Authorities'"—Conroy gives a shudder and a wide-eyed look of faux fear—"until all the legalities are worked out. Well. I learned a long time ago that some things in life are too important to be left to lawyers and bureaucrats."

A mischievous light comes into his eyes as he picks up a remote from the lectern. Clicks the Power On button. A wall of flat-screen monitors behind him blazes to life. Footage plays of Conroy and a couple of graduate students inside the Second Cave. They pick their way through ancient skeletons and crudely-made artifacts. Start setting up equipment around the painting.

"My team was able to gain access for just a few short hours. But during that time, we employed the very latest in high-resolution imaging technology. It's a process similar to that used in museums to reveal hidden artwork on canvases that have been painted over with other paintings. Only instead of canvas, we were looking at rock. But the principle is still—"

"Wait a minute!" interrupts a man in the front row. "Who let you into the cave?"

"Who said anybody let us in?"

"But—it's protected by armed security guards."

"I'm aware of that, sir. And your point is—?"

"So you broke in?"

"Such a rude phrase, with many negative connotations. But, yeah, we did."

"How did you do it?"

Conroy gives a lopsided grin. "It's amazing the things you can learn from the people of the Rain Forest."

He reaches inside his jacket. Removes a small blowgun. Quickly loads it with a tiny dart and aims in the direction of a wooden support beam off to the side of the stage. Phht— tock! Bull's-eye. The dart appears like magic in the center of the beam.

"Those big bad armed guards were probably too embarrassed to admit to sleeping on the job. Anyway. Forging on."

A murmur of discontent rises from the audience. Conroy ignores it.

Click.

A photo appears of the drawing from the First Cave. Although much of it is indeed worn away, the images are still striking.

"Not surprisingly," continues Conroy, "these images from the First Cave gave birth to all kinds of theories, some of them pretty wild. Even I was convinced that these were sketches of buildings with actual doors and windows, suggesting that mankind had a prehistory that had been lost to the ages."

Another murmur of disapproval ripples through the crowd, a little louder this time. His earlier theory still rankles.

"Our theory raised a lot of hackles in the scientific community. In fact, we were subjected to a level of ridicule that surprised us. Indeed, it would seem some of that derision remains alive and well to this day."

A voice cries out from the back of the hall. "No shit, Sherlock!" It's met with raucous laughter.

Conroy smiles and nods in apparent self-deprecation. When the laughter dies away, he says, "In the end, of course, there was no evidence to support our theory. It was just another guess as to what the drawing meant."

Click.

"Here's one of the photos taken by the Stanford team inside the Second Cave. We know from carbon-dating that this painting is precisely as old as the one in the First Cave. But there's a big difference between them: This one's been sealed in rock nearly all this time, and so is much better preserved.

"Though the style of the drawing is very different from the one in Kenya, it contains many of the same elements. Interestingly, it also appears to have been created by the hand of a young person, who we estimate to be ten to twelve years of age."

Conroy grabs a laser pointer from the podium. Uses it to underscore various features.

"Here are the blue balloons coming down from the sky." Conroy turns and gives the crowd an embarrassed grin. "I have to confess that I don't know what they are—which I'm sure will come as a shock to those who accuse me of having an answer for everything,. But don't worry. I'm sure I'll come up with the answer soon."

He turns back to the monitor. Points out more features.

"To continue; here on the ground are stick-figure people. And here is what looks for all the world like a small town. It's quite different from the town in the First Cave—which is what you would expect as they were no doubt different cultures living on either side of the world. And as you can see, much of the drawing has been obscured by a sand-colored pigment that was purposely applied over the original painting."

Conroy once again turns and faces the audience. He's no longer smiling.

"So now I ask my 'esteemed colleagues': How is it possible that these very similar drawings appeared on opposite sides of the world at virtually the same time so many thousands of years ago? And why have so much of both these drawings been deliberately obscured?" Conroy shrugs. "We don't know. We may never know. However, there are some things we do know. By using the imaging techniques I described earlier, we were able to penetrate the obscuration and get a clear rendition of what lay beneath. We originally tried this with the Kenyan painting, but it was far too eroded to get anything. However, the Placerville drawing is in much better condition."

As much as many of these people loathe Doctor Hamilton, a murmur of excitement rolls through the crowd.

A man sitting in the last row at the back of the hall leans forward, his interest piqued. No one could ever accuse Doctor Otis Larson of lacking style, however dubious it may be. The 45-year-old wears a red bow tie, a white dress shirt and a green plaid suit with elbow pads over his portly frame. Intelligent blue eyes peer from behind a pair of granny glasses. His balding pate is partially hidden by a few dark ribbons of hair in a half-hearted comb-over.

Conroy stares at the crowd with unsettling intensity. There's an edge to his words as he says, "What I'd like to show you now, are the results of the work done by me and my team inside the Second Cave..."

He pauses to let the information sink in. The room goes electric with anticipation. The silence is so complete, a dropped pin would sound like a firecracker going off.

Conroy turns back to the wall of screens.

"This...is what we found..."

Click.

There's a collective gasp from the audience as a super-high resolution photograph of the painting from the Second Cave fills the screen. Except now, just about all of the 'dust storm' is gone. Previously hidden details are revealed in stunning clarity.

"As you can see, we uncovered some new stuff," says Conroy with deliberate understatement.

A low, restless buzz starts to build in the room. It's not a friendly sound.

Undeterred, Conroy directs the laser onto the photo to emphasize his words.

"Like this, for instance."

Pointing the beam to a section that was previously obscured, his voice takes on the bite of victorious sarcasm.

"Somebody please correct me if I'm wrong, but this looks exactly like a village. With buildings. Some of them three and four stories tall."

Indeed, it does.

The buzzing turns into loud grumblings. Mixed in are a few cries of protest:

"Now just hold on a minute…"

"…hasn't been independently verified…"

"You're jumping to conclusions that aren't…"

In the back row, his elbows on his knees and his chin resting on his fist, Otis Larson smiles at the growing ruckus.

Conroy moves the laser to another part of the photo. "Oh, and looky here. A house. With doors. And windows. And—oh, my—could this actually be a picket fence?"

Indeed, it is.

The grumbling quickly builds to incoherent shouting. A dozen scientists jump to their feet like lawyers in a courtroom voicing objections.

"You're out of your mind!"

"We've had enough of your crackpot theories!"

"You doctored this painting to serve your own agenda!"

Conroy ignores the outcry. He talks loudly into the microphone to make himself heard.

"…And check this out: Down here, in the right-hand corner. This is my favorite."

He uses the remote control to zoom in.

"Look closely, boys and girls, and tell me what you see..."

As the magnified image comes into sharp focus, a disbelieving lull descends on the crowd.

There's no question what they're looking at.

A car.

The room explodes.

"Liar!"

"Charlatan!"

"What kind of idiots do you take us for?!"

Unperturbed, Conroy continues his presentation.

"You're looking at a boxy, independently-propelled vehicle, circa 60,000 years B.C. Obviously, it's like no make any of us has ever seen. That's because the technology used to build it evolved differently from our own, back in mankind's precivilization."

The shouting reaches a fever-pitch.

"You're insane!"

"We've had enough of your hare-brained theories!"

"Somebody get that lunatic off the stage!"

Things quickly get out of hand as shoving matches break out. Otis Larson's had enough. He shakes his head, gets to his feet and exits through a back door.

Conroy continues shouting into the mic. "...You'll notice that the car has an open top! Which makes it a convertible! How cool is that?!"

In the middle of the room, a large scientist with a full beard stands and hurls an unopened plastic water bottle at Conroy. It sails in a high, lazy arc toward the podium.

Conroy continues. "And if you observe very carefully, you can see that there are four passengers on board! Possibly a mother and father and two children on a family outing! Or it could even be two couples out on a double—unh!"

The bottle hits Conroy square in the back of the head, knocking him unconscious. He collapses to the floor.

One of Conroy's young team members, a small, shaggy student wearing old jeans and a tie-dyed sweatshirt, charges over to the bearded scientist and socks him in the jaw. The fellow shakes it off and the two men wrestle each other to the floor.

More objects are thrown at the stage. Other fights break out in the crowd.

As the conference dissolves into chaos, two other members of Conroy's team, their eyes wide with fright, run to their unconscious boss, pick him up, and carry him outside the building. They gently lay him on a grass meridian next to the street. One of them dials 9-1-1 on his cell phone while the other checks his pulse. Una is suddenly there, cradling Conroy's head in her lap. Her tears flow as she leans forward and gently presses her cheek onto his forehead. As they wait for the ambulance, blood seeps steadily from his wound, slowly drenching her skirt and Conroy's blue jacket with the frayed cuffs.

Here's another piece of the hindsight puzzle I found while digging through The Record:

Several years before the conference in New York, a mining-based corporation called New Haldron Industries sent a small fleet of unmanned spacecraft to the moon to do some exploratory drilling. Its purpose was to search for the presence of potentially valuable minerals.

Wouldn't you know it? The corporate 'moon shot' paid off, big time. It turned out that, hidden beneath the surface of moon, were large deposits of something called rare earth elements, or REEs for short.

See, back in BEFORE, REEs were really important. They were needed to make all kinds of stuff, everything from computers and televisions to rockets and jet fighters. Thing is, they were really hard to come by and really expensive, just like the name said—rare.

Until now.

It was just sitting there for the taking.

All you had to do was go to the moon and dig it up.

Which is exactly what New Haldron Industries did. It poured rivers of cash into the building of workhorse spacecraft. Giant machines designed specifically for mining on the moon were shipped into space. Because ninety-nine percent of the work was performed by machines, only a single flesh-and-blood human was needed at the excavation site to oversee them. The 'Moon Miners' job was to maintain and repair the equipment.

The Moon Miners were a breed unto themselves. They were chosen not because of (nonexistent) backgrounds in science and math, but for their ability to think on their feet. Basically, they needed to be able to solve all kinds of mechanical problems with duct tape and a hammer.

They also had to be able to deal with working in near total isolation for three years—the standard duration for the job. There was no direct contact with other people. Just radio and video transmissions from Earth and orbiting spacecraft.

They also needed to be able to withstand harsh living conditions. Home was a module the size of a walk-in closet that was combination bedroom, bathroom, kitchen, and workstation. Because machines recycled and purified oxygen and water, both tended to smell and taste on the rank side. Food consisted of military-type rations that would keep for the duration of the job.

What made it all bearable was the pay. A Moon Miner could make enough money in three years to live extremely well for the rest of his life.

As for getting back to Earth, each work site came with its own escape pod. These were bare-bones rocket ships of which 90 percent consisted of a powerful, computer-guided, solid-fuel thruster. The other ten percent was a stubby escape pod just large enough to accommodate the miner and a small amount of personal gear. It was equipped with enough oxygen, water, and food for the three-day trip home. The thruster was jettisoned shortly after blasting off from the moon. When the escape pod reached the Earth's vicinity, atmospheric friction slowed it down enough so that several large balloons deployed and the pod drifted to a soft landing at New Haldron Industries' giant new Space Port located in southern Nevada. The miner would then collect his paycheck, reenter polite society, and presumably live happily ever after.

The escape pods were programmed to lift off three years to the day from when the miner began his stint. That three year timeline was hardwired into the pods' control and guidance system. Woe be unto the Moon Miner who wasn't in his escape pod when it lifted off. He would be left behind to die a horrible and lonely death.

For maximum corporate efficiency, the Moon Miner, machines, supplies, and escape pod were deposited to the job site in one fell swoop by a disposable spacecraft built specifically for that purpose.

The lunar mining process itself was pretty straightforward. Excavating machines dug the ore out of the ground and packed it into metal containers about the size of a minivan. Every few weeks, an unmanned transport landed, dropped off empty ore containers, picked up the full ones and ferried them up to one of two Space Freighters that took turns orbiting the moon. These craft were as big as aircraft carriers. It took about six months to fill the hold. The freighter then departed for Earth, where it glided to a landing at the Nevada Space Port. Meanwhile, its sister freighter took its place in lunar orbit so that mining could continue without interruption. Plans were in the works to build more freighters as mining operations expanded.

Like the moon-mining machines, the Space Freighters were designed so that just about all the work was performed by computers and robotics. The 'crew' consisted of a single pilot whose job was to ensure everything ran smoothly.

On the last day of BEFORE, a 48-year-old Moon Miner named Spike Penovitch was ten days into his second three-year hitch. Which was really unusual—if not downright crazy. No Moon Miner had ever gone back for a second tour.

Even weirder was that Spike had volunteered to be one of a handful of miners working on the far side of the moon, a place where the idea of 'isolation' took on a whole new meaning. That's because the Earth is never in view, as opposed to being constantly visible from the near side of the moon. Plus all communications had to be relayed by satellite. The only time the Moon Miner had direct interaction with another person was when the orbiting Space Freighter came within direct line of sight.

{The Zachary Stone Chronicles}

MINING PIT
FAR SIDE OF THE MOON

His workday at an end, Spike steps into the airlock that's just big enough to hold a person wearing a spacesuit. He closes and seals the outer door, then hits a switch that causes air to surge into the chamber. As soon as the pressure's equalized with the module's interior, he opens the inner hatch and steps inside. He removes his helmet and hangs it on a hook in the wall. His iron-grey hair and beard are cut to the same quarter-inch length. He runs a weary hand across his bristly scalp and looks around at his cramped quarters.

"Home, sweet home," he murmurs to himself. There's no bitterness or sarcasm in his voice, just quiet acknowledgement of the Spartan conditions.

He extricates himself from the spacesuit, hangs it on another hook, then plugs in the oxygen feeder tube so that the suit's air tank will be fully charged for tomorrow. He strips off his undergarments—basically high tech long johns—and drops them into a small laundry box, which will automatically wash and dry them overnight.

Spike takes two steps in sweaty nakedness to the kitchen area where he fills a tall plastic cup with water, takes a long drink, then fills it again. He takes a whiff of an armpit and grimaces. He pours a few inches of water into a plastic bucket, grabs a sponge, then takes a seat at the communications console where he starts giving himself a sponge bath.

Half-way through his bath, the console starts to beep and squawk. The Space Freighter has cleared the lunar horizon and is trying to make contact. An image of the freighter's captain comes jerkily to life on the monitor.

A woman's voice comes over the speaker loud, clear, and irritated. "Penovitch, you stupid sack of shit!"

Unselfconscious in the extreme, Spike continues to sponge down his taught, wiry body. Doesn't even look at the screen as he grins and says, "That you, Angie?" His voice has a mild rasp to it.

"Who the hell else would it be?!"

Spike's grin widens. "I can't tell you how much I missed that sweet melodious voice of yours."

"What in the world is wrong with you, Spike?!"

"What makes you think something's wrong with me?" .

"Because no one in their right mind comes back here! I couldn't believe it when I saw your name on the roster."

Spike shrugs easily. "I needed a job."

Angie's incredulous. "Spike, you had life dicked! You made enough dough to never have to work again. You're supposed to be down on the big blue marble living the dream!"

Spike looks up at the computer screen and smiles sadly at the skipper of the Space Freighter. In her early 50s, Captain Angela Hardingway's olive skin is unlined, giving her a much younger appearance. Her dark auburn hair is cut short.

"Oh, darlin', I lived the good life like you wouldn't believe. For a year."

"A year? What happened?"

Spike shrugs again. "I ran outta money."

Angie shakes her head. "How is that even possible?"

Spike takes his time answering as he towels off. "I'm gonna tell you a story, Angie. One you haven't heard before."

Spike doesn't care that Angie sees him in his birthday suit. Angie doesn't care either, probably because she's observed this ritual more than once during his previous stint. She folds her arms over her chest and leans back in her chair. "Sure, Spike," she sighs. "Tell me one I haven't heard."

"My old man was a coal miner in West Virginia," Spike says, pulling on sweat pants and a T-shirt. "His favorite saying was 'Life is hard and then ya die.' Which pretty much summed up his own life. He drank himself to death before he was 60. His daddy did the same. I was well on my way to carrying on the family tradition when I got hired by a mining company that actually cared about its employees. They had a substance abuse program, which helped me keep things under control. But then they went belly up."

Spike frowns at the thought of what might have become of him before continuing.

"This was right around the time of the big discovery on the moon. I applied for a position with New Haldron like thousands of other guys, went through their screening process, and they hired me. Imagine that? Before I knew it, I was up here on a three-year hitch. Turns out the work isn't all that hard. Machines do all the heavy lifting. I just have to keep'em running. And being alone's never bothered me. I actually prefer it most of the time. Prob'ly why I never married. Plus I never was very good at being around people. It's only when I'm hammered that I get along with them. So moon mining turned out to be a good fit for me.

"After I made my nut, the company cut me loose as per the terms of the contract. Thing is, I've almost never been without a job. And I sure never had any real money. But suddenly I'm rolling in dough. And I don't have to work anymore. Everything's great, right? Unfortunately, in my case, this turned out to be not so good a recipe."

"How so?"

"I've always worked hard and played harder. But now what was I gonna do? Sit on my porch and watch the weeds grow for the next thirty years? Uh-uh. Not my style. So I decided to play."

"Let me guess: wine, women and song."

"A lot of wine. A lot of women. Not much song that I re-call."

"Still. To have burned through that much money in a year."

"Plus a lot of time at the gambling tables of Las Vegas."

"Ah. I'm starting to get the picture."

"Yeah. Lived like a king. Or so they told me. It's all kind of a blur. Then the money ran out. I reapplied with New Haldron. They took me back. And here I am."

Angie shakes her head in mild confusion. "Meaning—what, exactly?"

"The way I see it, I'm being paid—and paid very well—to detox for the next three years."

"So what's the plan after this stint is up?"

"The plan is three years a monk, one year a madman until I can't do it anymore."

"And you're okay with that?"

"I am. Except..."

"What?"

"When I'm not actually working up here, it can get kind of boring."

"So read. Or watch videos. That's what I do."

"I don't like to read. And I'm not big on movies. But I will say I always wanted to play a musical instrument."

"Let me guess. You had them deliver a baby grand to your palatial estate."

"A baby what to my what?"

"Nothing. Just trying to be funny. It sounds like you've got it all figured out."

"It's a game plan that works for me."

Angie sighs. "I suppose there are worse ways to live."

"That's for sure. Like my old man. So you see—'Life *isn't* so hard, and *then* ya die'."

"Well, I still think you're crazy to want to spend another three years in that smelly broom closet you call home."

"Trust me, I'm fine with it. How 'bout you?"

"What about me?"

"How're your girls?"

Angie's face softens at the thought of her two daughters.

"They're good. Sadie's starting her second year at the University of Washington. Studying to be an electrical engineer. Getting good grades. Bonnie'll be a senior in high school this year—or I guess I should say in a couple of days. She's staying with my folks until I finish my rotation. We plan to start looking at colleges in the spring. So, yeah, my girls are fine. They turned out to be great kids."

"I'm not surprised, considering their mom."

"Thanks. It hasn't been easy... I can't believe it's been ten years since Jack died..." Spike watches the tears come into her eyes behind her glasses. He doesn't want to see her cry.

"You're moving out of range, Angie. I'm losing your signal. We'll talk again on another pass."

Spike turns off the computer. Sits staring a moment at the blank screen, then reaches into a corner and retrieves the slightly-battered, second-hand banjo he picked up at a Goodwill store. He grabs a book lying on the floor, Banjo for Dummies. Opens it to page 2 and begins picking awkwardly at the strings. It sounds like metal shavings being dropped into a tin bucket.

STONE FAMILY RESIDENCE
LOS ANGELES
SUNSET

A warm, beautiful evening. The Stone family relaxes in their spacious backyard. Lydia is stretched out on a padded chaise lounge next to the pool enjoying a glass of wine. Zack and Jeffrey sit at a nearby picnic table drinking sodas and texting on their cell phones. Next to that, Eric grills four steaks on a custom-built barbecue. He and the boys wear shorts and t-shirts. Lydia has on a light cotton shift. All four are barefoot.

The sun has just set. A turquoise glow lingers on the horizon. Stars begin to appear. Crickets whirr.

Eric tongs the steaks off the grill and arranges them on a platter. He carries it over to the picnic table and sets it down with a flourish.

"Voila! Dinner is served."

"Cool," Zack says, turning off his phone. "I'm starving."

"We've got the turf," Eric says. "Now we just need the surf."

Lydia's already heading into the kitchen. "Coming right up. Boys, can you give me a hand?" Zack and Jeffrey get up and follow. Lydia returns a moment later carrying a platter on which rest three freshly-boiled lobsters. Even in the warm air, steam rises from the bright-red crustaceans.

Zack and Jeffrey bring up the rear bearing platters of baked potatoes, steamed broccoli, and a big wooden bowl of green salad. Everyone takes a seat at the table.

Eric eyes the feast before them and actually rubs his hands together in anticipation. "Okay, let's dig in!"

"Wait," Lydia says. They all stop in mid-reach as she refills her and Eric's wine glasses. "First, a toast." She raises her glass. Looks directly at Eric. "To your dad—the best husband and father in the known universe. I'm so proud of you." Tears appear in her eyes. She looks at her two boys. "I'm proud of all of you."

Eric gives his wife a warm smile and says, "Here, here." He takes a drink of wine and sets down his glass. "Now, let's dig in."

Eric and the boys attack the food.

Lydia slices off a small piece of filet mignon and chews slowly with eyes closed, savoring the meat. She swallows and says, "That. Is. Yummy."

"Amen," Eric says around a mouthful of steak.

One of the filets lies untouched on the platter—Jeffrey's. Lydia watches him as he takes a bite of baked potato.

"Jeffrey, honey? Are you sure you don't want some steak? It's really good."

"I'm sure." He spears a small broccoli crown with his fork. Pops it into his mouth.

Zack says to his brother, "No lobster. No steak. Are you going all vegan on us?"

"What if I am?"

"Nothing. Just that there's been studies that say plants experience pain when they're cut. Trees actually scream when a chainsaw—"

"Mooom!"

"Zachary, don't torment your brother."

"Sorry."

As Eric refills Lydia's wine glass, he gives Zack a wink. "I guess that just means more for you and me."

Zack smiles. Guides a forkful of butter-drenched lobster into his mouth.

"So, Dad," Jeffrey says as he works on a corn on the cob. "What are you going to be doing down in Mexico?"

"Mexico City's starting a major expansion of their subway system. My company won the contract."

"When do you start?" Zack says.

"The same day you start high school. I have to be on the job ready to go first thing Tuesday morning."

"Does that mean you have to leave tomorrow?"

"Not till tomorrow night. So you guys have to put up with me for one more day—or most of it, anyway. That being the case, what do you say we all go to the beach tomorrow?"

"Yay!"

"Cool!"

Later that night, in a small alcove off the main Control Room of the Jet Propulsion Lab in Pasadena, a team of three technicians and their supervisor were settling into the graveyard shift of their vigil.

An offshoot of NASA, the Asteroid Detection Tracking and Avoidance Department (ADTAD) was plugged into an international network of Earth-based telescopes and satellite dish arrays. Its purpose was to scan the skies for any object that might pose a threat to our planet.

After years of routinely cataloguing thousands of heavenly bodies that turned out to be harmless, things were about to change...

{The Zachary Stone Chronicles}

ADTAD

JET PROPULSION LABORATORY
PASADENA, CALIFORNIA
SUNDAY SEPTEMBER 6, 2026 10:25 PM

The young Technicians and their Night Supervisor sit in adjacent cubicles, each monitoring oversized computer screens on which live feeds of data stream continuously. It's a mind-numbingly boring job reserved for low level interns who must pay their dues before moving up the ladder.

It's about to get a lot less boring.

A soft yet persistent chiming sounds through the little room.

No one visibly reacts. It's just business as usual. The Techs rotate the handling of each new contact. The Night Supervisor calls out, "Josh? You're up."

Josh grumbles to himself. Sighs. Hits some keys. "Running Initial Tracking and Analysis program..."

After a moment, the results appear on his computer screen.

"That's weird..."

"What's weird?"

"This bogey just appeared out of nowhere."

"What was the point of origin?"

"Somewhere near Jupiter."

"No track before that?"

"No, sir."

"That is odd."

Josh leans toward his screen as more data comes in.

"This is even crazier."

"What's the matter?"

"The computer's telling me this thing's moving at thirty-three thousand miles a second."

"Impossible." The Night Supervisor gets out of his chair and walks over to stand behind the intern. "That's nearly a fifth the speed of light."

Josh gets out of his chair. "See for yourself, sir."

The Night Supervisor takes over his seat. His hands skitter across the keyboard like spiders on crack as he double-checks Josh's finding. He stops and stares at the screen in disbelief. Whispers, "...How can that be?"

The other two Techs have overheard and gather round to watch.

The Night Supervisor hits keys that open a program entitled Advanced Tracking and Extrapolation. "Let's see where this guy is going in such a hurry..."

It takes a moment for the results to come up. When they do, the Night Supervisor turns pale. "This thing's headed right for us."

Josh quickly does the math in his head. "...Which means it'll be here in less than three hours."

The Night Supervisor bolts from the chair and covers the distance to his cubicle in three strides. "I need to get the Director on the horn." He grabs his phone and hits a number on speed dial.

Josh sits back down in front of the screen as more data comes in.

"Sir?"

The Supervisor looks at Josh in irritation.

"Can't you see I'm on the—"

"It's slowing down."

The Supervisor stares at Josh as he takes in the implication of what that means.

The soft chiming in the room continues as the Director of the JPL answers his phone. The Supervisor speaks quickly. "Doctor Seifert, it's Sam Telfer, Night Supervisor at the Asteroid Detection Tracking and Avoidance Department. We have an emergency situation. I think you better alert the president ..."

That same night, in the high-tech heart of Seattle, Washington, another piece of the puzzle fell into place...

{The Zachary Stone Chronicles}

SEATTLE

Through large windows in a darkened room overlooking Puget Sound, the lights of the Space Needle and the Seattle skyline glimmer in the distance. The quiet is broken by a soft pinging, which grows steadily louder.

A bedside lamp flicks on. Kent Hatcher fumbles for his glasses. Glances at the clock—one in the morning. Picks up his smart phone and mutes the pinging. He stares at the screen a moment. Suddenly sits up straight.

The short, skinny, 55-year-old with the boyish face gets out of bed. Pulls his robe on over his pajamas, turns off the lamp, and pads down the hall to another room. He steps inside and closes the door. Soft track lighting automatically comes on, illuminating a home office unlike no other.

Kent walks to the center of the windowless room and stands over a dark touchscreen the size of a pool table. Several large monitors are mounted on the walls, their screens blank. He brushes a finger over the giant touchscreen. It and the other monitors come to colorful, blinking life.

Like a shaman conjuring spirits, his hands slide across the touchscreen with practiced ease. On the monitors, ghostly images, data streams, snatches of conversations, clips of video come and go.

Kent Hatcher, one of the smartest, richest, most successful people in the world, takes it all in. As usual, Hatcher Technologies will have a head start on learning what's happening in the world.

Within the hour, President Claire Crawford gathered most of her cabinet, the National Security Council, the Joint Chiefs of Staff and a handful of advisors in an emergency meeting.

Those who couldn't personally attend or were out of town were patched through by video...

{The Zachary Stone Chronicles}

WHITE HOUSE SITUATION ROOM
LABOR DAY SEPTEMBER 7 2026
4:05 AM

A large conference table occupies the center of a wide, low-ceilinged room. On the wood-paneled walls hang six large flat-screen monitors. High-ranking government officials are seated around the table.

The door opens. President Claire Crawford strides into the room and marches over to a chair at the head of table.

"Thank you all for coming in," she says as she settles into her chair. "Right now, I know as much about what's going on as you: That an asteroid appears to be on a collision course with the Earth."

A trim, handsome woman of 62, the president's brown eyes sparkle with intelligence. She's allowed her hair to go gray. It falls thick and full to her shoulders.

Crawford looks around the table at the sober-faced officials. Because of the short notice and high urgency of the matter, many are in various states of dress—or undress. Her Secretary of State wears a sport coat over his pajama top. The Secretary of Commerce has a serious case of bedhead. Vice President Jameson has a T-shirt under his jacket with a drawing of a hula girl on a beach with the caption, 'I Got Lei'd In Hawaii'.

The Joint Chiefs of Staff is a different story. By some military miracle President Crawford can only wonder at, all five members are in full uniform, every medal, every button, every crease in place. Clean-shaven, clear-eyed and alert, they look as crisp as freshly-cut stalks of celery.

"I know you've got a lot of questions and concerns, as do I. We're expecting an update any minute from the Jet Propulsion Laboratory in—"

An aide appears at her side. Leans down to whisper in her ear. She nods and says to the group, "Dr. John Seifert, the Director of JPL, has the latest information."

One of the flat-screen monitors comes on with a live feed from the JPL.

"Hello, Madam President."

The president wastes no time.

"What have you got for us, Doctor Seifert?"

Seifert, just this side of 50-years-old, gives his salt-and-pepper beard a scratch, then pushes his horn-rimmed glasses back to the bridge of his nose before replying.

"The first and most important thing you need to know is this: the object is not going to collide with the Earth."

This causes deep sighs of relief around the conference table. Someone stifles a low sob, "Thank God."

Seifert continues, "It is headed our way, but it's slowing down dramatically. We estimate it will arrive in the vicinity of the Earth at approximately 9:30 AM Eastern Time." He looks at his watch. "A little less than 5½ hours from now."

Another voice cuts in. "John, if I may interject..." Everyone's attention turns to another flat-screen monitor. This one has Otis Larson's image on it—the same man who was sitting at the back of the lecture hall during the Paleoanthropological Conference. Still in New York, he's been patched in. He wears a hotel bathrobe. At the bottom of the screen are the words Chairman – President's Council of Advisors on Science and Technology.

Seifert gives his colleague a quick smile. "Of course, Otis."

"You said this object is slowing down."

"That's correct."

"Which implies that it's traveling under its own power and guidance systems."

"Yes."

Otis's eyebrows furrow in concentration. "Which makes it highly doubtful we're dealing with an asteroid."

"I was getting to that. We believe it's a spaceship of some kind."

There are gasps from around the table.

"A spaceship...!?"

"Are you serious?!"

After taking a moment for people to settle down, President Crawford says, "You're talking about extraterrestrial intelligence."

"Yes, Ma'am."

"Obviously far more advanced than us."

"One would assume so."

President Crawford says, "So the question before us is; what will they do when they get here?"

Air Force General Jim Walters is the first to speak up. "A better question might be—what will *we* do?"

"Please clarify, General."

"Either they're going to be friends or they're going to be foes. If they're friendly, there's no question mankind will reap amazing benefits. But what if it turns out they're not so friendly?"

President Crawford senses that the meeting is veering toward issues of national security. She turns to the JPL Director and says, "Dr. Seifert, do you have anything else to add at this time?"

"No, Ma'am. We're monitoring the object as best we can. We'll issue updates as they come in."

"Thank you, Doctor." The JPL video feed goes blank. Crawford turns back to General Walters.

"What is it you suggest we do, General?"

"I'm all for hoping for the best, but it wouldn't hurt to be prepared for the worst."

"Are you saying we should nuke this thing out of the sky as soon as it arrives?"

"No, Ma'am. I'm saying let's be *ready* to nuke it out of the sky. Just in case."

Otis Larson speaks up from his monitor. "I appreciate your caution, General. But I can't imagine advanced beings traveling half-way across the galaxy to conquer us. Or murder us. Or enslave us. Or whatever else you have in mind."

General Walters responds, "I'm sure a lot of Native Americans thought the same thing when the first Europeans landed on their shores."

An uneasy silence descends upon the room. All eyes turn to President Crawford. She in turns looks at the Head of the Joint Chiefs and says, "General Walters, I want you and the other Joint Chiefs to work up a contingency plan. One that assumes a worst case scenario. Just in case."

She addresses the others in the room. "So far," she says, "we've somehow managed to stay a step ahead of the media on this, so things have remained quiet. I'm sure that will change at any moment. I suggest you all brace yourself for a day that will be like no other. Dr. Larson, I need you back in Washington ASAP."

"On my way, Madam President." Larson switches off his laptop. The live feed goes dark.

"As for the rest of you," Crawford says to those in the room, "consider this a full-blown national emergency. I want you all to stay on your toes. I'll be calling some of you back to the situation room as more information comes in. This meeting is over. Good luck."

President Crawford stands and strides out the door, staff in tow. The room erupts in a frenzy of activity as everyone begins barking orders at each other and into cellphones.

The President was right. It didn't take long for the news to get out. This was an event that would sooner or later affect every human being, so there was no point in trying to hide it.

The media had been busy in the night. That morning, the world woke to the reality-altering fact that an alien spaceship was headed toward Earth.

Needless to say, me and my family didn't go to the beach that day...

{The Zachary Stone Chronicles}

STONE RESIDENCE

DAWN

It's just starting to get light out as Zack pads down the hall in his pajamas. He knocks gently on the door of his parents' bedroom.

"Dad?"

No answer. He waits a moment, then knocks again, harder this time. "Mom? Dad?" There's a slight quaver in his voice. "Are you awake?"

The door opens. Eric is pulling on a robe while blinking sleep from his eyes. "Zack? What's the matter? Is everything all right?"

Zack can hear his mom stirring in the darkened room. "Eric, is something wrong?"

"I couldn't sleep," says Zack, his voice earnest. "So I got on my computer to do some stuff, but there were all these alerts and emails and newsflashes." He takes a shaky breath. "Mom, Dad, something's happening."

A short time later, Eric, Lydia, Zack and Jeffrey have gathered on the couch in their living room where they're glued to the flat-screen TV. The four sit unselfconsciously close together, the boys wedged between their parents.

On television, Clifford March, network news anchor for Broadcast and Communications Systems, or BCS, conveys the latest information.

"...Just moments ago, at around 9:30 this morning Eastern Time, an alien spacecraft went into orbit around the Earth."

All four jaws of the Stone clan drop in unison.

"What!?"

"Oh my God!"

"No way!"

The boyish-looking 45-year-old newscaster speaks earnestly into the camera. "This is what we've learned so far:

The craft first appeared 'out of nowhere' in the vicinity of Jupiter. This has led some scientists to believe that it arrived in our solar system by way of a wormhole, a theoretical warp in the fabric of space-time. In layman's terms, it's a kind of tunnel that allows objects to travel instantly between distant parts of the universe..."

As the broadcast continues, Eric and Lydia exchange quick glances, their expressions stunned and nervous.

Clifford March suddenly presses on his earpiece and says, "We're going live now to the Jet Propulsion Lab in Pasadena, California, where its Director, Dr. John Seifert, is making a statement."

There's a jumbled cut to a live feed from the JPL. In under six hours, the once church-quiet Asteroid Detection Tracking and Avoidance Department has undergone a seismic shift. Its operations area has moved from the little alcove into JPL's Main Control Room. Over a hundred people now bustle about NASA's nerve center. Technicians, government officials, astrobiologists, and uniformed military liaisons swarm the area in barely-controlled chaos. There is a constant stream of shouts and exclamations as orders are given and acknowledged. Giant flat-screen monitors are ablaze with multi-colored data. Phones and machines chirp and buzz.

Dr. Seifert is the one calling the shots now. He stands in front of a podium on a raised dais just off the Main Control Room. A handful of disheveled reporters jostle for space in front of him while straining to hear him speak.

"...The craft is a metallic sphere about 20 feet in diameter. Scientists think it's unmanned because it's too small and dense for anything living to be on board. It's orbiting the Earth at a height of about 200 miles. I use the term 'orbit' lightly because the word implies an object revolving around the Earth in accordance with the laws of gravity. But this vessel isn't following the rules."

A reporter shouts, "What do you mean by 'not following the rules', Doctor?"

"It's zipping this way and that without effort, as if it's operating on some kind of anti-gravity propulsion system."

The reporter's forehead crinkles in consternation. "I thought that only happened in science fiction."

A wistful smile appears on Seifert's face. "So did I."

Another reporter shouts, "Doctor, if the spaceship is unmanned, what's it doing here?"

"We think it may be a probe of some kind sent to gather data on the Earth, much like the probes we've sent to other planets in our solar system ..."

Eric's cell phone rings. He checks the caller ID before answering. "Yeah, Ted. ...It *is* amazing. Hard to believe... Yeah, I pretty much figured that. Of course... No problem... Thanks. You take care, too."

He switches off the phone and says to his family, "That was my boss. He said we're putting Mexico City on hold until we know more about what's going on." Eric shakes his head in mild bewilderment. "Gee, ya think? There's no way in hell I'd leave you guys unless I was totally sure you were safe."

Like us, people around the world stopped whatever they were doing and peered at televisions or computers or I-phone screens, anxious to know what was happening with the alien craft. The only folks moving around were first responders like police officers, firefighters, and medical workers.

But even they were nervous and distracted...

{The Zachary Stone Chronicles}

HOSPITAL ROOM
NEW YORK CITY
MORNING

Professor Conroy Hamilton wakes up alone in a hospital room. His head is wrapped in a white bandage. He looks groggily around. Notices the door is half open. He calls out, "Hello? Nurse? Anybody?"

Silence.

He eases out of the hospital bed. Lifts a robe from a hook. Pulls it on over green pajamas. Steps into the hallway and makes his way toward the nurses station. A clutch of doctors, nurses, and medical assistants is gathered around the counter watching a flat-screen television. Una stands among them as Dr. Seifert continues his new conference.

"...For now, I'm urging people not to panic. Thus far, there's been absolutely no sign of hostile activity on the part of the spacecraft..."

Conroy says, "'Spacecraft?'"

Una cries out, "Conroy!" and runs to his side. The rest turn as one to look at him.

"Professor Hamilton," a nurse says. "You shouldn't be up."

"I left your room to get a glass of water," says Una, holding one of his hands with both of hers. "I didn't plan to be gone more than a minute. Then I saw what they were watching... I'm so sorry I left you alone, Conroy." Una speaks with an odd, lilting accent but her English is excellent.

Conroy gestures at the TV. "What's going on?"

The nurse says, "Let's get you back to your room first."

Once Conroy is settled back in bed, a doctor checks the pupils of his eyes with a small flashlight. "Can you remember what happened yesterday?"

"Yes, unfortunately. The shouting. The ridicule... And then I wake up here."

"Somebody clocked you a good one with a water bottle," the doctor says. "You suffered a minor concussion. How are you feeling?"

"A bit of a headache, but I've been worse. Can I leave? "

The doctor gives Conroy a careful onceover before replying. "I suppose so, but I would prescribe bedrest for the next 24 hours."

Conroy says, "Sounds good to me."

Una says, "Our flight home is in two days. Will he be okay to travel then?"

The doctor nods. "I'm sure he will."

"So," Conroy says. "Will somebody tell me what's going on?"

The doctor says, "While you were unconscious, the world changed..."

MINING PIT

FAR SIDE OF THE MOON

Spike sits nude at the communications console plucking his banjo, his brow furrowed in concentration, when Angie's image jitters to life on the monitor. The instrument's round base is placed strategically over his crotch.

"Spike," Angie says, sounding a little breathless. "Have you heard the news?"

"Mornin', Angie," he drawls. He keeps fiddling with his banjo. Doesn't look up at the screen. "You mean our little visitor from points yonder? Yeah, I've been following it on the relay comsats."

"Isn't it incredible?"

Spike's tone is lackadaisical. "It's pretty interesting, all right."

"Anyway, I just got word that New Haldron is suspending all mining operations, effective immediately."

This gets Spike's his attention. He stops messing with the banjo. Looks at Angie's image. "Why?"

"People are worried. They want to go home and be with their families."

Spike's face clouds. He doesn't speak for several moments—unusual for someone who always has something to say about everything.

"Spike? Did you hear what I said?"

"What if you don't have a family to go home to?"

"I...don't know how to answer that. What I *do* know is that all personnel have been ordered back to Earth. A lunar shuttle is making the rounds. It's scheduled to pick you up in four hours. So gather up your shit and be ready to—"

"Save your breath, Angie." Spike's voice is surprisingly calm.

"Excuse me?"

"I'm not going anywhere."

For a moment, Angie's too flustered to respond. Finally she says, "What did you say?"

"You heard me. I'm staying here."

"But—you can't do that."

"Watch me."

"You know, technically, I am your boss. Which means I have the authority to—"

"Really, Angie?" Spike says, amused. "You gonna order me around from that freighter of yours? You gonna fire me? Banish me to the far side of the moon? Oh. Wait. I'm already here. You gonna have me dragged aboard the shuttle in handcuffs?" Spike laughs gently. "That's not gonna happen."

Angie's voice softens. "Spike…"

"Angie. Listen to me. Remember what I said? I've got no family. I've got no place to go. I'm flat broke. So what on earth would I do on Earth? Where would I stay? How would I eat? At least here, I've got three squares a day and a roof over my head and something to do. Not to mention it keeps me away from the booze."

"Staying behind isn't an option."

"Of course, it's an option. It also happens to be the best one I have. As soon as this whole alien spaceship thing blows over, I'll bet mining operations are back up and running before you can say—"

"Dammit, Spike, you'll die up here. Alone." There's a catch in her throat as she says this. "So, please. Get on the shuttle when it comes."

A brief silence. Then Spike says, "Look. Angie. I appreciate your concern. I really do. But I've made my decision. And I'm sticking with it, come hell or high water. So, thanks but no thanks."

"Spike, stop being so damn stubborn. Look, depending on what happens, who knows? Maybe, at some point down the road, you and I could—"

"You're starting to fade on me."

"I don't think so, Spike. I'm still well within—"

"Yep," Spike says as he fiddles with the controls. "I'm definitely losing you, girl.

"Spike, don't—"

Spike switches off the communications console. Resumes messing with his banjo, his forehead wrinkled in thought.

Although people dealt with the news of the alien craft in different ways, the majority accepted the fact that a profound change was coming, and that the human race was headed into uncharted waters. We strived to face this new reality with as much courage as we could muster.

{The Zachary Stone Chronicles}

The Stone family eats a silent, nervous lunch of soup and sandwiches in the dining room. In the adjacent living room, the television remains on with the sound turned low. Finally, Eric breaks the silence.

"How's everyone holding up?"

Jeffrey sets his half-eaten sandwich down and stares into his bowl of chicken noodles. Says quietly, "I'm scared."

Lydia reaches out and takes his hand in sympathy. "Oh, honey..."

Eric gets out of his chair, goes over to his son, and gets down on one knee so that he's eye-to-eye with him.

"It's okay to be scared, Jeffrey. We're *all* scared, some maybe more than others. Pretending you're not won't do anybody any good. The important thing to remember is to be brave. We need to face our fears the best we can and deal with whatever comes. Right?"

Jeffrey resolutely purses his lips together. Gives his father a solemn nod.

Even in those scary, unsettling times, life managed to go on. Most people went about their daily business as best they could, as if staying with a familiar routine would keep them from going crazy with worry.

But there was something else mixed in with all this.

Something strange.

It's hard to describe. It was really subtle, but I definitely remember having this weird sense of inevitability about what was happening.

And it wasn't just me. I heard other people talking about it. It was this odd sense that we somehow expected this to happen. It's not hard to figure out why.

For generations, we'd been exposed to tons of science fiction books and movies about aliens arriving from outer space. It was like the possibility had been coded into our DNA.

So when an alien craft did show up, it wasn't this huge, terrible surprise. In fact, a lot of people put a positive spin on it. They said things like 'It's the fulfilment of mankind's destiny'; and that 'As a conscious and intelligent race of beings, we're finally going to take our proper place in the cosmos'.

I'll just leave it at that for now...

{The Zachary Stone Chronicles}

SITUATION ROOM
THE WHITE HOUSE

Later that day, President Claire Crawford, her cabinet, and the Joint Chiefs of Staff watch Clifford March's latest broadcast. Also present is newly arrived Otis Larson.

Clifford speaks into the camera. "...In a moment, we'll be going again live to the Jet Propulsion Lab to get the latest updates from Dr. Seifert. Until then, in related news, we've just learned that all lunar mining personnel have been successfully removed from the moon and are en route back to Earth. All, apparently, except one. For reasons not made clear to us, a miner named Spike Penovitch has refused to evacuate. Instead, he's decided to finish up his three-year contract on the other side of the moon."

Otis Larson murmurs quietly to himself, "What a strange thing to do. Poor man..."

Clifford continues delivering the news. "...Angela Hardingway, the pilot of the Space Freighter currently in lunar orbit, has volunteered to temporarily remain behind in a last-ditch effort to try and convince him to—"

Clifford stops in mid-sentence. Presses his earpiece. "Okay, we're going back live to Pasadena where Doctor Seifert has new information."

The screen switches to the live feed from the JPL, where Dr. Seifert is once again at the podium. Although there's even more people working in the control room than before, things have settled down from the frantic disarray in the earlier broadcast.

Seifert speaks. "Just moments ago, the alien craft ceased its erratic orbit around the globe. As soon as it did, the object sent a quick burst of energy back toward the spot near Jupiter where it first showed up. It then descended rapidly to a spot 102 miles above the Earth, where it remains in a stationary position."

A reporter speaks up. "Doctor, can you tell us where over the Earth the spaceship has parked itself?"

"Beijing."

In the Situation Room, Crawford and General Walters exchange a look of concern.

Another reporter jumps in. "Any theories as to what the energy beam means?"

"We think it's a communication signal of some kind."

"What do you think it's communicating?"

"It would seem logical that it's reporting back to whoever sent it about what it found here on Earth."

"What's the spacecraft doing right now?"

"It's gone completely dormant. No activity whatsoever."

Another reporter pipes up.

"Any ideas on why it's gone dormant?"

"If I had to hazard a guess, I'd say it's waiting."

"What's it waiting for?"

Seifert hesitates before answering. "I honestly don't know... But I think we'll soon find out."

A brief but poignant silence fills the room. Dr. Seifert continues. "Those are the latest developments. We'll make more information available as it comes in. Now if you'll excuse me, I need to get back to..."

In the Situation Room, President Crawford motions for an aide to mute the broadcast. She quietly scans the faces around the table, then pronounces a single word.

"Beijing."

This causes most of those in the room to frown. The military men flat-out scowl.

Crawford zeroes in on her Chairman of Advisors on Science and Technology.

"Doctor Larson. Any thoughts as to why the spacecraft has chosen to park itself over Beijing?"

Otis peers through his granny glasses down the length of the conference table at his boss. Twiddling a pen, he responds, "Beijing is the most populous city in the most populous country on Earth. If beings from another world want to establish contact with the human race, that would seem to be the most logical place to do it. If we were in the aliens' shoes, we'd probably do the same thing."

"Thank you, Dr. Larson." Speaking clearly and forcefully, she addresses the table in general. "The situation before us is this: Thus far, the aliens—or I should say, the alien craft—has not harmed a single human being. They seem to be merely observing us. I take that as a sign they may very well be friendly."

She sets her mouth in a determined line.

"That said, unfortunately it appears first contact will take place in China. If the aliens establish friendly relations with the Chinese, what does that mean for America? Would the Chinese try to cut us out of any agreement made with the aliens and reap the benefits for themselves?"

Somber nods around the table from, mainly from the men and women in uniform.

"We have our own national security to consider," continues Crawford. "We need to take into account all scenarios, good or bad, of what the future may hold for us. For instance, what would happen if the Chinese gained access to weapons technology so advanced it's beyond anything we can imagine?"

An aide appears at the president's side with a note. She quickly scans it, looks up and says, "Chinese security forces have just restricted the movement of all foreigners in and around the capital until further notice. Tiananmen Square has been cordoned off."

She turns to the Director of the CIA and orders, "I want to know every move China makes."

"I'll get right on it, Ma'am," he says.

Crawford stands up, indicating the meeting is over. As people grab up their notes and laptops, Larson ventures a question. "What happens now?"

"We wait," answers the President.

"What are we waiting for?"

"For whatever comes next."

STONE FAMILY RESIDENCE

The Stone family is once again perched side-by-side on the couch, watching Clifford March wrap up the live feed of Dr. Seifert's latest updates.

"...So it appears that the Chinese will be the first Earthlings to greet our interstellar travelers. Rest assured BCS will have a full team on the ground there to bring you live coverage..."

Eric and Lydia glance nervously at each other over the heads of their sons.

That night, Eric and Lydia lie in bed together talking quietly in the darkened room.

Lydia says, "What do they want with us? Why can't they just leave us alone?"

"Shhh." He pulls her close. "It's going to be all right."

Just hearing him say these words calms her down. She's quiet for a few moments. Then she says, "What do you think's going to happen, Eric?"

Eric takes a breath. "I have no idea. And in a lot of ways, I don't care. I know that sounds strange, but what's happening is totally out of our hands. I can't afford to care.

If it comes down to it, of course I'll do everything I can to protect you and the boys. But beyond that, all we can do is hope."

"And pray."

"You know I'm not a religious man...but I don't think a little prayer would hurt."

Lydia cuddles close to him in the darkness. "I love you, Eric Stone. No matter what happens, never forget that. I love you and the boys more than anything else in this world."

Less than 24 hours later, a new, much bigger kid appeared on the block...

{The Zachary Stone Chronicles}

PART TWO

IT BEGINS

CONTROL ROOM

JET PROPULSION LABORATORY

A steady buzz fills the room as specialists work around the clock trying to unlock the secrets of the Probe.

A soft but persistent chiming sounds through the crowded room.

The place goes completely silent.

Dr. Seifert hurries over to the main Detection and Tracking Console. The Technician there is already running Advanced Tracking and Analysis programs.

Seifert wastes no time. "What've you got?"

The Technician says, "There's a new visitor on the way. Trajectory and velocity identical to the Probe. Coming straight for us."

The Technician hits a few more keys, then stops and stares at the computer screen. He whispers, "Jesus..."

"What is it?" asks Seifert.

"Looks like the Probe called in his big brother."

According to The Record, when the new spacecraft arrived, it took up a position near the Probe over Beijing. As unhappy as President Crawford was that the first meeting between humans and beings from another planet would apparently be taking place in China and not the United States, President Chan of the People's Republic of China was feeling quite the opposite...

{The Zachary Stone Chronicles}

IMPERIAL HALL
PRESIDENTIAL PALACE
BEIJING

President Li Chan stands at a window looking down on Tiananmen Square, which is quickly filling with citizens. He wears black horn-rimmed glasses and a conservative business suit. The fact that he never smiles projects an air of perpetual seriousness. His subjects find his studious mien fitting and proper for a leader, making him one of the more popular presidents in recent Chinese history. He's very much aware that the arrival of the aliens will be the watershed event in human history, one that will reverberate down through the ages. He's determined that China will own it.

On his orders, a platform—the Official Alien Reception Zone—has quickly been erected in the center of the Square. And on that platform, Chan is determined to be the first human to greet the extraterrestrial beings.

Less than an hour after positioning itself over Beijing, the new vessel began slowly descending toward the Earth, as if the aliens didn't want to waste any time in getting to know us...

{The Zachary Stone Chronicles}

58

SITUATION ROOM
THE WHITE HOUSE

The room is occupied by the president, her cabinet, the National Security Council, the Joint Chiefs of Staff, and a handful of aides. All are in deep consultations with each other or with someone on their cellphones.

One of the monitors on the wall is tuned to BCS with the sound turned low. Otis Larson has been keeping an eye on it A sudden flurry of activity gets his attention. He calls out to an aide. "Turn that up!"

Clifford speaks urgently to the camera. "...just received word that the spacecraft is preparing to land."

Everyone in the room turns to the monitor as Clifford says, "...We're going live now to Beijing where Peter Ross, our Chinese Bureau News Chief, has the latest."

The image switches to veteran foreign reporter Peter Ross. At 58, he's thin, has wispy brown hair and a flat nose. He holds a microphone close to his mouth.

"Clifford, we're standing just outside Tiananmen Square, which is as close as the Chinese authorities will allow us to get. The square has been cordoned off to all foreigners, including the press." For emphasis, the news camera focuses on a line of scowling Chinese police a couple of feet behind him.

"Because the Chinese are running the show," Peter continues, "the rest of the world will have to take a back seat." There's a jaded tone to Ross's delivery, suggesting he's seen it all and then some.

"For what it's worth," Peter says, his words dripping with sarcasm, "the state-owned Xinhua News Agency has magnanimously offered to let some news networks tie into their video feed. Luckily for us, BCS is one of them."

A roar goes up from the crowd behind Ross, nearly drowning him out. He presses his ear-piece with one hand. Brings the microphone close to his lips with the other.

"Something's obviously happening in the square, Clifford."

The image on the monitor switches back to Clifford March in New York.

"President Chan's entourage has just entered the square, Peter. We're going to cut over now to the Chinese cameras."

A drone equipped with a high-definition video-cam floats above a half-million Chinese packed into Tiananmen Square. Nearly all of the spectators clutch small red flags of the People's Republic of China.

An area large enough to accommodate a large spacecraft has been roped-off in front of the hastily-built platform of the Official Alien Reception Zone.

The presidential convoy of black limousines arrives at the roped-off area and stops. A camera crew leaps from the lead limo and begins recording as President Chan emerges from the second limo. Bodyguards spring from the third limousine and surround the president. The remaining limousines disgorge government officials and aides.

Dozens of video monitors the size of drive-in movie screens have been positioned throughout the square so that the president's every move can be seen by the throng. At the sight of their leader, the cheering of the crowd doubles in volume. Chan waves solemnly back.

Chan climbs a set of stairs up onto the platform. The bodyguards and entourage stay a respectful distance back as Chan makes his way to a podium where he leans into the microphone and announces, "Welcome, fellow citizens!" Five hundred thousand Chinese erupt in cheers. Chan then looks skyward and says, "And welcome, space travelers!"

The crowd looks up as well and roars its approval. Waving flags transform the square into a flickering sea of red.

Chan waits for the mass of people to settle down before addressing them. "Our visitors will be here soon. And we—the Chinese people—will give them a reception that will echo down through the centuries!"

More cheers from the crowd.

PLAZA HOTEL
NEW YORK CITY

Conroy and Una watch the same broadcast from the bed of their suite. On the covers between them is a pizza box with the pie half gone. Their eyes are glued to the giant flatscreen TV as they chew on wedges piled high with pepperoni and mozzarella.

On TV, Clifford March says, "Peter, can you hear me?"

Peter's voice comes through over the ruckus of the crowd. "I can hear you, Clifford, just barely."

"The people at JPL say the craft is descending; that it should be visible to the naked eye at any moment."

The TV image switches back to Peter Ross in Beijing. He searches the sky while speaking into the mic. "No sign of it yet, Clifford. I must say there's an incredible sense of excitement in the air. Everyone here is aware they're moments away from bearing witness to the next step in mankind's destiny, whatever that may be. I have to confess I'm getting goosebumps myself, which I hardly ever—"

"Sorry to cut you off, Peter," interrupts Clifford. "But something's happening on the reception platform. We're going back to the Chinese feed."

On the platform in Tiananmen Square, a general of the People's Liberation Army has emerged from the entourage behind President Chan talking into a cellphone. He ends the call,puts it in his pocket, then gently touches the president's arm to get his attention. The general speaks to him while pointing excitedly at the sky. Chan smiles and looks up.

The many thousands of people watching this exchange on the giant screens realize arrival must be imminent. They turn silent as a million eyes scan the sky for the first glimpse of the craft.

In The White House Situation Room, a nervous tension charges the air. Everyone stares at the large monitor on the wall. Some of those sitting at the table unconsciously grip the arms of their chairs as if bracing for a collision.

Otis Larson realizes he's been holding his breath. He exhales and quietly says, "Here we go..."

Tiananmen Square remains strangely silent as everyone cranes their neck skyward, straining to see the spaceship. Suddenly a young man points and yells, "I see it! I see the spaceship!" His shout electrifies the crowd. All look to where he's pointing...

There.

A speck in the sky.

So high up it looks like a BB held at arm's length.

Hundreds, then thousands catch sight of it. An excited murmur rustles through the gathered masses.

As the craft steadily descends, the nervous whispering of the crowd gives way to a rising crescendo of oohs and aahs. But that starts petering out as the vessel comes more into focus. This is because of the craft's appearance. Those expecting a sleek, futuristic-looking spaceship are disappointed.

Because what's coming into view is something that looks like a bloated airplane made out of old plumbing fixtures. But instead of wings, on either side of the fuselage are what look like massive faucet heads the size of motorhomes, their spigots turned toward the Earth. The clunky, cylindrical fuselage is about hundred yards in diameter and two hundred yards long. In front of the stubby 'wings' is apparently the cockpit. The enormous 'windshield' is composed of a reflective material tinted obsidian-black. A half-dozen oval-shaped portholes extend back about a hundred feet from either side of the windshield. At the rear of the craft, there is no 'tail' to speak of. Instead, the fuselage abruptly ends in a gaping opening sealed with a blue, fabric-like material. The bottom half of the fuselage is studded with what appear to be sensors, all pointed toward the Earth. The top half is barren of such apparatus.

The vessel has a weathered, burnished look to it. Except for the tinted windshield and portholes, it looks like it was constructed out of hammered bronze.

Clifford March's voice comes over the live image of the craft.

"Peter, can you hear me?"

Peter's voice likewise cuts in over the image. "I can hear you, Clifford."

"Any first impressions of the spaceship?"

Peter hesitates before responding. "I have to say, Clifford, I was expecting something...more. It's not my idea of what a vessel from outer space should look like."

"Why is that?"

"As a life-long fan of science fiction, I guess I expected something with a little more...style. This thing looks like it fell off the work bench at a high school machine shop. It's clunky and it's graceless. It's hard to imagine a machine that looks less likely to fly."

"And yet, fly it does."

"Well, technically, because of its anti-gravity propulsion system, it levitates."

"Which means the craft doesn't have to be aerodynami-cally designed. It can be any shape at all."

"You're right about that. This hunk of machinery is a case in point."

That was the most incredible moment. Everyone in the world knew this was it. That we were finally going to meet the aliens! All of the tension and anxiety that had built up over the last few days was coming to a head...

{The Zachary Stone Chronicles}

As the ship continues to descend, it slowly twists this way and that, as if tweaking its flight path in preparation for landing. The mass of onlookers erupts in spontaneous cheers, happily welcoming mankind's fellow life forms in the cosmos. A half million red flags wave.

As the exultant mayhem erupts around him, Peter Ross says, "This is a pretty incredible reception, Clifford. It's like Elvis, the Beatles and the Pope all rolled into one. Are you tracking this?"

Clifford replies, "We've got cameras in several locations outside the square..."

As the craft looms ever larger as it continues its descent, Peter says, "I've got to tell you, Clifford—watching something this huge maneuver without any apparent effort goes against your instincts. Even weirder, it's descending in total silence. There's no rumble of engines. No blast of rockets..."

In the center of the Square, President Chan stands ram-rod-straight at the podium, staring up at the spacecraft, which is now about three hundred feet from the ground. The cheering of the crowd steadily increases.

But then, the craft slows to a complete stop. It hovers in the air, perfectly still and silent.

A minute goes by.

The spacecraft doesn't move. Just continues to hover a hundred yards above the ground.

Another minute goes by.

The cheering of the crowd diminishes. The flags wave less enthusiastically. This is not what they were expecting.

The drone circles in closer to the vessel, being sure to keep a non-threatening distance between them.

Another minute goes by. Still no movement of the spacecraft.

The flags cease waving. The cheering dies out altogether. An uneasy silence falls over the crowd.

Watching the broadcast, President Crawford says, "Why did it stop?" She looks down the table at her science expert. "Doctor Larson? Your thoughts?"

Larson puts his fingertips together in a contemplative pose. "I think it would be premature, if not patently futile, for human beings to indulge in speculation on alien protocols and procedures for initiating first contact with another species."

"In other words, you don't have a clue."

"Precisely."

All cameras remain focused on the massive, immobile spacecraft as Peter says, "Uh, Clifford? Can you hear me?"

"Yes, Peter."

"Isn't this the part where an alien emerges and says, 'Take me to your leader'?"

"I don't know how to answer that. I'm sure the aliens have their own way of—Okay, hold on... It looks like something's happening with the spacecraft."

Something is beginning to flow out of one of the two giant spigots. It's a material that's neither solid nor liquid, but has properties of both. An iridescent and shimmering blue, it spills slowly from the sky. Rippling and billowing, it flashes every shade of blue imaginable.

"Are you watching this, Clifford?"

"We see it."

The two jaded reporters lapse into awed silence as they watch the otherworldly substance slide down the sky.

After a moment, Clifford says, "Could it be a means of transport? Like an elevator? Or an escalator? To bring the aliens down to the surface?"

"Beats me," Peter says. "Do the rocket scientists at JPL have any ideas?"

"Their silence is deafening. I think they're as mystified as we are."

Moving like liquid silk, the material continues to pour from the spaceship in a controlled descent. It slows as it nears the ground.

Peter says, "It's almost here, Clifford. Just seconds from reaching the Earth."

"Okay," Clifford says, "we're going back to the live feed from Tiananmen Square so we can be there when this... stuff—whatever it is—reaches the ground..."

The mood of the crowd in Tiananmen Square has shifted. The uneasiness has passed. There's more ooh-ing and ahh-ing at the rippling, scintillating blue column. It finally touches down on the cobblestones of the square 50 yards from the raised platform of the welcoming committee.

A minute goes by. Nothing else happens.

A restless buzz starts to build in the crowd.

President Chan senses the crowd's growing impatience. It's possible the aliens expect him to make the next move.

Another minute goes by. Still nothing. The crowd grows increasingly restive.

Chan decides to act.

He steps away from the podium and descends the stairs to the square, where he pauses to take in the enormity of the situation. It's not every day one is called upon to act as mankind's official greeter to beings from another planet.

Chan adjusts the knot in his tie. Smooths his hair back. Takes a deep, calming breath. Begins walking in dignified strides toward the blue column.

Whatever happens this day, no one will ever accuse the President of China of being a coward.

It's a different story for the camera crew as they nervously continue filming Chan while staying several feet behind him.

Peter's voice is tense as he says, "It looks like this is it, Clifford. The moment all humanity has been waiting for..."

Clifford responds in an awed whisper. "We're going to go silent now, and let this historic moment unfold without interruption..."

Chan comes to a halt a few feet from the diaphanous blue column. He stands calmly looking up at the spaceship hovering directly overhead three hundred feet above him.

Silence once again settles over the vast throng of people, a collective holding of breath for whatever's coming next.

Chan raises his arms up over his head, palms open. To anyone—or anything—watching, the gesture is unmistakably welcoming.

In a ringing voice, Chan says "On behalf of the People's Republic of China, I welcome you to our beautiful planet. On this glorious day, we look forward to beginning a long and mutually beneficial relationship with—"

That's when several things happen in rapid succession, all recorded by the camera crew:

The spacecraft above begins moving in a small circle. The undulating blue column moves with it as it hangs suspended from the giant faucet. A hatch fifty yards square slides open in the center of the vessel's underside. Directly in front of the hatch, what looks like a giant searchlight switches on, its beam trained on Chan. He's immediately drenched in a sickly, sepia-toned light. All of his clothing instantly dissolves. Every last bit—shoes, socks, suit, underwear, watch, eyeglasses—falls away from his body in wispy tatters, leaving him completely naked. There's not even time for shock or embarrassment to register on his face. Instead, his eyes close, his body goes limp and a smile appears on his lips, as if he's dreaming pleasant dreams. Before he can hit the ground, President Chan is encapsulated in a gelatinous blue material. As soon as that occurs, the blue-wrapped Chan accelerates swiftly up to the spacecraft where he disappears into the open hatch.

This all takes place in a matter of seconds.

Every one of the hundreds of thousands of people packed into Tiananmen Square stare up at the spacecraft in open-mouthed shock.

World-weary reporter Peter Ross who's seen everything says, "Holy shit!"

Conroy drops a half-eaten triangle of pizza back in its box. He rises from the bed and slowly approaches the television, his eyes suddenly dark.

"Oh, no..." he whispers.

Alarmed, Una goes and stands close to him. She gently places a hand on his shoulder. "Conroy? What is it?"

Conroy doesn't answer. Continues to stare at the TV as if in a trance.

Una watches him with growing concern. "Conroy?"

The spacecraft is close to completing the circle, the blue pillar keeping steady pace with it.

But now something else becomes apparent: As it moves, the pillar has been leaving something in its wake—a continuous, 300-foot tall, extremely thin sheet of translucent blue material. It shimmers in the sunlight.

When the spacecraft completes the circle, it comes to a momentary halt. When it starts moving again, four things happen: It veers out of the circular pattern into a spiral one; It also begins to ascend; The spigot reverses operation, reeling the blue pillar and the thin sheet of material back up into the ship; It then begins cascading out of the other spigot and down to the ground.

The three camera crew members stand motionless, staring up at the spaceship in shock. Having been so caught up in watching what happened to President Chan, they automatically recorded everything that transpired.

 Now they see the yellowish beam coming toward them. They drop their equipment and run for it.

They don't make it. As the beam catches up to them, they undergo the same transformation: Stripped. Encapsulated. Whisked into the sky like souls traveling to heaven.

The dropped camera continues to record for a few seconds. A sideways image of the square from ground level appears on all of the giant screens. As the beam sweeps over it, the camera dissolves into a lumpy pile of brown grit. The screens go dark, as do billions of television monitors around the world tuned to the Chinese feed. They're down for only a moment as somewhere a program director cuts over to the drone camera, which is focused on the raised platform.

The world gets a bird's-eye view of President Chan's entourage of high-ranking civilian and military personnel scrambling to get down the stairs and away from the platform before being cut off by the giant sheet.

They're too slow. Moments later, a couple of dozen blue balloons soar up to the spacecraft.

The line of presidential limousines is next to get caught in the yellow beam. Every one of the vehicles is quickly rendered down to a pile of grainy dust.

Meanwhile, the spacecraft continues to ascend into the sky while moving in an ever-widening spiral.

A thousand feet below, the beam passes over the drone. It immediately dissolves into a tiny cloud of dark sand and sprinkles to the ground.

The giant screens go black for good.

A half-million people all attempt to flee the square at the same time.

STONE FAMILY RESIDENCE

Zack, Jeffrey, Eric and Lydia huddle together on the couch, staring at the black screen of the television.

Lydia says, "What just happened?"

It's a scene simultaneously playing out billions of times around the world as confused and frightened families gather close, trying to make some kind of sense out of what they just witnessed.

For the sake of their sons, Eric and Lydia do their best to remain calm. Lydia looks at her husband, swallows and says, "What do you think we should do?"

Eric says, "I never thought I'd say this, but I sure hope the government steps in and—"

An image sputters to life on the television. Even though the Chinese feed from Tiananmen Square is gone, numerous other news organizations are still up and running, including BCS.

Peter Ross appears onscreen. He's being jostled by thousands of citizens bolting from the square. "Hey! Watch it!"

Clifford March has to shout to be heard over the commotion.

"Peter, can you hear me?!"

Peter presses on his earpiece. "Just barely."

"Are you all right?! What's happening?!"

In Beijing, Peter and his crew duck into a stone alcove where they're partially shielded from the fleeing crowd. Their camera continues to roll. It's focused tightly on Peter as hundreds of people sprint past.

"Are you watching this, Clifford?"

"We're watching."

"As crazy as this sounds, some kind of...levitation process—for lack of a better phrase—is gathering up thousands of people from Tiananmen Square. They're being systematically encased in something resembling blue pods or capsules, and then transported up to the ship."

Clifford is in disbelief. "Did I hear you right?"

"See for yourself." Peter points up at the sky. The camera follows, focusing on a steady stream of thousands of blue balloons rising up in a long spiraling line.

Clifford manages to utter, "Jesus..."

"But I have to say, Clifford, amazingly, it appears no one is being physically harmed. As people are enveloped by these bubbles or coverings or whatever they are, they immediately go into some kind of suspended animation. From the looks on their faces, it seems to be a pleasurable experience, not a painful one."

Conroy stands in front of the TV staring at it. Una sits very close beside him. She reaches out and takes his trembling hand.

Conroy speaks quietly. "God, Una, I had it totally backwards... The blue balloons weren't descending from the sky. They were *ascending up into it.* No doubt to another alien ship, so long ago. All those people..." He swallows hard and whispers, "This changes everything..."

In Beijing, Peter again presses on his earpiece as Clifford asks him, "What's the spaceship doing now?"

Peter looks up and squints as the camera focuses on the spacecraft. "You know those two giant spigots or faucets or whatever the hell they are on either side of the vessel?"

"Yes."

"They seem to be working in tandem now."

"What do you mean, 'in tandem'?"

"One spigot works as the outtake pipe, the other as the intake. As the spacecraft moves, the blue material is continuously spilling to the ground from one side of the vessel, while being simultaneously reeled back up on the other side. Meanwhile, the yellow beam dissolves everything in between except people, who are whisked up to the ship in blue balloons. It's the craziest thing I've ever seen."

"Did you say 'dissolve'?"

"I don't know how else to put it. Hold on, hold on..."

The camera pans back down to ground level. "Okay, can you see this?

Onscreen in the near distance, buildings dissolve one after the other. Simultaneously, their inhabitants are encased in balloon-like pods and levitated up to the spaceship.

The camera focuses back on Peter. "I'm watching it happen with my own eyes, Clifford, and I still can't believe it..."

A clattering hiss can be heard in the background, as if it's raining coarse sand.

"What's that noise?" says Clifford.

"It's the sound of buildings crumbling to the ground. It's getting louder, so you're going to have to speak—"

Peter's cameraman interrupts him. Urgent words are muffled. Peter looks to his right and his eyes go wide.

"Okay, the yellow beam is curving around. Looks like it's headed our way."

The camera points in the direction Peter's looking. Buildings dissolve at a relentless pace. Buried infrastructure isn't spared. Basements, subways, tunnels—all melt quickly away. The noise grows louder by the second, sounding now like a giant truck dumping a continuous load of pebbles.

The carnage is heading directly for them.

"Shit!" Peter yells. "We're right in its path! Run!"

The television image goes blurry as Peter and his crew make a mad dash for safety. Peter's breathless voice is heard. "This way! Hurry! Oh, God, this is gonna be close..."

His heavy panting is drowned out by the roar of what sounds like a waterfall of gravel hitting the ground.

Peter's terrified voice cuts through. "Look out! Here it comes! Get out of the way! Shit—!"

The noise drops rapidly away. The image on television suddenly becomes a static close-up of a curb, as if the camera has been dropped.

"Peter...?" says Clifford. "Peter, can you hear me?"

Silence.

"Peter! Are you there?!"

Several moments go by. Then the television image begins to move, as if someone is picking up the camera.

"Yes, Clifford, I'm here." Peter comes into focus. He stands on a wide boulevard. In the background are rows of apartment buildings. His jacket is torn and smeared with dirt. There's a scrape on his forehead. He taps the mic. "Can you hear me?"

"Yes." Clifford breathes a sigh of relief. "Yes, we can hear you just fine. Thank God, you're all right."

"Yeah, we're all just peachy keen here." Peter's voice is shaky. He's aware of it and brushes some of the dirt from his coat, trying to calm himself and regain his trademark jaded composure. He's successful for the most part.

"Talk about close calls. We missed getting hoovered up by inches. We had to literally dive out of the way."

"Can you describe what happened?"

Peter's world-weary persona is back. He flashes a cynical grin and says, "How about if I just show you..."

The camera follows Peter as he takes a couple of steps to his left. "Check it out."

The camera turns to see what Peter sees. What was once a neighborhood of crowded tenement buildings and perpetual traffic jams is now a barren landscape. All that's left are trees, grass and shrubbery. A few stone archways and patches of cobblestones remain, but even they look like they've been ground down with a giant file. The scene is made even more eerie by the fact that everything appears ever so slightly warped, as if being viewed through plastic sheeting.

"Jesus Christ..." exhales Clifford.

"Clifford, I'm standing here watching 5,000 years of Chinese culture, art and architecture crumble before my eyes like it never existed. How is that even possible? Entire city blocks—gone. Every resident transported away. You can see all the way over to what was the center of Tiananmen Square. But the only sign of life here now is a handful of dogs and cats wandering around in a daze. Animals that were peoples' pets just minutes ago. Now they're on their own."

Peter looks skyward and says, "As for the spaceship, it's climbed so far up I can't see it any more. There's just an endless line of blue bubbles spiraling upward until they blend in with the sky and disappear."

Clifford says, "This is just...incredible."

"It gets even more so. When you look at the devastation, do you notice how it doesn't quite come into focus? That everything seems slightly distorted?"

"I do notice," Clifford says. "Why is that?"

"It's the weirdest thing. When the yellow beam went by, the outtake spigot laid down some kind of barrier between the dissolved zone over there and everything on this side of it. It's mostly transparent, sort of like looking through a rain-streaked window."

Peter bends down and picks up a stone. He throws it at the barren landscape but the stone comes to an abrupt halt a couple of feet away as it hits the invisible barrier and slides to the ground.

"What in hell...?" Clifford says.

Peter steps forward and runs his hand over the filmy alien material.

"This stuff is obviously thin enough to see through. It's not rigid. It gives a little, but the more you press on it, the greater the resistance. Just for fun, I'm going to give it the old Peter Ross slice-o-matic test."

"Be careful, Peter."

That grin again. "Little late for that, dontcha think?"

Peter takes a pocketknife from his jacket and opens it. He slashes several times at the barrier but it remains intact. Then, in an attempt to puncture it, he pushes the point of the blade against the material, grunting with exertion as he does so. After a moment, he puts the knife back in his pocket and leans forward to inspect the result.

"Not even a scratch. Whatever this stuff is, it's really strong."

"But why a barrier?" Clifford says. "Why keep us away from an area that's been scraped clean?"

Peter shakes his head. "You got me, Clifford. I can't make any sense of what's happening here. On the one hand, I've never seen physical destruction so total as this. Beijing is being systematically atomized. On the other hand, I haven't seen anyone killed, or even injured. Even during the stampede from Tiananmen Square, no one got trampled. In fact, if anything, people are being treated with remarkable... *tenderness.* If the aliens are planning on doing us harm, I haven't seen any evidence of it.

"Obviously, we're being gathered up. But to what end? Maybe it's for our own good. They could be here to help us. Maybe they know something we don't, like the Earth's going to break apart, or the sun's going to go supernova, and they want to relocate us to someplace safe.

"I guess what I'm saying, Clifford, is; if this is an alien invasion, it's the most gentle one you could imagine."

From off camera comes a distant sound of massive quantities of coarse sand and pebbles raining down. Alarmed, Peter says, "I think it's coming back around."

"Speaking of relocation, Peter," Clifford says, "this might be a good time for you and your crew to get out of there."

"I think you're right," Peter says. "It looks like we need to beat feet again, only..."

"Only what?" Clifford says.

Peter squints as he describes what he sees. "The yellow beam has changed. It's moving faster and is much wider; the distance between the barrier next to me and the new one being deposited across the way has increased by a couple of hundred yards."

Peter looks into the camera. "There's no way we can outrun it this time."

"What are you saying?"

"It looks we're going to be taking a little trip."

Peter steps out of view of the camera. He can be heard talking to his crew.

"Peter?" Clifford says. "Are you there?"

Peter moves back in front of the camera. "I'm still here, Clifford. We've decided to keep the camera rolling until the last possible second, so that we can relay as much information to you as possible..." That smile again. "...before we're hoovered up."

The dry rattle of raining gravel dramatically increases.

"But—can't you take cover? Get down into a basement or something?"

"We've already seen that doesn't work." Peter turns and looks behind him at the oncoming whirlwind of dust and grit, which is now just a couple of hundred feet away. Trailing behind it, thousands of blue bubbles rise skyward. "It's coming fast." He glances back at the camera, speaks to his cameraman. "Are you getting this?"

The camera tilts up and focuses on buildings dissolving one after the other.

Peter can be heard shouting over the roaring hiss of the falling remnants. "It's almost on us, Clifford. It's been good working with you." Then, his voice breaking a little, "Betty, if you're watching this, I love you! Tell the children I love them and that I—"

The screen goes black.

The camera cuts back to Clifford in New York. Tears fill his eyes. It takes him a moment to speak. When he does, his voice quavers.

"Okay. Well, uh, obviously, we've lost contact with Beijing. I'm not sure what..."

The picture begins to waver and the sound fades in and out. Clifford speaks to somebody off camera. "Hey! What do you think you're doing?!"

A muffled voice responds.

Clifford says, "You can't do that!"

After a moment, he turns back to the camera and says, "Okay. Well. Apparently some of our technicians have abruptly decided to quit. They just went home. So if our signal starts to—"

Once again, the screen goes black.

President Crawford and everyone else in the Situation Room sit staring at the darkened screen with ashen faces. Vice President Jameson is the first to break the silence.

"What in the name of God just happened...?"

Crawford leans back and speaks to one of her aides sitting in a chair behind her. "Contact the Communications Office and find out if any of the other news organizations are still on the air. If so, tell them I plan to address the nation in ten minutes."

The aide hurries out the door.

General Walters, his face pale and twisted, barks, "Madam President, we've got to shoot the damned thing down now! Hit it with everything we've got, including nukes, before it can do any more harm!"

Visibly agitated, Otis Larson says, "President Crawford, if I may speak?"

Crawford nods. "Go ahead, Doctor Larson."

Larson turns to face General Walters, who's sitting across the table from him. "General Walters, with all due respect, what you're proposing would be nothing less than global suicide."

"Didn't you just see with your own eyes that we're under attack?!"

"But are we? Like the reporter said, no one appears to have been injured or killed. All we know for sure is that human beings are being transported up to their ship, and very gently at that. Technically, I'm not sure that qualifies as an attack."

Says Crawford, "What would you suggest we do, Doctor?"

"Before we go blundering into a self-inflicted holocaust, we need more information. And I know just the person who can give it to us."

"And who might that be?"

"A paleoanthropologist named Conroy Hamilton."

Walters makes a face. "A paleo-what-ogist?"

"I watched him give a presentation in New York. He seemed to know quite a lot about these blue bubbles. He might have some insights on how to proceed."

"Yeah, that's a great idea. Let's bring in another egghead and have some meetings on 'how to proceed'. Meanwhile, the population of Beijing is being annihilated."

Exasperated, Larson says, "We just went over that. They're not being—"

"Madam President!" cries General Walters, jumping to his feet. "How many more people have to disappear up into that spaceship before we start defending ourselves?!"

Larson jumps to his own feet. "But we still don't know what their intentions are! And it's insanity to risk Armageddon until we've made a serious effort to do just that!"

The aide returns and makes a beeline for the president. He whispers in her ear, "Ma'am," he says, "several networks are still online. And BCS is expected to return to the air shortly. But there's also this." He hands her a note.

Crawford scans the document and frowns.

Meanwhile, the general and the scientist continue to argue. "You're a fool, Doctor! Every second we waste sitting around trying to study a hostile vessel while it—!"

"And you're crazy if you keep insisting we—!"

"Both of you—shut up!"

Both men are shocked into silence. Everyone at the table stares at the president. No one has ever seen her really angry before. She holds up the document.

"Word's coming in from around the country that people are panicking. There are reports of rioting in several major cities."

She lets that sink in, then says to Larson and Walters, "I've heard you both out. Here's what I've decided: I agree with Doctor Larson. To our knowledge so far, no one's been killed or injured. If we attack an advanced race of beings with deadly force, the chances are enormous that we would make a bad situation exponentially worse. So there will be no attack from us at this time. I also agree with him in that we need more information. We need to try to find out what they're doing and why they're doing it. We've been flying blind. That has to change. "

President Crawford directs her attention to Larson. "Doctor Larson, I want you to find this scientist you spoke of, and find him fast. Every resource we have will be at your disposal. Let's hope he knows something that could be useful to us.

"I also want to learn as much as we can about this...dissolving process. How does it work? Can it be stopped? Slowed? Maybe even reversed somehow? Gather the best people you can, put your heads together and get me some answers. Understood?"

"Yes, Madam President," Larson says.

Crawford turns her attention to Walters. "General Walters, as soon as the JPL is able to plot an accurate path of the alien craft, I want our most sophisticated military reconnaissance satellite to do a flyby of it. Let's try to get a look at what's going on inside that vessel. In the meantime, I want you to keep a full barrage of nuclear missiles targeted on it. If things go south, I want to be able to launch at a moment's notice. Understood?"

"Yes, Madam President," Walters says.

President Crawford turns her attention to everyone else in the room. "I'm going to address the nation in a couple of minutes and try to calm a frightened country. But before I do, I want to say that we're facing a threat unlike anything we've ever experienced. So I'm asking all of you here to think, people. Use your brains like never before. I want you to think not just outside the box; I want you to transcend the box. Or become one with the box. Or become the unbox. Whatever it takes. Because I think it's very possible that the survival of the human race may depend on how well we use our God-given intelligence."

The flat-screen on the wall sputters back to life. All eyes turn to Clifford March. He's regained some of his composure.

Clifford asks someone off-camera, "Are we back on? Okay, good." He turns to face the camera, a stern look on his face. "I just wanted to say that we're back on the air thanks to a skeleton crew that's remained on the job. We have new footage from drones taken moments ago from outside the city limits of Beijing. This is what it reveals..."

Onscreen, where large numbers of modern high-rises were standing less than an hour ago, there are now rolling mounds of gritty sand.

"As you can see," Clifford says, "the city has virtually disappeared. But, oddly, if you look closely, you can see that the greenbelt areas are untouched."

The camera zooms in on parks and trees and grass, all unscathed.

"That large rectangle of green you see in the middle of the devastation is the Beijing Zoo. All of the lush landscaping remains intact, but the cages and pens holding the animals have disappeared. Hundreds of animals are roaming free."

The aide sitting behind President Crawford receives a text. He reads it, leans forward and says quietly, "Madam President, they're ready for you."

Crawford gets to her feet and goes out the door, a couple of aides in tow.

The image on the monitor has switched back to Clifford.

"In the meantime," he says, "we've been in contact with the Jet Propulsion Laboratory. It hasn't been able to pinpoint the new course of the spacecraft because its flight path keeps changing. They'll let us know as soon as it's stabilized, but that it could take time, anywhere from a few hours to a few days."

Clifford goes quiet, presses on his earpiece, looks up and says, "I've just received word that President Crawford is going to address the nation..."

STONE FAMILY RESIDENCE

At the Stone residence, the family hasn't budged from the couch as they watch the same broadcast.

Zack asks his parents, "Why are all those people being sent up to the spaceship?"

Eric is shaken at what he's just seen, but does his best to sound reassuring. "That's what they're trying to figure out."

"Do you think it'll happen to us?"

Eric shakes his head no. "I don't think so. They're all the way over on the other side of the world."

Jeffrey says, "All the animals are going free."

Lydia is also doing her best to maintain a calm façade. "It sure looks that way, honey."

"That's a good thing, right?"

Lydia smiles at her sensitive younger son. "I don't see how it couldn't be."

On television, Clifford says, "...We're going live now to the White House."

The image switches to President Crawford sitting at her desk in the Oval Office. Her hands are folded in front of her. She looks calm and composed. Her eyes are clear and serious.

"My fellow Americans," she says, her voice solid and un-wavering. "As most of you know by now, large numbers of Chinese citizens are being transported up to the alien craft. We don't know *how* the aliens are doing it. We don't know *why* they're doing it. But what we *do* know is that, thus far, *no human beings have been harmed*. Therefore, at this time, we don't consider this to be an overt act of hostility. Indeed, it's been suggested that maybe a calamity is about to befall the Earth and they're moving us out of harm's way. For the moment, we have no way of knowing if that's the case. Meanwhile, we're continuing to watch the situation in China very closely. Obviously the aliens are highly intelli-gent beings. We're hoping that means they're also compas-sionate ones."

A glint of steel enters her eyes and her voice hardens.

"But make no mistake: If, at any time, we obtain irrefut-able proof that our fellow human beings are being harmed in any way, I will order an immediate and devastating at-tack upon the spacecraft. We will use any and every means available, including nuclear weapons, to bring it down. I pray it won't come to that, but we're prepared if it does."

Eric and Lydia glance at each other, a spark of fear in their eyes.

"I'm not going to sugarcoat things," the president continues. "The human race has entered uncharted waters. We're going to take this as it comes, one step at a time. As the situation evolves, we'll respond accordingly. And please know that, whatever happens, we'll do our very best to keep you informed.

"In closing, I urge the American people not to panic. Rest assured that, as I speak, we have the best and brightest minds from every field of knowledge working on this around the clock. We'll get through this together.

"I implore you to remain calm and to be strong through these trying times. May God bless the United States of America, and may God bless our world and keep all her people safe."

The screen goes fuzzy as the station attempts to reconnect with Clifford in New York.

Jeffrey looks at his parents with wide eyes. "Are we all going to die?"

Alarmed, Lydia looks back at him and says, "Jeffrey, don't even think that!"

Eric stares at his son with all the sincerity he can muster and says, "No, Jeffrey, we're all not going to die."

He can feel his wife watching him. He briefly meets her eyes then looks away.

On the night of the President's speech, I have to admit Jeffrey and I were pretty scared.

Though they tried not to show it, our parents were scared, too.

For that matter, the whole world was scared.

That night, we crawled into bed with mom and dad. We all huddled together until we finally went to sleep.

Early the next morning, a knock at the door woke us up. Which was weird. Who would be going around knocking on doors when an alien invasion was underway?

My dad wasn't going to answer it. He whispered for us to just stay put until whoever was there went away.

But they didn't go away. They kept knocking and ringing the doorbell.

Then we heard a voice cry out.

Another piece of the puzzle was about to fall into place...

{The Zachary Stone Chronicles}

"Hello? Mr. Stone? I'm looking for Eric Stone. It's very important that I speak with you. It'll just take a minute of your time. The welfare of your family could be at stake."

This gets Eric's attention. He gets up and goes to open the door. He's greeted by a tall, muscular man in his 30s wearing a crew cut and a dark suit and tie.

Eric eyes the man warily. In a voice that's not exactly rude but not quite polite, he says, "I'm Eric Stone. What do you want? And what's this about my family?"

The man nods toward a limousine parked at the curb.

"My employer would like to have a word with you."

"And who might that—?"

But Crew Cut has already turned and is walking toward the limo.

Eric watches him for a moment as he considers going back into the house and shutting the door. But a stranger can't say something like the 'welfare of your family could be at stake' and then just walk away unchallenged.

He follows the man to the vehicle where Crew Cut opens the door and stands holding it open for him. Eric hesitates.

A mild voice comes from inside. "Please get in, Mr. Stone. Every minute counts."

Eric slides onto the plush leather seat. Crew Cut shuts the door. Eric turns and finds himself staring at a familiar face. Not someone he knows personally, but from television news stories, articles in newspapers, profiles in magazines over many years.

"Do you know who I am?" the man says.

"You're Kent Hatcher. One of the richest people in the world."

Hatcher's smile is surprisingly warm. "Correction. *Formerly* one of the richest people in the world. The global economy is in freefall, of course. The arrival of visitors from another planet will tend to do that. But I'm glad you're aware of who I am so we won't have to waste time verifying my credibility."

Eric quickly goes over in his mind what he knows about the diminutive man with the glasses and the boyish face:

—One of the highest IQs ever recorded.

—Founder of Hatcher Technologies, a giant business software company whose products are sold around the world. Rumors would occasionally surface that—to protect HT's stock price—Hatcher had embedded highly-sophisticated code into his systems that gave him a private backdoor into numerous computer mainframes. Supposedly, this phantom code served as a built-in early warning system in which he would automatically be alerted to any event that adversely impacted the world's financial markets.

—Widowed at the age of 35 when his beloved wife died of cancer. No children.

—The latest rumor to surface about Kent Hatcher was that he and a team of experts were building a super computer that would leave all other calculating machines in its dust.

Still. For all the man's achievements, what Crew Cut said to lure Eric out of the house was uncalled for.

There's a slight edge to Eric's voice as he says, "What's this about my family?"

"It wasn't intended as a threat, Eric. Just the opposite, in fact. But I've learned people sometimes respond better to a carrot when it's disguised as a stick."

"What do you want?"

"I'm here to offer you a job."

The last thing Eric expected to hear. "A job," he repeats.

"Pretty crazy, huh? The world could end at any moment and I'm out on a recruiting mission."

"What kind of job?"

"I need someone to oversee the construction of an underground bunker. You're one of the best in the world at doing just that."

Eric quickly puts it together. "If you're thinking about burrowing underground to escape the aliens, it's been made pretty clear that it won't work."

"Has it, though? I've got people working on it. They say they've found a way to defeat their collection and dissolution beams. But we'll have to go deep. That's where you come in. Interested?"

Eric thinks a moment, then, "Yes. I'm interested. But first I want to know what—"

"I know you have a lot of questions," interrupts Hatcher. "Everyone does. Unfortunately, we don't have a lot of time to discuss things. We need to work fast to get the shaft and bunker built to the proper specifications. Plus I'm short-handed on the people I need to pull this off. Which is why I'm personally going around trying to hire folks like you so you'll know that I'm serious. So I hope you don't mind if I just cut to the chase."

"I'm listening," Eric says.

Hatcher speaks quickly and clearly, as if he's given this talk more than once. "How would I pay you? Cash is useless. Gold and diamonds soon will be. So what's left? How about this: A safe haven for you and your family in the bunker when the spacecraft passes overhead."

"*When* it passes overhead? Not 'if'?"

"My team was able to determine its flight path. We're ahead of the curve on that. It's not easy to beat JPL to the punch. The spacecraft is moving in a pattern that will eventually allow its beam to travel over every square inch of the Earth."

"So? When it gets close, we'll just move out of the way. Those people in Beijing didn't have any warning. Everyone else does."

Hatcher frowns and looks into Eric's eyes. There's an ominous tone in the mild-mannered genius's voice when he says, "I'm afraid it's not that simple."

Eric feels a chill go through his body. His every instinct is telling him to do this man's bidding.

With his eyes locked on Hatcher's, he nods and says, "Okay. I'm game. But I'll need to talk it over with my wife."

"Of course." Hatcher looks at his watch. "I'll give you five minutes."

"Five minutes?"

"Time is of the essence. In fact, construction's already begun. My jet's fueled and ready to go. I'll fill you and your wife in on the drive to the airport. And if for any reason you decide not to come, I'll let you off. But you'll have to make your own way back home."

"Understood." Eric opens the door and starts to get out, but then stops and says, "You say you've got a jet waiting. Where is this construction site, anyway?"

"Ever been to Argentina?"

Eric raises his eyebrows in puzzled response but doesn't say anything. He heads back to the house where Lydia and the boys are watching him from the doorway.

KENNEDY INTERNATIONAL AIRPORT

Pandemonium reigns. Uncertainty about what's happening has everyone on edge. People are either trying to get home to be with family, or they've decided to flee to some remote location they're convinced will be a safe haven. Many flights are delayed or cancelled, only adding to the stress.

After waiting in line for what seems like forever, Conroy and Una step up to the ticket counter for their non-stop flight from New York to Rio de Janeiro. Conroy is relieved to see that it's on time.

When the ticket agent runs Conroy's passport through the scanner, he glances quickly up at him, then looks over at two men in suits standing off to the side and nods.

Conroy says to the ticket agent, "Is there a problem?"

A voice from behind. "Conroy Hamilton?"

Conroy turns around to see the two men standing before him. Both are tall and muscular. One of them has a shaved head.

"Yes?" Conroy says.

Shaved Head shows a badge. "United States Secret Service. Would you come with us, please?" A command, not a request.

"What's this about?"

"Some people would like to ask you a few questions."

"What people?"

"You'll see soon enough."

"Am I under arrest?"

"No, you're not under arrest."

"What if I refuse?"

"Then you *will* be under arrest."

"But we haven't broken any laws. We're just trying to get home."

"I'm sorry, sir, but it's a matter of national security."

"What about my wife?"

"She's authorized to come with us if she wants."

"Of course I want," says Una, her dark eyes flashing angrily.

"Come this way, please."

The ticket agent steps away from the counter and uses his security pass to open a door.   The two Secret Servicemen escort Conroy and Una down a flight of stairs and through another door that leads out onto the tarmac where a small government jet waits.

"Wait a minute. We're getting on another flight?"

"Correct."

"Where are we going?"

"I'm not at liberty to say. But it's definitely not Rio."

This gets a grin from the other agent.

Crew Cut is at the wheel of the limousine as it cruises down a Los Angeles highway. The sprawling metropolis is usually choked with cars. But today, traffic is eerily sparse.

The four members of the Stone family watch Kent Hatcher warily. There's that disarming smile again. "You're probably wondering, 'Of all places, why Argentina?'"

"It crossed my mind," Eric says.

"It'll become clear in a moment. But first, I should give you some background."

Hatcher settles into the plush leather seat. "One of the reasons I've been successful in life is by trusting my own instincts. When the Probe first showed up, I had a really bad feeling about it. A lot of other people did, too, but not for the reason I did."

Zack says, "Why did it give you a bad feeling?"

"The fact that the probe went about its business without giving any indication as to whether it was friendly or hostile. It was totally indifferent to us, like we weren't even here. I thought, why come all this way and not initiate contact of some kind? I mean, we are the dominant species on the planet, right? But then, the more I thought about it, the more I became convinced that the aliens definitely knew we were here but, for some reason, weren't trying to communicate with us. That bothered me.

"Another reason I've been successful is that I hire only the best and brightest people. If JPL is Edison, my team is Einstein. I ran my misgivings by them. They all agreed it was odd, if not downright suspicious. So rather than take a 'wait and see' attitude like the rest of the world, we decided to be get proactive.

"I've always tried very hard to be as prepared as possible for worst case scenarios. Once the variables are known, I move fast.

"During the last couple of years, my team built the most powerful super-computer in the world. We're light years ahead of the machines at JPL."

"What's a super-computer?" Jeffrey asks.

"It can do a million trillion mathematical instructions a second."

"Oh," Jeffrey says, as if that cleared that up. Eric and Lydia exchange a brief smile.

"Anyway, when the Probe first arrived, we ran hundreds of simulations about what it was up to, while continuing to refine new data as it came in.

"The results were mixed. The computers didn't quite know what to make of the Probe. But then suddenly the spaceship arrives and starts vacuuming up humans.

"That changed everything.

"Because, for one thing, it confirmed that the aliens absolutely do know we're here. And yet they're still not bothering to try and talk to us. I didn't take that as a good sign. Neither did the computers. They concluded that we should do everything in our power to avoid getting transported up to that ship. They didn't—or couldn't—specify why. Just that something was really wrong with this whole equation.

"So we went to work to try and find a way to defeat their collection process. My people are convinced they found it. It includes building this bunker. I'll fill you and the others in on the details on the way to Argentina. If you decide to come, that is."

Zack is impatient. "You didn't answer your own question: Why Argentina?"

Lydia says, "Zachary. Mind your manners."

"That's okay, Ms. Stone." He turns to Zack. "I'm getting to that. What it comes down to is making sure we have the time to build the bunker. Obviously, it wouldn't make sense to get halfway through construction just to have that spaceship come zooming overhead and hoovering everyone up. We needed to pick a site where we would have the maximum amount of time to build it. So the logical next step was to determine two things: where the ship would eventually end up, and how long would it take to get there.

"We put the computers back to work. We entered every bit of data we could on the vessel's movements. The craft only recently settled into a pattern steady enough that we could plot its course. According to our calculations, taking into account all variables and extrapolations, in exactly fourteen days, it will end up in Argentina."

Says Zack, "That just seems weird."

"We thought so, too. But it turns out there's a good reason for it—at least from the aliens' point of view."

Hatcher shifts gears. Suddenly becomes more serious. "I'm going to tell you something. About what we learned. It's...disturbing. I don't mean to frighten you, but it's just a matter of time before JPL arrives at the same conclusion, and then it will be common knowledge. You four will just happen to be in the know a little sooner."

Hatcher flips open a storage area under the seat and takes out a small globe of the world.

"Rather than try and explain it, I've found that it's easier to show people."

He places his fingertip on the globe.

"Here's Beijing..."

The Stone family leans forward as one to watch...

THE WHITE HOUSE

Otis Larson and several other cabinet members monitor network and cable news outlets. Clifford March of BCS seems to have breaking news. Otis turns up the volume.

"...We're going now to Doctor Seifert at the Jet Propulsion Laboratory. Doctor?"

"Thanks, Clifford."

Seifert is looking haggard, having been dealing non-stop with the crisis. "One of the key questions we've been scratching our heads about is: Where are all those people going? The spacecraft is fairly large, but it's nowhere near big enough to contain all the humans being funneled into it. Well, that question has been answered..."

The image switches to that of the space ship.

"This was taken moments ago by one of our most powerful Earth-based telescopes. As you can see, the vessel is undergoing a change..."

The craft can be seen with good clarity. What's different about it is a large, sac-like growth protruding from the rear of the vessel.

It wasn't there before.

"If we do a time-lapse video, you can see this new addition begin to grow."

The video plays. The blimp-sized sac slowly swells like a balloon being filled with water.

"This is where we think people are being held in a state of suspended animation. It seems to be made out of the same super-material as the barrier. It brings to mind one of those rubber water storage bladders used by the military. Only the scale of this one is off the charts. At its present rate of expansion, it won't be long before the bladder is many times larger than the spacecraft..."

Hatcher's limousine pulls into one of several private airports that are scattered around the Los Angeles area. Things are calmer at these lightly-used hubs. Just a few craft coming and going. The limo continues across the tarmac and stops next to an idling Boeing 737. The jet is devoid of any markings.

"Okay, we're here," says Hatcher. He looks from face to face. "Decision time. You've heard my spiel. What's it going to be?"

Lydia, Zack and Jeffrey all look at Eric. They each give him a solemn nod.

"We're in," Eric says.

Hatcher smiles. "I'm glad. Welcome aboard."

Crew Cut opens the door. They all pile out of the limo and climb a set of metal stairs to the jet. An attendant stands waiting at the open hatch.

Hatcher slips into the cockpit. When the Stone family boards the plane, they're surprised to see most of the seats are taken. Then Eric hears familiar voices cry out.

"Hey! It's Eric Stone!"

"Hi, Eric!"

"We thought you'd get invited along on this gig."

Eric hasn't smiled in days. He does so now as he recognizes several coworkers. There are even a few rivals from other companies, which doesn't bother him in the least. "Aaron. Jason. Max. Charlotte. It's good to see you all!"

Most of the workers are accompanied by their families, which explains why the plane's so full.

The jet is already taxiing toward the runway. The pilot wastes no time. His voice comes over the speakers, "Prepare for takeoff."

As soon as the plane makes the turn onto the main runway, the pilot engages maximum thrust. The engines scream. The jet is airborne in seconds.

I remember looking out the window of the jet and watching the land fall away.

The only home I'd ever known soon became a distant blur. I had no idea if I would ever see it again. I looked at my parents. My mom was crying but trying not to show it. Jeffrey was asleep in her lap. My dad just sat quietly beside her, holding her hand.

We had no idea what the future held, but I remember getting the distinct sense that the people onboard were ready to do whatever it took to get us through that trying time...

{The Zachary Stone Chronicles}

The main entrance gate to The White House slides open. A black SUV turns in. The gate closes immediately behind it.

Shaved Head and the other Secret Service agent sit in the front of the vehicle. Conroy and Una are in the back, where they exchange a nervous look.

Says Conroy, "What are we doing at the White House?"

The agents remain silent. Stare straight ahead. The SUV follows a short road to the side of the building and disappears down a ramp. Deep in the bowels of the structure, the SUV comes to a halt. The two agents get out and open the back doors. Conroy and Una hesitantly emerge. Several heavily-armed Marines in combat fatigues eye them warily.

The agents begin walking quickly down a wide, tall hallway made of reinforced concrete. One of them calls back, "I'd advise you to stay with us. You wouldn't want to get lost down here."

Conroy and Una scurry to catch up.

Moments later, the four turn down a short, windowless corridor.

"Look," Conroy says. "I may be an expatriate, but I'm still an American citizen and I know my rights. You can't just..."

The agents come to a halt in front of a solid metal door guarded by two more Marines. One of them checks the credentials of the agents, then looks at a clipboard. He nods to the other Marine, who pulls open the door. The two agents remain at the entrance. Shaved Head smiles with sudden warmth and gestures for them to proceed in without them. As Conroy and Una walk past him, he whispers, "Good luck to you."

From inside the room comes the voice of President Crawford. "Professor Hamilton. We've been expecting you."

Conroy and Una come to an abrupt stop and exchange a look of disbelief.

The Marine closes the door.

According to The Record, Conroy Hamilton was happy to try and help President Crawford and her team get to the bottom of the mystery of the blue balloons. He was as curious as anyone about what it all meant.

Otis Larson wasted no time. Within hours of his arrival at The White House, Conroy found himself sitting in on brainstorming sessions with some of the top minds in the world. Most of these sessions were done by video-conferencing.

One was held with a group of British scientists who had come up with a unique

Otis, Conroy and a handful of assistants sit at a conference table facing a wall of blank flat-screen monitors. One of them comes to life with the image of a man with large teeth and wooly sideburns.

Larson shuffles through a stack of papers in front of him. "...Next up, we have Professor Arnold Dutton of Oxford University."

Larson is businesslike and to the point. He looks at the monitor and says, "Professor Dutton, what have you got for us?"

Dutton speaks with a strong English accent. "I and my colleagues have developed a theory on how the dissolution process works."

Larson glances back down at his papers. "And your specialty is..."

"Micology."

Larson stops what he's doing and looks up. "Micology," he says, his voice flat.

"Quite. It's the study of—"

"I know what it's the study of, Professor." Larson's normally upbeat personality is starting to fray. "Mushrooms and fungi. My question is; how in the world does that relate to the alien dissolving process?"

"Because that's precisely what fungus does; it dissolves things. My team and I think they're using a strain known as Saprophytic Fungi. It degrades any compound and disassembles any molecules that aren't naturally combined in nature—which would mean just about everything produced by the hands of man. What's so impressive about this particular strain is that it appears to have been genetically engineered to the nth power, so that it acts like a super fungus. As we've seen, it renders everything down to its most basic components at lightning speed. Everything else that's still in a naturally-occurring state, such as trees, grasses, plants, remains intact. It's quite a marvel, really."

"Yeah, it's a marvel, all right. Professor, correct me if I'm wrong, but wouldn't such a fungus have to be specifically... attuned to the Earth's unique flora and fauna?"

"Oh, without question."

"So...if that's the case, wouldn't this fungus have to have originated on Earth?"

"I can't imagine how it could possibly be otherwise."

"Which would mean...the aliens have paid a visit to our planet on an earlier occasion. Possibly much earlier..."

Larson and Conroy shoot each other knowing looks.

"I suppose I would have to assume that be to the case," says Professor Dutton. "But I'm afraid the field of space travel is quite out of my realm of expertise."

"Do you and your team have any ideas on how to neutralize this super fungus?"

"Unfortunately, Doctor Larson, we haven't a bloody clue."

And that was where Hatcher's team had the advantage. They'd been studying the dissolution beam with all the analytical power of their super computer. They couldn't figure out how to actually neutralize it, but they were confident they'd come up with a way to at least dilute its effectiveness.

Meanwhile, after we'd been in the air for what seemed like most of the day,

Hatcher stands in the middle of the aisle and picks up the intercom microphone.

"May I have your attention, please."

Most of the passengers were sleeping, or trying to. Everyone now comes fully awake.

"We're close to beginning our descent to Argentina. I thought I would take this time to fill you in on some of the details about what it is we'll be doing there. Then, if you have any questions, I'll do my best to answer them.

"We've been able to pinpoint where the spacecraft is predicted to complete its collection process. It's a small city on the Pacific coast called Bahia Blanca. The jobsite is located in the desert about fifty miles from there.

"I picked this location for two reasons. One: we need to be reasonably close to the spacecraft's termination point so that we'll have the maximum amount of time to finish the job. And two: it's far enough out in the country to not raise suspicions. As for cutting through the red tape, I happen to be on good terms with some highly-placed officials in the Argentinian government. In return for the use of the land, I reserved space for them and their families in the bunker."

Hatcher leans against a seat and continues.

"Personally, I don't care for the prospect of getting sucked up by an alien spaceship without my consent. I don't think anyone does. In fact, I find it pretty damned infuriating. So I put my people to work to try and find a way to stop it, or to at least disrupt the process enough so that when the dissolution beam arrives, we'll be able to 'slip under the radar'.

"We've all seen the footage of people deep underground apparently getting extracted just as easily as if they were standing in plain view on the surface. From that, we concluded that no matter how far below ground you are, you're still going to get transported up to that space ship.

"Emphasis on the word 'apparently'. Because we had an accurate map of the ship's path early, we were able to run some experiments. We placed different kinds of materials directly in the path of the beam to see if everything dissolves at the same rate. They don't. The differences are very small, but steel dissolves just a little bit slower than Styrofoam.

"Therefore, if different materials are stacked in layers atop one other, the dissolution process slows down ever so slightly. Apparently, the beam has to recalibrate itself for each kind of substance. It's just a tiny fraction of a second, but it's there.

"In conjunction with that, careful observation of the aliens' collection process has demonstrated that their craft doesn't linger over an area. It zaps it with its dissolution beam and moves on.

"So. Armed with those two tiny but critical pieces of information, our calculations show that if enough varied material is piled overhead, the rate of dissolution will slow down just enough so that whatever is beneath it will ride out the passing over of the dissolution beam without being affected.

"In Argentina we've dug a pit hundreds of feet deep. In this next phase, we'll construct the bunker. It will be just big enough to accommodate everyone working on this project, plus their immediate families. It will also be stocked with enough food, water and bottled oxygen to wait out the passing over of the dissolution beam. It will also contain generators, computers, medicine, chemicals, blueprints, machinery—in short, much of what we need to begin the task of rebuilding the world. It's going to be a tight fit. Pretty much every cubic inch of bunker space has been accounted for, but I know we can pull this off.

"As soon as the bunker is built, we'll start layering dozens of different types of material over it, all the way up to the surface. There'll be a mine shaft for ferrying people and equipment to and from the bunker.

"Because we have only fourteen days to complete this project, everyone will have to work as if their life depends on it—because it probably does.

"As the time for the passing over nears, everyone will head down to the bunker. Once we're all safely inside, the entry will be sealed. On the surface, three small robotic front-end loaders, each about the size of a Volkswagen bug, will then backfill the shaft with more of the varied material. They'll be programmed to do this crucial task quickly and efficiently. Once that's done, we wait for the arrival of the dissolution beam. It will be moving fast and will pass over in a matter of seconds.

"Shortly thereafter, the vessel will wrap up its collection process in Bahia Blanca. Once that's done, we expect that it'll head back to wherever it came from.

"As soon as we open the bunker doors, excavating machines positioned at the front will immediately start digging us out. We'll follow them back up to the surface and get to work rebuilding the world."

These last words send a shiver of excitement through the planeload of scientists and engineers. They break into spontaneous applause. When it dies down, a frown appears on Hatcher's face.

"One last thing," he says with deep seriousness. "It's just a matter of time before the rest of the world becomes aware of the magnitude of what's happening. And when they do, when they learn that Argentina—and Bahia Blanca in particular—is the last safe haven on the Earth, thousands of desperate people are going to make their way down here any way they can. They'll be holding onto the tiniest shred of hope that a last-minute miracle will occur.

"And—who knows? Maybe that will happen. Maybe some eleventh-hour reprieve will take place. Scientists working elsewhere in the world might come up with a way to defeat the aliens. Or the spacecraft could suffer a breakdown and they have to abort their mission. Or they might decide they've collected enough of us and go their merry way.

"I certainly hope something like that happens. But I'm not counting on it. I'm a realist, and I've got to work with what I've got.

"But my greatest concern is not about the aliens. I'm worried that if word gets out about what we in particular are doing in Argentina, things will get very ugly very fast. We'll be overrun by panic-stricken people. And they'll probably be armed.

"And so for that reason, it's absolutely imperative that every one of us keeps this project a secret. That means no contact with anyone outside the jobsite. Our survival—and the survival of our very species—depends on it."

Except for the drone of the engines, it's deathly quiet in the cabin. Then the pilot's voice comes on over the speaker. "Mr. Hatcher, we're beginning our descent. Please prepare for landing."

"So," Hatcher says. "That's our plan. Any questions?"

A voice from the back of the plane. "How soon can we get to work?"

Hatcher smiles. "The second we're on the ground."

AGRA, INDIA

DAWN

On the banks of the Yamuna River, the Taj Mahal glows an ethereal pink as it greets the rising sun. The city of two million is unusually quiet. Information on the precise movements of the spaceship is still incomplete, but there are rumors that it's on a course that will bring it close to Agra. No one knows quite what to do. Should they stay put? Should they run? And if they do run, in which direction lies safety?

No use worrying about that now.

Because the rumors are wrong.

The spaceship is not just going to come 'close to Agra'.

In moments, it will pass directly overhead.

Early risers see it coming high over the horizon. It appears as a tiny glistening nugget of bronze metal. The shimmery blue sac trails behind it. The sight is completely unhinging.

People point and shout, sounding the alarm. Hundreds, then thousands of residents pour from their homes still in their bedclothes. Shading their eyes with trembling hands, they peer up at the vessel bearing down on them. There are cries of fear as they watch the edge of the translucent barrier spool with seamless precision up to the intake spout while feeding simultaneously back down to the Earth from the outtake spigot.

Anyone and anything caught between the two barriers will be hit with the yellowish dissolution beam.

The spacecraft continues its collection process with machine-like efficiency. When it passes over the most heavily populated section of the city, a gritty hiss fills the air as structures begin dissolving by the hundreds.

The Taj Mahal, the centuries-old monument to undying love, so painstakingly crafted from the finest ivory-white marble, melts away in seconds, collapsing into shapeless mounds of gray rubble.

That's when the panic hits. The people amassed in the streets run in mindless fear.

But there's nowhere to go. No place to hide. Every second, tens of thousands of blue bubbles soar skyward from the crumbling city, automatically merging into a fast-flowing cerulean river headed up to the alien vessel.

It's over with shocking swiftness. As the dust and grit settles, all that's left are a few dozen bewildered-looking cows wandering among the ruins.

Mr. Hatcher wasn't kidding when he said we'd get to work 'the second we're on the ground'.

Right after landing on the brand new airstrip, everyone was assigned a job—and I mean everyone. I was put to work driving a golf cart ferrying ice water, coffee, and power bars to anyone who needed them—which kept me totally busy. Mom and Jeffrey went to work in the kitchen. Mom was a really good cook and helped with food preparation. Jeffrey was one of several kids whose job was carting trays of dirty dishes from the meal hall back to the industrial-sized dishwasher, then ferrying clean dishes to the kitchen.

Dad, of course, helped Mr. Hatcher oversee the building of the bunker.

People alternated 12-hour shifts, so the place never stopped bustling. Jets landed around the clock bringing in food, water, building supplies, and construction equipment.

Meanwhile, the spaceship continued its systematic circumnavigation of the Earth...

{The Zachary Stone Chronicles}

ISTANBUL, TURKEY

It's a hot, windless day in the ancient city that connects Europe and Asia. Amplified by loudspeakers, the cries of dozens of Mullahs ring out, calling the faithful to prayer. Every one of the hundreds of mosques in the sprawling metropolis is packed to overflowing with Muslim worshipers.

A flash of movement high in the blue sky.

...A far off hissing—the sound of distant buildings crumbling.

The spaceship is suddenly overhead.

The dissolution beam has arrived.

In seconds, Topkapi Palace melts away; the Grand Bazaar collapses with a gravelly rustle; the massive Hagia Sophia Mosque disintegrates into a colorful mix of dust and pebbles.

One by one, the Mullahs are silenced as the sky is darkened by millions of blue bubbles.

There was a communications center at the jobsite that scanned the airwaves for information. We'd been there just a couple of days when word spread that the Jet Propulsion Laboratory had some important announcements to make. Our technicians patched the satellite feed in to television monitors scattered around the grounds. I happened to be in the meal hall at the time. Mr. Hatcher and my Dad were sitting close by. The news was broadcast over BCS, which was still up and running...

{The Zachary Stone Chronicles}

ARGENTINA BUNKER JOBSITE

Zack sits in a folding chair staring at the monitor. His dad and Kent Hatcher sit close by watching the same broadcast with intense interest. A couple of dozen engineers are also present.

Clifford March speaks into the camera. "...As we go live now to Doctor Seifert for what he says are some very important updates. Doctor?"

The camera switches to Doctor Seifert sitting at his desk. "Thank you, Clifford. It took some time, but we finally have an accurate picture of the alien craft's flight path. What threw us is that its speed kept changing, sometimes dramatically so. It took us a while to figure out why. What we learned is that when the craft approaches a heavily populated area like a major city, it slows down quite a bit so that it can properly process a large number of people. Think of a chainsaw cutting through a tree when it suddenly comes upon a knot of dense wood. The cutting rate slows down as the blade makes its way through. The craft then speeds back up as it passes over sparsely populated areas like a desert, or an ocean, where it can reach a velocity of well over two hundred miles an hour..."

THE WHITE HOUSE

President Crawford, her cabinet, the Joint Chiefs of Staff, plus dozens of high-level government officials and their aides crowd the Situation Room watching the same broadcast. It's standing room only for most. Otis Larson has a seat at the conference table. Conroy Hamilton stands directly behind him.

All eyes are on the monitor as Seifert continues. "...It's important that we got this right because all of us—all of humanity—has a stake in it. To help people visualize what's happening, we've put together a short presentation."

Seifert gets up from his chair and steps over to a giant screen on which a video begins to play. A computer-generated image shows the Earth as a giant blue, white and brown marble hanging suspended in the vastness of space.

"When the spaceship appeared over Beijing, we here at JPL—like everyone else in the world—were hoping it would land, friendly contact would be established, and humanity would ride off into the sunset singing kumbaya with our new benefactors from another world.

"As we've all learned, it didn't turn out that way. Instead, the alien craft began its collection process."

The video zooms in on the sprawling Chinese capital.

"At first, we thought—I should say we *hoped*—that they would just target a few random cities, collect a token number of humans as specimens to take home and study, and leave the rest of us alone. But that didn't happen. They didn't go home. They didn't stop collecting."

An animated version of the spaceship circling over Beijing begins to play.

"As you can see, after nearly touching down in Tiananmen Square, the craft began ascending while moving in a spiral pattern. With each pass, it shifted farther away from its starting point. Eventually, the spacecraft settled into a flight path 102 miles above the Earth. The dissolution beam maxed out at 598 miles wide and is holding steady, while the barrier continues to be reeled up on one side of the ship and simultaneously redeployed down the other side. From where things now stand, we believe the spaceship is at its maximum collection capability."

Seifert takes a sip of water and continues.

"Speaking of the barrier, materials scientists have been studying it as best they can. It's tricky because they only have so much time to do their work before the dissolution beam spirals back around to them. To avoid getting collected, they have to flee in rocket helicopters to a safe zone 598 miles away to continue their work at another spot.

"They've concluded it's a graphene barrier, which is a sheet of material that's only one molecule thick. But what a molecule! It's engineered beyond anything we can imagine. It's semi-transparent, it's weightless, and it's impenetrable.

Seifert's voice takes on an ominous tone.

"On top of that, we've learned something...disturbing about this ever-shifting barrier that—for better or worse—we feel obligated to share with you. Essentially, the barrier is acting as a very effective seal for keeping people from going into the dissolved part of the world. Correspondingly, the area where people still exist is shrinking at the same rate. In other words, it appears the barrier was designed to keep us contained, so that no one can escape the dissolution beam. When the vessel reaches its final destination, it will have scoured every square inch of the Earth. If the spacecraft stays on its present course, that will happen in eleven days."

Seifert hesitates a moment. Looks down at his desktop. Takes a deep breath, trying to gather himself. Finally he looks up. Stares intensely into the camera.

"What this means is that eleven days from now, every structure built by the hands of man will have turned to dust; and every person on the planet will have been transported up to the ship."

MINNEAPOLIS, MINNESOTA

In a middle-class suburb of the city, a young couple watches the broadcast while tightly holding hands. Their house is small but neat and clean. The furnishings are sparse but tasteful. 24-year-old Cindy Franklin is home on maternity leave from her job as an administrative assistant to an executive at a bank. Nearly nine months pregnant, she shifts her body for the nth time on the couch, trying to get comfortable. Soft blond curls frame her face.

With his ink-black hair, her husband Bill makes a handsome contrast. At 25, he's a rising star at the local office of a nationwide CPA firm. They've been married just over a year.

On Cindy's last visit to the obstetrician, he told her she was doing everything right, from diet and exercise to getting enough rest, and that she could expect to give birth to two healthy baby boys any day.

That visit took place on the Friday before Labor Day weekend.

"Bill," Cindy says, tears in her voice, "why is this happening? We're good people. We give to charity. We go to church. We're just getting started in life."

"I don't know, darling," Paul says gently.

"It's not fair! What are we going to do?"

Bill puts his arm around her and holds her close. His voice is firm yet scared. "Somebody has to fix this. Either the government. Or the military. Or God. Somebody."

ARGENTINA BUNKER JOBSITE

Zack and the others continue watching the same BCS broadcast in the meal hall.

Clifford March has become noticeably paler. He speaks quietly. "Doctor Seifert, you used the phrase 'when it reaches its final destination'. Where would that be?"

Seifert has a ready answer. "Bahia Blanca. A city of 300,000 on the coast of Argentina."

Clifford is surprised at Seifert's rapid response. "How can you be so sure?"

Seifert gives a quick sad smile. "Actually, there's a perfectly logical reason for it—if you're the aliens. You'll see what I mean in a minute." He turns to the screen. "Let's go back to where the collection process started—Beijing." The Chinese capital occupies the center of the screen. Seifert takes a laser pointer from his shirt pocket and uses it to highlight the movements of the spacecraft. "As you can see, the vessel is moving in an ever-expanding spiral. Now watch ..."

Seifert speeds up the film so that the space ship moves quickly over the Earth in a counter-clockwise spiral.

"This is the path of the vessel so far." On the screen, the spacecraft circles over a large section of China, then cuts 600-mile-wide swaths through Mongolia, then more of China, then a slice of India, followed by the two Koreas, then up through Japan before swinging down again through Southern Russia, Tibet, Malaysia, and The Philippines. It veers back up and over another swath of Russia, then down through Turkey.

Seifert freezes the image and turns to face the camera.

"If the vessel stays on its present course—and we have no reason to believe otherwise—it will continue on to the other side of the world."

Seifert turns back to the giant screen and presses a button on the remote that switches the view to the other side of Earth. This includes much of the Pacific and Atlantic oceans, most of North America in the upper left quadrant, a swatch of East Africa on the right, and all of South America in the middle.

The city of Bahia Blanca lies dead center.

"This is the path we expect it to follow." He restarts the video at the speeded-up rate. The animated vessel continues to spiral around the globe.

"As you can see, the vessel will spend a fair amount of time moving across open ocean. Up until that point, the continental United States will have been spared. That's going to change."

Seifert aims the pointer at the upper left-hand corner of the screen. "72 hours from now, after crossing the Pacific Ocean, the vessel will appear over the North American continent. It will be moving at an angle of 32 degrees above equatorial latitude in a northeasterly direction. On this pass, British Columbia will take the brunt of the dissolution process, but the beam will be wide enough to take out everything north of Portland, Oregon—which means Seattle will be the first major American city to be dissolved."

Seifert uses the laser to draw a line across the northwestern corner of the US mainland.

"After that, with each new circuit around the Earth, it will cut a fresh swath across America 598 miles wide. The bulk of the country will be dissolved in the next three passes."

He uses the laser to illustrate cutting three 600-mile wide strips across the country. On the last one, a wide strip of land stretching from New Mexico and Texas in the west and from North Florida to Washington, D.C. in the east is taken out.

"On its fifth and final pass over our country, the dissolution beam will take out the rest of Florida. West Palm Beach will be the last area in the country to be dissolved."

Seifert turns to face the camera.

"On that date, Sunday, September 20th at around seven in the evening, the last citizen will be gathered up from American soil..."

There's a catch in Seifert's voice as he says this. The scientist clears his throat and carries on.

"The spacecraft will continue to circle the Earth. South America will be the last continent to go. As the vessel nears the completion of its task, our computer models show that the craft's spiral pattern will quickly begin to shrink."

The speeded-up animated sequence shows that, as the vessel circles closer to Bahia Blanca, the continuous ribbon of the dissolution zone becomes narrower.

"The vessel will move in tighter and tighter circles, similar to what happened in Beijing, only in reverse. Finally, we estimate that sometime in the afternoon on Friday, September 25 Argentinian local time, the last of the human species will be gathered up."

Seifert's words coincide with the animated spacecraft doing several quick, final revolutions over the center of the city until it's completely dissolved. The screen on which the video was playing goes dark.

Once again, it turned out Mr. Hatcher was right when he said that it was 'just a matter of time before the rest of the world becomes aware of the magnitude of what's happening.'
That time had arrived...

{The Zachary Stone Chronicles}

ARGENTINA BUNKER JOBSITE

Zack and the others continue watching the broadcast in the meal hall.

Seifert turns around, sets the video remote on a table, and stares into the camera.

"And so, Clifford," Seifert continues softly, "to answer your question: 'How can we be so sure that a city in Argentina will be the spaceship's final destination?'"

Seifert smiles. Shakes his head in quiet amusement, as if he's just heard the punchline of a stupid joke.

"Bahia Blanca just happens to be *on the exact opposite side of the Earth from Beijing*. Geometrically, it's the natural ending spot for their collection process."

The amused look vanishes from Seifert's face. He turns off the laser pointer. Places it back in his shirt pocket. Folds his arms and says, "And there you have it."

There's a long moment of silence. Finally, Clifford clears his throat and says, "But... Doctor Seifert, is it possible... that, even in the short amount of time we have left, some-one—a genius?—working quietly somewhere, or a group of scientists doing the same, can figure a way out of this?" Clifford speaks haltingly, struggling to keep the desperation out of his voice while expressing the hope of every person re-maining on the planet. "Someone who can come up with a... a breakthrough of some kind... something that will bring a stop to all this?"

Seifert steps back and half-sits, half-leans against the corner of his desk. He removes his glasses. Massages his eyes. Releases an all-encompassing sigh. Finally, he sets his glasses back on the bridge of his nose and looks into the camera.

"Anything's possible, Clifford. But realistically?" He gives a little shrug. "At this point, if there was going to be a break-through, I think it would have happened by now." Seifert scratches his jaw. "Then again..."

"Then again what, Doctor?"

Seifert's brows come together.

"There's this...rumor that just won't go away..."

"What rumor is that?"

"That there's a group of Americans digging some kind of specialized bunker in Argentina; that they think it will pre-vent them from being transported up to the space ship..."

Kent Hatcher jumps to his feet. "Shit!"

Everyone around him is startled by the man's shout. No one's heard him swear before. Hatcher runs a worried hand through his hair while watching the monitor. "I was afraid of this."

Eric exchanges worried glances with a couple of other engineers, then says to Hatcher, "I don't see what's so..."

"Things just took a huge turn for the worse," snaps Hatcher.

Hatcher stalks off as he pulls out a cellphone. Punches in a number. Begins speaking to someone in quick, angry Spanish, the words growing fainter as he moves away.

Eric glances at Zack. He senses his son's distress and waves him over. Zack walks over to the chair vacated by Hatcher and sits down. Eric silently puts a comforting arm around him as the two continue watching the broadcast.

Clifford says, "Do you think there's any truth to the rumor?"

"Hard to say," responds Seifert. "Somebody somewhere may have figured out something we didn't. And if that's the case, more power to them. It could mean a shot at survival for the human race as we know it."

There's a long pause. Clifford finally breaks it. "So, Doctor Seifert..." he begins somewhat awkwardly.

Seifert senses the other man's discomfort. Tries to put him at ease. "Yes, Clifford."

Clifford's at a loss. "There are a lot of frightened people out there." A self-deprecating smile. "Myself included. Any... suggestions, or advice, about what they should do until..."

"—Until we're all hauled off to the giant bladder in the sky?"

Clifford nods.

"Yes," Seifert says. "Pray."

"I didn't think you were a religious man."

"I'm not. But if there was ever a time when the human race needed a miracle, this is it."

Clifford doesn't respond.

"Look," Seifert says. "I apologize if I sound flippant. I guess that's just my way of dealing with what's happening. For what it's worth, I'll tell you what my own thoughts and feelings are on this whole business."

"I'm sure a lot of people would appreciate that."

THE WHITE HOUSE

In the Situation Room, everyone is glued to the monitor as Seifert walks around and sits down at his desk. He begins speaking calmly and reasonably.

"The aliens are obviously very intent on collecting everyone on Earth. Why they're doing this, no one knows. But I think it's important for folks to realize that a lot of very smart people—religious leaders, philosophers, scholars, some of the best thinkers in the world—don't for a second believe this is bad news. On the contrary, many of them are convinced that the aliens have come here as a force for good, to save us from some imminent cosmic calamity, like a nearby star going supernova; that they're here as our guardians and protectors."

Seifert allows that to sink in for a moment before continuing.

"Not only that, there's another, more metaphysical argument; that this whole collection process is another step—a hugely important step at that—to help mankind along on our evolutionary journey; that— much as the butterfly emerges from the cocoon—humanity will reappear in some spectacular new incarnation. So instead of being afraid, maybe we should all be excited. Grateful, even. I happen to be a glass half-full kind of guy, so I'm to go ahead and give the aliens the benefit of the—"

The screen turns to 'snow'. The audio becomes an electronic hiss. Those in the room stare blankly at the monitor.

President Crawford says, "What happened?"

Otis speaks up. "My guess is that right about now, a whole lot of people are walking away from their jobs."

"Turn it off," orders the president.

An aide presses the power button for the television, plunging the room into silence.

JET PROPULSION LAB

Seifert is still talking to the camera, unaware he's off the air. The cameraman calls out, "Doctor Seifert? I'm afraid we've lost out signal."

"Oh," says Seifert.

"What do we do now?" says the cameraman.

"I guess we can do whatever we want." Seifert scratches his jaw. "Feel free to go home."

"I think I'll do just that. My wife has been steadily freaking out. It's time to be with her. What about you, sir?"

Seifert speaks quietly. "I've been divorced for several years now. The kids are grown and live out of state. My job was the only thing keeping me going. I don't know what I'm going to do. It doesn't seem right to just walk away from here when everything's coming to a head. You know what I mean? So I think I'll hang around here a little longer."

The cameraman nods with understanding.

BCS TELEVISION STATION
NEW YORK CITY

The bank of video monitors in front of the Station Manager has gone dark. He presses buttons and turns control knobs to no avail. Finally he peels off his headset and pushes his chair away from his desk. He calls across the room to Clifford at the anchor desk, "I'm afraid that's it, Clifford."

"It was just a matter of time," Clifford says. Someone turns off the bright television lights. He rises from his chair and makes his way toward the Station Manager. "Does this mean I'm out of a job?

"That would be my guess. Go home and be with your family."

Clifford gives him a wistful smile. "You're forgetting I'm single. Not even dating anyone at the moment. That's why I've stayed on the job. So everyone else could be with *their* families."

"Sorry. I didn't mean to—"

"Forget it," Clifford waves his hand easily.

"What are you going to do?"

"I haven't really thought about it." Clifford places his hands on his hips. Looks around the studio as technicians shut done operations for good. "September's such a great time of year in New York. I love this town. I think maybe I'll take some long walks in the city. Something I haven't done in a long time..."

THE WHITE HOUSE

After the abrupt cutoff of the broadcast, there's more tension than usual in the Situation Room. Crawford notices that the vice president seems particularly stressed.

"Joe? Are you all right?"

Jameson stares in her direction for a long moment but doesn't seem to see her. Finally, he begins to speak in a quiet voice. "That video put me in mind of something I saw a long time ago..."

Even though he's talking softly, his words are clear and unhurried, and carry to every corner of the room.

"When I was a young man still in college, I spent a summer up in Alaska working on a fishing boat. The captain used a sonar-based gadget called a fish-finder to locate salmon, herring, smelt, walleye—you name it, we fished it. Whenever he found a good-sized school, a skiff would launch, pulling with it the leading edge of a long net made out of industrial-strength nylon. The net had floaters along its top. The bottom of it extended more than a hundred feet below the surface, well under the main body of fish. A nylon rope had been threaded through it.

"The skiff would move in a big circle around the fish, surrounding the school as the net played out from the boat. When the skiff arrived back at the boat, we hooked the nylon rope to a winch, which then pulled it tight, cinching the bottom of the net closed, like the drawstring of a purse.

"Another winch pulled the net toward the boat. When it came alongside, you could look down and see literally thousands of fish, all wriggling and squirming and jumping like mad. It looked like the ocean was boiling. A few of the lucky ones managed to leap out of the net just before it was hoisted over the deck. There, we opened the drawstring just enough so that the fish could be poured in a controlled flow through a hatch down into the hold of the ship.

"At first, I remember feeling kind of sorry for the fish, being gathered up like that. It just seemed so...callous. Barbaric, even. But those feelings didn't last long. It was just a job, one that paid damn well to a financially-strapped student. We pulled in dozens of nets that summer, all teeming with fish..."

One of the other members of the Cabinet blurts out, "What are you suggesting, Joe—that the aliens have come all this way, gone to all this trouble, to harvest us? That we're going to end up on the alien equivalent of a Weber grill? That's just plain crazy!"

Jameson's smiles. "I guess what I'm saying, Bob, is that if the fish in our nets had the power of reason, they probably would have thought the same thing as you."

An uneasy silence settles over the room. It's marred only by the drumming of President Crawford's long fingernails on the conference table—a sign she's not happy.

Otis Larson says, "If I may speak, Madam President?"

A curt nod from Crawford.

"I think it would be a mistake to jump to any conclusions about what the aliens want from us. We just don't know. Not yet, anyway. Also, I think it's important to keep something in mind: by getting transported up to the spacecraft, at least we'll be in the hands of a highly advanced civilization. And that certainly couldn't be any worse than what's in store for any so-called "lucky ones" who somehow manage to escape being collected. Think about it. Because of the dissolution beam, there won't be any infrastructure left on Earth. No buildings. No roads. No power plants. No clothes. No crops. Civilization will go up in a puff of smoke. The "lucky ones" are going to get knocked all the way back to square one."

"Doctor Larson is right," Vice President Jameson muses sadly. "There won't be any computers. Or tools. Or books. No instruction manuals on how to do or build or plant anything. No information on what's safe to eat and what's poisonous. There won't even be a square one to go back to. I'd say anyone lucky enough to avoid being collected will find themselves knocked all the way back to square zero..."

"Any way you look at it," Larson says, "the human race is stuck between a rock and a—"

President Crawford suddenly slaps her hand down on the conference table. "That's enough. Everybody out."

Uncomfortable glances are exchanged around the table—Is the president losing it? Jameson looks at Crawford and says, "...Ma'am?"

Her voice rising, the President says, "Except for Larson, Hamilton, and General Walters, I want everyone out of this room *now*!"

"Yes, Ma'am!"

There's a mad scramble to vacate the room. As soon as it's clear, President Crawford turns to Conroy, who's still standing behind Otis's chair, and says in a commanding voice, "Take a seat, Mr. Hamilton."

Conroy obeys, taking the chair next to Otis.

"Okay, Mr. Hamilton, just what the hell is going on?"

Perplexed, Conroy shakes his head. "Madam President, I'm afraid I don't quite know what you—"

"You've studied these so-called 'blue balloons' more than anyone. I'm about two seconds away from giving General Walters the order to nuke that thing out of the sky. Give me one good reason why I shouldn't."

Panicked, Otis jumps in. "With all due respect, Ma'am, we've been over this! We'd be kicking a hornet's nest of highly advanced—"

"Shut it, Larson," the President says, not bothering to look at her Science Advisor. "Go ahead, Professor. I'm waiting."

Conroy stares boldly back at the President. He spreads his hands and says, as if it's the most obvious thing in the world, "I can give you dozens of reasons." His voice becomes husky with belief and passion. "They're all *smiling*."

It's Crawford's turn to be perplexed. "Who's smiling?"

"The people in the cave paintings." Conroy reaches for his laptop. Opens it. Hits a few keys, which quickly brings up the two cave drawings side by side. As he does so, he continues to talk. "I'm convinced that mankind went through a similar experience 60,000 years ago, as recorded on the cave drawings. We pulled through it then, just as we'll pull through it now."

He turns his laptop around so Crawford can see it. He zooms in on various stick-figures.

"But what's convinced me that we're in no real danger is that, without exception, every person in both of the cave paintings is smiling. If they were crying and screaming and trying to run away, I'd say by all means, go ahead and shoot the sucker down. But that's not the case here. We're talking big, happy-face smiles. Like they seem to know something *good* is happening."

Crawford studies Conroy for a moment. Raising a skeptical eyebrow, she says, "Emphasis on seem, Professor."

"Yes, Ma'am," Conroy says. "Still, I think it's worth taking into account."

President Crawford ponders this a moment. Pursing her lips together, she releases a pent-up sigh of anger and frustration. Turning to General Walters, she demands, "What's the status on the flyby, General?"

"I've had the best and brightest working on it around the clock. Now that the craft's trajectory is stabilized, we should be able to—"

"Damnit, Jim, I didn't ask for details! In three days, Americans are going to start getting sucked up into that spaceship. I want a look inside that thing before it happens. 72 hours, General. Can you do it?!"

General Walters is usually the one doing the shouting. He stares at his Commander-in-Chief with newfound respect. His voice level and confident, he answers, "I can do it, Ma'am."

Crawford nods curtly. "Good." Her laser stare swerves back to Conroy. "Congratulations, Hamilton. For better or worse, you just bought the aliens three more days. And I hope to god it's for better. We're going to get an up close and personal at these beings from another planet. And if we don't like what we see, there'll be hell to pay."

Conroy and Otis exchange a quick look of relief.

Crawford turns back to the General. "Get to it, General."

Walters stands and crisply salutes. "Ma'am." He gathers his belongings and heads for the door.

Assuming the meeting is over, Conroy and Otis also stand and begin collecting their folders and laptops.

"Not so fast, gentlemen."

The two men freeze. They look at her in surprise, then sit back down.

As soon as Walters is out of the room, she says, "Your president has an assignment for you."

Otis and Conroy glance warily at each other.

"While the flyby is still being readied," Crawford continues, "I want you two to work on a contingency plan."

Otis gives her a dubious look. "A contingency plan? I'm not sure I..."

"I'm talking about in case things turn out bad," Crawford says. "And I mean really bad. Worst-case-scenario bad." Her voice turns earnest as she looks at Conroy. "I've been briefed on your theories, Professor Hamilton. Many in the scientific world think you're a crackpot. As for myself, in light of recent events, I'm not so sure that's the case. I'm referring to what you call mankind's 'precivilization'... the people who were here before us, so many years ago... Our very distant cousins. Apparently they had a thriving civilization. Then they vanished without a trace. No one knows where they went."

Her worried gaze fixes each man by turn as the words pour from her heart. "Except for two crude cave paintings, there's no record of anything they did. We don't know what they accomplished. What their hopes and dreams were. We never will. It was all taken away, as if they never existed."

Her voice hardens. "That's not going to happen to us. Not on my watch. Or maybe I should say our watch."

Caught up in her speech, Otis says, "What do you want us to do?"

"You two are the geniuses of the group. I want you to find a way to preserve as many of the accomplishments of mankind as possible. Our culture. Our works of art. Our inventions. Our history, warts and all. I want you to do this so that, in case things do go wrong, we can at least leave some proof behind that we were here. We existed. This is what we did. And if somehow we do leave some descendants behind who manage to survive and propagate the species, maybe in the distant future, they'll come across this...record of human civilization. Our record..."

Crawford's voice catches. Her eyes mist up. After a moment, she clears her throat and says, "So. Are you game?"

They reply in unison. "Yes, Ma'am."

Crawford allows herself a smile. "Good. You'll have all the resources that I can muster at your disposal."

"We'll do the best we can, Ma'am," Conroy says.

"One more thing," Crawford says. "I want to keep this secret."

Otis looks at Conroy, who shrugs as if it makes no difference to him.

Otis nods and turns back to the president. "That's fine with us, Madam President. But...do you mind if I ask why?"

"If word gets out, I'm afraid it would be taken as a sign of surrender. That we've concluded our situation is hopeless; that we know we're doomed and are giving up. We don't need that."

"I think we understand."

President Crawford stands up, as do Otis and Conroy. "Okay, gentlemen. Whatever you come up with, I want it ready to go by the time of the flyby. That gives you 72 hours. Any questions?"

Conroy says, "I have a question, Ma'am. Actually, it's more of a favor."

"What is it?"

"My wife Una would like to go back home to be with her people while all this is happening. Is that possible?"

"Consider it done."

"Thank you, Ma'am."

The president turns to Otis. "How about you, Doctor Larson? Any questions?"

Otis grins. "Zillions. But we'll figure things out as we go along. Right, Conroy?"

Conroy smiles cockily. "Geniuses are always up for a challenge."

With the exact route of the ship now universally known, the cities coming up in its path had plenty of warning. But even knowing the day and time when the craft would arrive didn't change much of anything. Most people had nowhere to evacuate to and were resigned to take their chances on going for a ride in one of the blue bubbles.

Other folks remained hopeful that some genius somewhere in the world would come up with a last-minute plan to thwart the collection process. They kept moving, determined to stay a step ahead of the vessel's dissolution beam any way they could, if only to buy a little more time for that genius to appear.

Which could still happen.

Meanwhile, the only viable prospect for escape was still under construction. Me and my family were lucky enough to be a part of it.

Except now, there might be a problem. Minutes after the end of the last BCS broadcast, Hatcher called an emergency meeting with all his department heads. Hatcher was pretty sure that word had leaked out. In which case, events could turn disastrous...

{The Zachary Stone Chronicles}

ARGENTINA BUNKER JOBSITE

Hatcher meets with his foremen and women in a barebones conference room inside a prefab trailer. The furnishings consist of card tables and folding chairs.

"I called this emergency meeting because I'm afraid the cat's out of the bag," Hatcher says. "The only way I was able to get permission from the Argentinian government to build the bunker was by promising a few high-ranking officials and their immediate families a place inside it. I just learned that a few days ago, apparently there was an 'end-of-the-world party' with a lot of drinking and crying and carrying on. Someone slipped up and word about us got out."

Hatcher pauses to let that sink in. Eric Stone and his fellow workers look at each other with concern.

"Fortunately," Hatcher continues, "Argentina is a large and sparsely settled country. We're pretty much a needle in a haystack. But the possibility, however small, of our location being found out has always been a huge concern to me.

"My contacts in Buenos Aries don't know our exact position. I was going to keep it from them until the last possible minute. But now, after that broadcast, folks are going to suspect we're here. I'm worried people will start actively looking for us. They may even have already started to search. And if they find us, all bets are off."

No one says anything. Hatcher gives a weary sigh and smiles sadly.

"I've tried to prepare for as many contingencies as possible. Our location being exposed was one of them. In the event that we need to protect ourselves, our families, and—most importantly—this project, I've taken measures to do so." Hatcher rises from his chair. "Follow me, please."

He takes them outside and leads them over to an open-air pit several hundred feet across. At the bottom, the bunker is taking shape.

"As you know, the construction of the bunker is progressing rapidly. We're well ahead of schedule. As soon as it's completed, we'll cover it with the different layers of fill." Hatcher gestures at small mountains of different material ringing the pit.

"After that, though, our weak point will be the access shaft to the bunker. So what I want to do is erect a ring of blast walls around what will be the entrance to the shaft." Kent indicates a nearby area about the size of a basketball court. "We'll leave a few narrow gaps between them so that we have access to the outside."

Hatcher gestures at three small remote-controlled front-end loaders that are positioned close to smaller mounds of the same materials.

"In case we come under assault," continues Hatcher, "we need to be able to hold off our attackers long enough so that the shaft can be backfilled. For that reason, I've taken steps to provide us a last-ditch line of defense."

They all steal uncertain glances at each other. A tall fit engineer in his 20's named Nelson speaks up.

"Uh, sir, what does that mean, exactly?"

"If all of you would come with me."

Hatcher leads them to a nondescript shipping container sitting off by itself in the sand. On closer inspection, the boxcar-sized structure is made of solid steel.

"Some of you aren't going to like what you're about to see," Hatcher says. "But this is the reality we've been dealt."

He punches a security code into a numbered pad on the door. There's a metallic click as the lock disengages. Hatcher pulls the handle.

"...Holy shit," someone breathes.

The steel door swings wide to reveal a long row of neatly stacked M16 rifles and cases of ammunition. Everything is brand new.

No one says anything as the implication of what they are looking at sinks in.

Finally Nelson speaks in an incredulous whisper.

"Wait a minute... You expect us to shoot people? When all they're trying to do is escape the spaceship? Just trying to survive, like us?"

"Like I said," Hatcher says, "this would only be as a very last resort. I seriously doubt that it will ever come down to—"

"This isn't what I signed up for," Nelson says.

There's a sudden edge to Hatcher's voice. "You signed up to preserve the human species. This might be what it takes."

"But at what cost? If it comes down to slaughtering innocent people 'to preserve the human species', maybe we're not worth saving."

"Look. Nelson. You're one of the few single people here, right? You don't have a family looking to you for protection, no matter the cost. So maybe the stakes just aren't that high for you."

Hatcher softens his tone as he speaks to the rest of the group. "I know this is hard for some of you to accept. But, like it or not, the fact is the story of mankind is survival of the fittest. And it is one long cruel and brutal slog. So in that regard, we're not so different from our ancestors who—"

Nelson turns his back on the group and starts walking away.

"Nelson. What are you doing?"

Nelson stops and turns. "I'm going to get my gear."

"Where on Earth would you go?"

"Bahia Blanca."

"For god's sake, why?"

"I'll take my chances with the rest of the poor devils out there."

They all watch him as he continues toward the living quarters.

A large foreman with a thick mustache and tattoos on his massive forearms says, "Should we stop him?"

Hatcher lets out a frustrated sigh. "No. If that's what he wants, let him go."

A few minutes later, while making his rounds in the golf cart, Zack sees Eric coming back from the meeting.

"Hey, Dad!"

Eric continues walking. Appears not to have heard Zack, who shouts again.

"Dad! Hey, wait up!"

Eric stops as Zack approaches. "It's pretty hot out here, Dad. Do you want some ice water? Or a soda? Or..."

Zack notices the faraway look in his father's eyes. He instinctively knows something is troubling him. "Dad? Are you okay?"

Eric pulls himself together. "I'm fine, son." He reaches into the golf cart. Places his hand affectionately on the back of Zack's neck. "I'm fine..."

CENTRAL INTELLIGENCE AGENCY
LANGLEY, VIRGINIA

Otis and Conroy practically have to run to keep up with Mr. Green, their long-legged, fast-walking escort. They move down a brightly-lit hallway, passing numerous unmarked doors, their footsteps echoing off the marble floor. A few employees scurry about, a worried frown on every face.

Mr. Green stops abruptly at one of the anonymous doors. He enters a code on a numbered pad, turns the doorknob and pushes it open.

"Here you go, gentlemen," Mr. Green says. "Your workshop."

A large windowless space. A couple of desks and chairs. Brand new computers with oversized monitors. Mounted on an adjacent wall is an interactive whiteboard the size of a ping pong table. Off to the side, massive shelves brim with all manner of tools, wires, mechanical parts. Next to that, a long empty workbench stands ready for whatever Otis and Conroy can conjure up.

Mr. Green nods at the two computer terminals. "You've been given access to the government's most powerful computers, all at the touch of a button."

He points out a strange-looking telephone sitting on one of the desks. There's no number or keypad.

"The President has given you carte blanche. If you need anything, and I mean anything at all for whatever it is you're working on, just pick up that phone, and the United States government will do everything in its power to procure it for you."

In a far corner is a living area. A couple of king-sized cots with thick pads and pillows and plenty of blankets. A small but well-stocked kitchen. A dining table with two chairs.

Mr. Green points to a closed door. "Through there is a bathroom with shower." Mr. Green gestures toward the kitchen. "You're welcome to cook your meals in here if you want, but there's a strong preference that you order food from the cafeteria. It's actually pretty good. The cooks will whip up anything you desire and have it delivered hot to your door."

Conroy says, "Why don't they want us to cook?"

"The President would prefer you use that time to work on your project."

He hands each of them a card. "If you feel the need to step out of the building for a dose of fresh air, the code for the door is on this card."

The two pocket their cards.

"Any questions?" Mr. Green says. "If not, I'll be on my way."

Otis glances at Conroy, who shakes his head no. "I think we're good for now."

"Very well." Mr. Green goes to the door and punches in the code. As he's about to leave, he glances back at them and says in all seriousness, "Good luck, gentlemen."

Conroy nods back. Replies softly, "Thank you, Mr. Green."

After Mr. Green exits, the two men wander around their new digs.

Otis muses, "The accommodations aren't half-bad."

"It's not the Ritz Carlton, but it'll do," Conroy says. He stops and turns to Otis. His voice is playfully stilted as he says, "So. Doctor Larson. Have you managed to come up with any ideas on how we're going to save mankind's legacy?"

Otis replies in kind. "Well, Professor Hamilton. As a matter of fact, indeed I have. I've been thinking about it ever since the President gave us this assignment."

"Oh? And what did you come up with?"

Otis heads over to the whiteboard, removes his jacket and drapes it over the back of a chair. His flippant tone vanishes as he suddenly turns serious. "I'm envisioning a survival kit."

Conroy's interest is piqued. "A survival kit."

"Yes. I'm talking the *ultimate* survival kit. A package custom-tailored to ensure the preservation of the record of human civilization. It's still in the planning stages, of course, but let me show you what I mean..."

He flips a switch to activate the whiteboard. Picks up a stylus and begins to draw.

I learned from The Record that, as the Russians tracked the spaceship on its approach to Moscow, they came this close to firing nukes at it. But, like the United States, they were afraid that if they did, the aliens would respond with overwhelming force. So, in the end, like in most cities, those with the means and the will to flee did so. Citizens with nowhere to go hunkered down in their homes, waiting for the inevitable...

{The Zachary Stone Chronicles}

MOSCOW, RUSSIA
MIDNIGHT

The streets are deserted except for a few lost, vodka-swilling souls wandering the boulevards like drunken ghosts. Still, Red Square remains brightly, defiantly illuminated. Powerful spotlights shine on dozens of oversized Russian flags and banners, all rippling in a breeze. The red stars atop the spires of the Kremlin burn steadily in the night. The candy-colored domes of St. Basil's Cathedral are lit up like a giant psychedelic birthday cake. A recording of the Russian national anthem blasts continuously across the square from dozens of massive speakers.

...Another sound intrudes—a gravelly hiss that quickly grows very loud, overwhelming the anthem—the dissolution beam. Its approach is hidden by the night.

The speakers go abruptly silent.

One bleary-eyed denizen sways in the shadow of the Kremlin wall, watching in amazement as the ancient city dissolves into grit and dust. A movement from above catches his eye. Looking up, he can just make out streams of balloons, appearing black in the darkness, zipping skyward from the carnage. As the Kremlin Wall suddenly melts beside him, he joins his comrades on the journey to the spacecraft.

Then all the spotlights go out.

Pretty much all communication channels in the United States were down for a full day after the last BCS broadcast. Thankfully, emergency backup systems kept the power on in much of the country. People were so starved for information that they left their computers or televisions on with the sound muted, watching the electronic snow, waiting, hoping, praying for a news update to appear.

Thanks to the dedication of a few selfless transmission specialists in the nation's capital, a signal was about to go out across the country…

{The Zachary Stone Chronicles}

THE WHITE HOUSE

In the Situation Room, President Crawford huddles with Vice President Jameson and General Walters.

"…If it comes down to it," Crawford is telling them, "I want to be able to hit them with everything we've got all at once. It might be our only chance to take them out with a surprise attack."

"Understood, Ma'am," says the General.

"I want the launch codes pre-entered into the—"

An intercom buzzes on the table in front of Crawford. Annoyed at the interruption, she hits the speaker-phone button and snaps, "Yes?"

"Madam President, you wanted to be informed if Communications was able to get the EBS online."

"And?"

"It's up and running. They're waiting for you now in the Oval Office."

She practically jumps out of her seat.

"Thank God! I'm on my way."

She grabs the jacket draped across the back of her seat. Pulls it on while heading out of the room, trailed by a couple of aides. She shakes out her hair out while walking briskly down the hallway. She doesn't have to break stride when she reaches the door to the Oval Office as an aide pulls it open for her.

"Where are they?" she says.

"Over here, Ma'am."

Crawford smiles brightly at a crew of a half-dozen men and women, all in their 20s. The men have a couple of days of stubble on their faces. The sleeves of their dress shirts are rolled to the elbows. The women's skirts are wrinkled, their make-up rubbed off, their hair tousled. Everyone's eyes are red from lack of sleep.

Crawford goes over to them and shakes hands and gives hugs. "You did it!"

Tired but happy smiles all around "Yes, Ma'am."

"Great work, people! Thank you!"

The hard-working crew beams at the President's praise.

A harried-looking woman in her 30's hovering near the presidential desk calls out in a firm but gentle voice, "We're ready for you, Madam President."

"Of course." Crawford heads over to her. The woman pulls the chair out for her. "Thank you, Paula."

Crawford sits. A television camera is positioned on the other side of the desk facing her. A cameraman stands at the ready. Paula takes a place beside him.

"Okay, the tone is going out now. We'll let that run for a minute or so to get people's attention..."

Across the country, a harsh tone sounds on millions of televisions, radios, computers and smart phones. It's accompanied by the recording of a man's voice:

"This is the Emergency Broadcast System. This is not a test. Repeat—this is not a test. Please stand by for an important message from the President..."

In Minneapolis, Bill and Cindy Franklin try to rest in the shade of an elm tree in their backyard. Sweaty and flushed,

Cindy reclines on a padded lounge chair. She's so very pregnant, it would seem impossible for her to get any bigger.

Bill's in a lawn chair next to her, watching her with concern. In a gentle voice, "Can I get you anything, sweetie? Some more water? A pillow?"

"No, I'm all right," she lies.

They hear the attention-grabbing tone leaking from open windows up and down the street.

"What's that noise?" Cindy says.

An upstairs window flies open in the house next door. A man in his twenties with a blonde crew-cut leans out and shouts down at them. "Hey, Bill! Cindy! Turn on your TV! The President's coming on the air!"

"What?!" The two look at each with wide eyes. Jim gets up from his chair. Helps Cindy up from the recliner. They shuffle inside where they turn up the television's volume.

"This is the Emergency Broadcast System. This is not a test. Repeat—this is not a test. Please stand by for an important message from the President..."

THE WHITE HOUSE

The cameraman tweaks the focus as President Crawford composes herself at her desk. Smooths a wrinkle out of her jacket. Folds her hands on the desk in front of her. Clears her throat.

"Stand by," Paula says. "Three... Two..." She mouths the word 'one' and points at Crawford.

MINNEAPOLIS

Bill and Cindy are settled on their couch in front of the TV as the image of President Crawford sitting calmly at her desk in the Oval Office appears. She speaks in a firm voice.

"My fellow Americans: Before I begin, I would first like to apologize to you for taking so long to reestablish communication with you. It's been a little over 48 hours since network and cable stations suddenly went off the air. Communications specialists have been working around the clock to get us back online. I'm told the connection isn't perfect, but that it will do for short broadcasts, like this one will have to be.

"As you know, our world was recently turned upside down by the arrival of the alien ship. For several days now, human beings have been systematically collected and transported up to this vessel. Yet, as far as we can determine, no one has been physically harmed during this process. Accordingly, I and the National Security Council have chosen to refrain from initiating hostilities against the aliens. Some of my most trusted advisers convinced me an attack on such an advanced race of beings would be nothing short of global suicide. That said, we need to know what's going on inside that ship. We need to know what's happening to our fellow human beings, because it's going to happen to us all..."

ARGENTINA BUNKER JOBSITE

Loudspeakers blare the president's words throughout Hatcher's compound.

"...To that end, our military has been working diligently on the guidance system of the most sophisticated spy satellite ever built. That satellite is now executing a tricky series of maneuvers in an attempt to get close enough to the spaceship so that, hopefully, we can get a glimpse of what's going on inside.

"The satellite is now less than 24 hours away from rendezvousing with the spacecraft. I've been informed that any data it gathers will have to first be processed by computers at the National Security Agency here in Washington so it can be turned into a format that can be understood by laymen. That information will then be transported by special courier to the White House. Accordingly, there will be a slight delay until I and the National Security Council are able to view it..."

JET PROPULSION LABORATORY

It's gone mostly dark in the windowless Control Room. Dr. Seifert and a handful of technicians stand in a cluster, quietly sipping coffee and soft drinks while watching the President's speech on one of the giant monitors.

"...As soon as that happens," continues the President, "if we are able to learn anything new about the aliens, I just want to say to you—the American people—that I give you my solemn promise as your president that I will immediately report back to you and let you know what—if anything— we find. We are all equally affected by these cataclysmic events, and you're entitled to know exactly what's happening on that ship."

The picture wavers. The sound fades in and out. The screen is trying to turn into 'snow'...

Crawford looks off camera where someone is speaking to her. She nods in response and her gaze swivels back to the camera.

"Okay, it looks like we're losing our signal. I'll say good-bye for now. But before I go, I just want to say that, come what may, we're all very much in this together. And that's when America is strongest, when we come together as one. God bless the United States of America."

During the last sentence, just before the screen goes dark, Crawford's voice cracks ever so slightly.

ARGENTINIAN HIGH DESERT

Nelson walks at a steady pace across the arid landscape. On his back is a makeshift pack made of canvas and rope. In it is enough food and water to last several days, courtesy of Kent Hatcher. Tied to the top of the pack is a blanket roll. It's not exactly a goose down sleeping bag, but is enough to keep him warm during the cool nights of the high desert.

Nelson walks with his head held high. His conscience is clear. He knows he did the right thing.

THE PYRAMIDS
CAIRO, EGYPT

The spaceship passes high overhead in a sere blue sky. Even structures made of rock are not invulnerable to the dissolution beam. The Pyramids erupt in a brown cyclone of dust, as if a giant sand-blaster is raking over the ancient blocks. Numerous inner chambers collapse upon themselves, rendering the tombs of ancient Egyptian kings into nothing more than a few immense piles of shapeless rocks.

The Sphynx, heavily scored by the same force, is reduced to an unrecognizable hunk of stone.

As the vessel crosses over Cairo, thousands of earthen buildings instantly dissolve into a vast sandstorm from which rises a blue, fast-moving river of balloons. The gritty hiss of the crumbling structures muffles the cries and lamentations of ten million souls...

MINING PIT
FAR SIDE OF THE MOON

Spike sits at his communication console talking with Angie. She asks, "Did you watch the President's speech?"

"I got it off one of the relay satellites."

"I can't believe this is happening."

"That's some crazy shit going on, all right. How're you holding up?"

"I'm hanging in there," Angie say. "Except..." Her voice catches. "...Except I'd give anything to be home with my daughters."

"You mean they haven't they given you the green light to get your ass back down to Earth?"

"At first, I voluntarily stayed behind in case you changed your mind. But then everything was put on hold and I was ordered to stay put. They don't want to do anything that might provoke the aliens—like having a freighter filled with moon ore go zipping past."

"How are your girls doing?"

"Like everyone else, they're freaking out. Communications are screwed up. Power's going down in a lot of parts of the country. I'm so worried..."

"Angie, listen to me. If your girls are one tenth as tough as their Mom, they're going to be just fine, and that's a fact. Comprendo?"

"Spike, I'm losing you. Catch you on the next orbit?"

"Later, alligator."

"After awhile, croco..."

Angie's voice fades as the freighter slips beyond the curvature of the moon.

Spike picks up his banjo. Plucks a few strings. Makes a sour face at the sound—pretty bad. He sets his mouth in determination and continues to torture the instrument.

ATHENS, GREECE

...Something moving quickly high over the city in the hot afternoon sun.

Keeping pace with it on the ground is the dissolution beam. Because Athens is a dense, flat city—no forests of skyscrapers, most buildings no taller than a few stories—the impression is that of an invisible tsunami roiling through the metropolis. A fast-moving stream of blue bubbles rises continuously from the chaos of destruction.

When it reaches the Parthenon, the edifice erupts in a giant smear of white powder. When the dust settles, the ancient pillars lie collapsed in a tangled, sand-blasted heap.

ARGENTINA BUNKER JOBSITE

Work proceeds at a brisk pace. Over-sized cranes, back hoes, and dump trucks jitter back and forth across the open pit like dinosaurs on speed. At the bottom of the earthen cavity, steel I-beams are being erected. The bunker is beginning to take shape.

On the rim of the giant manmade crater, Eric and Kent are bent over a work table going over a blueprint. They both wear hardhats and steel-toed work boots.

Eric is speaking. "...The tensile strength of the steel is more than enough to ensure the bunker's structural integrity."

"You're doing a great job, Eric. At the rate things are going, we should have a couple of days to spare."

"That's what I've been shooting for. I think we're going to need as much wiggle room as we can get."

EUROPE

Moving steadily south, the dissolution beam begins cutting a 600-mile-wide swathe through the heart of Europe. London and Berlin are just within range of the westernmost and easternmost edges of the beam, respectively. Amsterdam lies in the middle, directly under the spaceship.

Because all three cities exist at roughly the same latitude, they begin to dissolve simultaneously. The spacecraft slows considerably so that it can process the three densely-packed streams of bubbles pouring up through the hatch. The giant bladder attached to the tail of the alien craft steadily swells.

The proud citizens of never-conquered London are not exactly inclined to go gently into that good night. When the dissolution beam arrives and begins pulverizing their city, Londoners are defiant to the end. Spilling from pubs and flats, they fill the streets and public squares. The Parliament Building. Big Ben. The British Museum. Buckingham Palace. All collapse in quick succession. Millions of enraged Londoners shake their fists at the heavens while shouting every epithet known to man. A great and unified roar fills the sky.

But as the river of blue bubbles rising from the rubble swells, the Londoners' roar diminishes as the citizens are gathered up. It soon disappears altogether, replaced by the sound of coarse sand raining to the ground.

In Berlin, the Brandenburg Gate and the Reichstag crumble to gray dust.

In Amsterdam, the museum that houses the largest collection of Van Gogh paintings in the world, dissolves into a shapeless pile of rocky granules.

ARGENTINIAN HIGH DESERT

It's been two days since Nelson left the construction site. He's tired and dirty. Most of his food and water is gone. He stops to get his bearings. Squints into the distance.

There. A hazy cluster of buildings on the horizon.

Bahia Blanca.

He smiles.

Nelson resumes his trek but doesn't get more than a few paces when his attention is drawn to a dust-covered jeep making its way toward him over the hard-packed sand. He stops to watch as the vehicle approaches at a leisurely speed. It carries two men.

The jeep pulls up with the driver nearest to him. Both men are in their twenties. Normally their hair and week-old beards would be raven black but desert dust has tinged them sepia brown. They appear to be wearing military fatigues but everything in the jeep is covered with so much dust it's hard to tell. The driver has a long bandana tied around his forehead. The passenger wears dark sunglasses. Hanging from his neck is a pair of good-quality binoculars.

The engine idles quietly.

The driver smiles but his eyes are wary. "Buenos dias, senor."

"Buenos dias."

"Que pasa?"

As brilliant an engineer Nelson may be, he never learned any languages.

"Ahh, do you speak English?" he says.

"Si," the driver says. "Yes. I speak some English. Americano?"

"No, Canadian," Nelson lies. "Are you with the army?"

The passenger grunts a laugh. The driver sighs and says, "There is no army. No air force. Everything has fallen apart. Since the space people." He points up at the sky while keeping his eyes on Nelson's. "What is a Canadian man doing so far out in the Pampas?"

"Camping."

"Camping?"

"Yes. Si."

"Where did you camp?"

"On the other side of that ridge." Nelson points in a direction different from the way he came.

The driver turns to the passenger and speaks some Spanish, apparently translating the exchange. The passenger doesn't say anything. Just stares at Nelson, his face a stone mask behind the sunglasses.

The driver turns back to Nelson. "But, senor, there is something I do not understand."

"What don't you understand?"

"Why someone would have such poor equipment for camping." He gestures at the jerry-rigged backpack and blanket roll. "And why someone would choose to wear shoes like that—" he points at Nelson's feet "—instead of hiking boots."

Nelson glances down at his steel-toed work boots. Looks back up. Locks eyes with the driver.

The driver smiles. "But, you know, this could be a good thing."

Nelson grows more leery. "Why would that be a good thing?"

The smile is still in place, but the eyes have turned hard.

"I think with boots like that, you have made a trail that will be easy to follow."

In a flash, Nelson realizes what he's done. *I've put the bunker in danger.* In desperation, he lunges for the keys in the ignition.

A pistol appears in the hand of the passenger. Nelson freezes. The passenger leans toward him. Presses the barrel against his temple.

The driver speaks calmly. "My friend truly does not want to shoot you, gringo. But if you don't move away from this car rapidamente, that is what he will do."

Nelson backs away from the jeep. The driver puts the vehicle in gear. Begins driving slowly in the direction from which Nelson has come. He leans out the side of the vehicle, scanning the ground for footprints made from steel-toed work boots. The passenger keeps his eyes and the pistol trained on Nelson.

Nelson can only watch helplessly as the jeep moves slowly deeper into the Pampas.

One by one, the grand cities of Europe are vaporized and their occupants whisked up to the spacecraft. Brussels. Frankfurt. Prague. Paris is up next.

Paris!

Poor magical, magnificent Paris. As the City of Light starts to dissolve, its citizens behave quite differently from their London counterparts. Instead of hot-eyed rage, Parisians gather quietly in the tree-lined boulevards and squares. Every church bell begins to ring. As the dissolution beam nears the heart of the city, anguished cries rent the air as, one by one, beloved landmarks disintegrate:

THE ARC DE TRIUMPHE.

THE EIFFEL TOWER.

NOTRE DAME CATHEDRAL.

Tears fill the eyes of every Parisian. Strong men weep unashamedly. Then, hesitantly at first, the entire population starts singing La Marseillaise. Their voices grow stronger, more passionate in a heartfelt lamentation for their fair city. The anthem resonates across the vast, majestic metropolis.

The Louvre Museum is completely deserted except for one man. Security Officer Pierre de Nevers, 29, stands in full uniform before Leonardo da Vinci's Mona Lisa, his hands folded in front of him. Imbued with a deep love for art from an early age, he tried his hand at painting but met with minimal success. Still, he wanted above all else to stay in close proximity to the great masterpieces that touched his very soul. The best way of doing that was to join the museum's security force. For Pierre, safeguarding these art treasures wasn't just a job, but a calling bordering on religious fervor.

From outside comes the growing chorus of people singing La Marseillaise. It's followed moments later by what sounds like a waterfall of pebbles striking the ground. It drowns out the singing. Pierre can't help himself. As tears stream down his cheeks, he reaches out and gently places his hand on the Mona Lisa. Two seconds later, it dissolves to dust.

ARGENTINA BUNKER JOBSITE

The exterior steel shell of the bunker has been completed. A couple of front-end loaders have begun the tedious but crucially important job of spreading alternating layers of different materials over the shelter.

Close by, massive cranes hoist 20-foot-tall slabs of steel-reinforced concrete into place in a circle around the entrance to the shaft.

Hundreds of feet below ground, Eric Stone and his crew work nonstop to finish the bunker's interior. Men and women in hard-hats and earplugs labor to the whine of power saws and the staccato of hammer guns. Forklifts scurry between dwindling piles of construction material. The last cement footings are poured, the final steel I-beams installed.

The heavily-laden 20x20 foot platform of an industrial elevator slows to a halt at the open doorway at the bottom of the shaft. Forklifts immediately start unloading its wares: Tanks filled with compressed air; chemical toilets; cases of bottled water; power bars; energy drinks. There's also a large variety of seeds, plus a couple of years' supply of freeze-dried and canned food—enough to see people through the expected early hard times until they can get crops planted and harvested. All is transported to the back of the bunker where other goods are packed tightly together: tools of every kind; generators; gasoline; batteries; a couple of small, battery-powered SUVs; an ultra-light aircraft.

ROME. THE ETERNAL CITY.

150,000 of the faithful jam St. Peter's Square. They kneel side-by-side, heads bowed, eyes closed, hands pressed together in prayer. A million more overflow into the surrounding streets. Most are dressed in black dresses or black suits as if in mourning—which, in a very real sense, they are. For their country. For their families. For themselves.

The Pope stands on the balcony of the Vatican dressed in flowing white vestments, leading his flock in reciting The Lord's Prayer in Italian:

"Padre Nostro, che sei nei cieli, Sia santificato il tuo nome..."

The words are chanted with an electrifying passion

In the distance, the dissolution beam begins to ravage the city:

The Roman Forum—gone.

The Coliseum—gone.

Some of the people look around in fear. The Pope continues praying in a voice that is commanding yet soothing.

...E non ci indurre in tentazione, Ma liberaci dal male. Amen."

More startled cries as:

The Trevi Fountain—gone.

The Pantheon—gone.

The Pope begins reciting the Hail Mary. His voice doubles in intensity and volume:

"Ave Maria, piena di grazia, il Signore è con te..."

The praying mass of people now realizes without any doubt that this, their final plea for divine intervention, will go unanswered.

Directly in front of them, the Sistine Chapel crumbles to the ground.

As the Vatican dissolves around him, the Pope's voice rings out with power and resolve.

"...Santa Maria! Madre di Dio! Prega per noi peccatori, adesso e nell'ora della nostra mort! Am—!"

Swooooosh! The Vatican—gone.

Cries of terror engulf the Square as the sky fills with blue balloons.

THE WHITE HOUSE

In the Situation Room, most of the wall-mounted screens have gone dark. The ones still working show sputtering images from drones and closed-circuit security cameras of European cities dissolving.

President Crawford, Vice President Jameson and General Walters sit at the conference table staring numbly at the footage.

Crawford speaks quietly. "Reports are coming in that half of Europe is gone."

"Jesus..." Jameson manages to whisper.

"I spent my honeymoon in Paris," says Walters, trying—and failing—to sound matter-of-fact.

Crawford says "Mine in Rome."

"Let's have a look at the real-time map," the President says.

"Yes, Ma'am." Walters hits a few keys on his laptop, causing one of the darkened wall monitors to come to life as an animated map tracking the progress of the spaceship's dissolution beam. The portion of the Earth processed so far has been digitally-colored a dull brown.

This consists of over half the planet.

The 598-mile-wide beam continues its relentless journey. It's now moving down through the middle of Africa. It's like watching a giant ribbon winding steadily around the globe.

President Crawford stares quietly at the image. After a moment, she says, "It's my understanding that our turn's coming up."

"Yes, Ma'am."

"Show me."

Walters hits a few more keys. This speeds up the movement of the spaceship as the vessel follows the path calculated by JPL's computers. After leaving the African continent, the dissolution beam advances quickly across the Southern Atlantic Ocean, then over Antarctica, then heads back up the globe on a northeasterly bearing. It zooms across thousands of miles of Pacific Ocean before making landfall on the coast of British Columbia. There, the six hundred mile-wide beam angles up into southern Canada, but not before its southernmost edge cuts across the northwest corner of the United States.

The city of Seattle turns a dull brown.

Crawford's lips purse into an angry line. Before she can say anything, Walters pauses the video and says, "I know what you're thinking, Ma'am—'Where's the flyby?'"

"And your answer is?"

"We've been tracking this thing every second of every day. The conditions have never been right for our satellite to get close enough to rendezvous with it. It's been frustrating as hell. But. I'm happy to tell you that's about to change."

He turns to the animated map and backs the cursor up to a spot over the western Pacific Ocean and freezes it in place.

"When the spaceship crosses this long stretch of open ocean, it will be moving very fast but also at a very steady velocity. So steady that we should be able to sync the orbit of our satellite with the path of the alien vessel long enough to get up close and personal."

"And this will happen when?"

Walters glances up at the blood-red digital clock on the wall. "Approximately six hours from now."

ARGENTINIAN HIGH DESERT

As night falls, the two dusty rogue soldiers continue backtracking Nelson's footprints. The passenger walks ahead of the jeep at a steady pace, his eyes glued to the ground. His sunglasses are perched atop his head. He stops, turns, and says to the driver in Spanish, "I'm losing the light. We should bed down for the night and start again first thing in the morning."

The driver says, "I agree." He turns off the engine, removes the bandana tied around his forehead and uses it to wipe the sweat and dust from his face. He grabs a plastic gallon jug of water, takes a long swig and tosses it to his compadre, who does the same. He chucks two bedrolls out of the jeep as they prepare to settle in for the night.

THE WHITE HOUSE

The chairs in the Situation Room are occupied by the few senior administration officials who are still around. Everyone else has gone home. A couple of stressed-out aides hover close by, clutching clipboards and laptops. President Crawford sits at the conference table in front of the real-time map. On her left is Vice President Jameson.

At the far end of the table, General Walters sits deeply engrossed in his laptop. The other Joint Chiefs huddle around him, equally transfixed. The strain is finally taking a toll on these once squared-away soldiers. Their uniforms are wrinkled, their cheeks unshaven, their eyes red from lack of sleep.

On the monitor, the spaceship advances across the Pacific Ocean toward the west coast of the North American continent. According to data readout in a corner of the screen, the vessel is traveling at a steady 220 miles an hour.

President Crawford drums a jittery tattoo on the table with her pen. She glances at the digital clock on the wall. It's been exactly six hours since Walters updated her on the flyby status.

Her voice frayed with irritation, Crawford calls down the table.

"General?"

General Walters looks up from his laptop and locks eyes with her. For a person who never seems to smile, a corner of his mouth turns microscopically up.

"It's happening as we speak, Madam President."

PART THREE

THE FLYBY

ONE HUNDRED MILES ABOVE THE PACIFIC

In a delicately choreographed maneuver, the spy satellite slowly approaches the spacecraft from above and behind it. Continuously firing small directional jets, it eases down and to the left, closing to within a mile of the vessel.

For two minutes, the satellite keeps pace with the alien ship while bringing all of its instruments to bear on it.

As planned, this one and only shot at a rendezvous causes the satellite to lose orbital velocity. It starts plummeting to Earth in a controlled freefall. Moments later, just before slamming into the sea, it beams its findings to the cluster of giant satellite dishes at NSA headquarters in Washington, D.C.

ARGENTINIAN HIGH DESERT

The two Argentinian soldiers continue carefully tracking Nelson's boot prints through the desert sand. The sun beats mercilessly down on them.

The man wearing sunglasses is stooped over studying the ground. He's moving less confidently than before. He stops and stands up straight, stretching his back. He looks back at Bandanna driving the jeep a few steps behind.

Sunglasses says in Spanish, "I don't know, Amigo. I think I've lost the trail."

Bandanna turns off the jeep and climbs down. He wipes gritty sweat from his neck with the bandanna. Bends over to study the ground. "Could this be a scuffmark?" He straightens and looks at a slight incline in front of them. "It looks like he came down that hill..."

Bandanna follows what he thinks is the trail. Sunglasses stays with him.

When they reach the top of the rise, they both stop and stare. Rising out of the desert a half-mile away are the bunker's blast walls. Sunglasses raises the binoculars to his eyes. A smile appears through his sand-encrusted beard.

"It's them! The Americanos and their secret hideout."

Without another word, the two men hurry back down to the jeep, jump in, swing the vehicle around and roar back in the direction of Bahia Blanca.

WASHINGTON, D.C.

A government car speeds through the deserted streets of the nation's capital.

THE WHITE HOUSE

Her arms crossed in front of her chest, President Crawford paces the floor of the Situation Room. She neither looks at nor speaks to anyone, just stares at the ground. The others in the room stand in small clusters talking quietly.

A Marine guard opens the door. "Madam President; a Mr. Bennett from the National Security Agency."

"Show him in."

A short, thin man in his mid-forties strides into the room. He's wearing a black suit, white shirt, no tie. His movements are quick and precise. He carries a thin laptop.

Crawford says, "Come in, Mr. Bennett. We've been expecting you." She notices he's quite pale. "Are you all right?"

"No, Ma'am, I'm not all right," says Bennett, his voice tight. He taps his laptop. "You need to see this right away."

Worried glances ricochet around the room.

Crawford remains calm. "Have a seat and we'll get started."

Bennett sits down and opens the laptop. Just as he's about to boot it up, Crawford says, "Can you sync your computer with the wall monitor so we can all see it?"

Bennett freezes. He glances uneasily at the nearby aides.

"Is something wrong, Mr. Bennett?"

"Pardon my hesitation, Ma'am, but I'm thinking you might want to clear the room except for those on a need-to-know basis."

"The time for secrets is over, Mr. Bennett. Everyone here has a need—and a right—to know what's happening."

"As you wish, Ma'am." Bennett turns on the computer. He speaks quickly and efficiently.

"You're about to see footage that was taken less than a mile from the spaceship. The resolution was very low, but our computers did a great job of refining and enhancing it. There's a lot of data we don't understand; it would take years for our scientists to comb through and analyze it. Obviously, we don't have that kind of time. The primary mission of the flyby was to try and find out what's happening to our fellow human beings up there; to determine if the aliens are friend or foe."

Bennett hits a few buttons on the laptop. Everyone turns to watch as one of the wall monitors comes to life.

"The flyby came in from behind and to the left of the vessel. The duration was just under two minutes."

An image of the giant bladder fills the screen.

"Here's the expanding sac. It's filled with hundreds of millions of blue balloons, all packed together in neat rows and grids. Not an inch of wasted space. Our analysts think it's made of the same material as the graphene barrier."

The images change as the satellite moves from back to front of the spaceship. From this distance, there appear to be lots of sensors mounted on the bottom of the craft pointed toward the Earth. Strangely, there's hardly any instrumentation on the top half.

"Because the cameras aboard the satellite covered just about the entire electromagnetic spectrum, enough energy waves made it through the craft's exterior shell so that they were able to pull in data and even some visuals of the vessel's interior.

"One of the first things we learned is that these aliens like it hot. The temperature inside is a steady 134 degrees with 100 percent humidity. The atmosphere is composed of equal parts methane gas, carbon dioxide, and nitrogen. It's extremely dense, and seems to be more liquid than gas."

As the view zooms in on the spacecraft, the images move from left to right. There are a lot of strange-looking objects whose function can only be guessed at.

"Most of what we're looking at—we have no idea what it is. Our analysts think it could be the energy sources for their antigravity propulsion system and their dissolution beam."

The images continue to track by.

"Coming up on the left, you'll see the giant hatch where all the balloons come in. It appears that they're immediately ushered onto some kind of ultra-high tech conveyor belt that propels them back to the holding sac at lightning speed. Normally, this would be a very busy place. But as you can see, there's no activity at the moment. That's because the ship is traveling over a large area of empty ocean, so no balloons to collect."

Vice President Jameson says, "So where the hell are the aliens? On a coffee break?"

"Not exactly." There's a tightness in Bennett's voice that causes Crawford to look over at him.

Bennett clicks the pause button and gives the people in the room a look that chills them. "Ladies and gentleman, you're about to meet your first alien."

Everyone's frozen to their seats staring at the screen. Some lean forward in their chairs in anticipation of what's coming. Others grip the armrests and lean back, as if preparing for a physical blow.

Bennett hits the play button.

...Something's lumbering into view from the left.

Hard to make out exactly what.

As soon as it's centered in the frame, Bennett freezes the image and zooms in.

Gasps and smothered cries fill the room. They're staring at a creature that looks as if it had been designed by Hieronymus Bosch on acid.

The first thing they notice is that the thing is big. Its 'head' resembles a giant melon 15 feet in diameter. But instead of being uniformly spherical in shape, it looks like it's been afflicted with Proteus syndrome—the 'Elephant Man' disease. It's bulbous. Bloated. Misshapen. Its 'skin' is a slimy, mottled green, like that of rotting fruit. The only recognizable feature of what might be a face are what appear to be three 'eyes' that are the size of dinner plates set in a triangular shape. The eyes are disturbing. They have a vacuous, expressionless look, like those of a great white shark. Other than that, there are no other recognizable facial features such as a nose or a mouth or ears. Gills would not look out of place on the alien, but there's no sign of them.

The head is seamlessly attached to a 'body' that looks like a jellyfish thirty feet long, twenty feet wide and ten feet thick. The gelatinous 'skin' is semi-transparent. What most likely are the creature's veins and internal organs are clearly visible.

Protruding from either side of the body is a long, slender appendage. At the end of each appendage are what appear to be several 'fingers' of various widths and lengths. These tentacle-like limbs look both delicate and strong, and are no doubt capable of a number of tasks.

Extending from the back end of the body is another, much larger and longer appendage. This one would appear to be the workhorse of the three. It's thicker and more sinewy than the other two, and has the muscularity of a giant python snake.

"Man," says Vice President Jameson, "those things are uuuhhhg-ly."

General Walters tries to chime in with a bit of humor. "They make E.T. look like Miss America."

Bennett's voice is a grim monotone as he says, "Before I show the rest of the footage, I must warn all of you; what you're about to see is not pretty."

"We're all adults here, Mr. Bennett," says Crawford, annoyed at the man's heavy-handed warning. "Please continue."

"Very well."

Bennett hits a button on the remote. The footage of the flyby resumes.

The spy satellite's camera pans slowly toward the front of the spacecraft. It passes more strange machinery whose function can only be guessed at.

Mr. Bennett provides commentary on what they are looking at.

"The scientists who chose the path for the flyby assumed that the control room would be at the forward-most part of the ship. Accordingly, they configured it so that the camera would spend the most time focused on that area. Their educated guess would seem to be correct."

The spy satellite moves adjacent to, and in tandem with, what is the alien equivalent of the cockpit, its sensors recording what's inside. The video zooms in on what must be the ship's helm. Because the camera is now able to look through the enormous semi-transparent 'windshield' as opposed to the solid metallic body of the vessel, the resolution of the footage is suddenly much improved.

A large alien—possibly the ship's captain?—is in the center of the cockpit. It's partially surrounded by a large, horseshoe-shaped surface covered with strange, glowing hieroglyphics. The creature's two tentacles move across it with smooth dexterity. In response, huge 3D holographs of the Earth from various angles and distances appear and disappear like magic. The giant snake-like limb on its behind is neatly curled up. Weirdly, the alien's method of propulsion appears to be similar to that of a Manta ray; there's a thick membrane all around the bottom edge of its jellyfish-like body. Its undulating, wing-like motion allows the creature to glide effortlessly around three feet off the floor.

But then, a few feet beyond the 'captain', another alien comes into view. Bennett zooms in on it.

"This will put to rest any doubt as to why they came here," he says flatly, not enjoying at all what he's about to show.

The truth was finally about to become known. Man's place in the universe would now be revealed...

{The Zachary Stone Chronicles}

This other alien holds a blue balloon with its large, snake-like limb, handling it with the utmost gentleness. So far, so good.

But then something strange happens...

The limb passes the balloon over the top of the creature's rotting-melon, Elephant Man head to where the three eyes can see it. The appendage on either side of its body rise and approach the balloon. With great tenderness, one of the 'fingers' at the tip of each appendage slide down the length of the balloon on each side, deftly slicing it open. The balloon material sluffs to the floor, where it is quickly sucked down a drain to be recycled.

Held in the grasp of the large limb is a completely nude, unconscious Asian man in his 20s. With the material no longer encasing him, he quickly comes out of his state of suspended animation. The man's eyes open. He's groggy at first, then looks around to get his bearings. As he does so, he begins coughing violently in the hot, viscous atmosphere.

As the man hacks and coughs, the limb raises him back up over the top of the alien's head, where an opening several feet across has appeared. This would be the creature's mouth. As he's lowered down to the palpitating orifice, it begins secreting a blotchy, pink slime. The man panics and struggles to escape, but the two appendages hold him firmly in place. As he's pushed into the opening, everywhere the pink slime touches his body the flesh falls away. He makes one last weak effort to break free, but his hands are turning skeletal. As the "mouth" closes around him, his head is becoming a bleached skull.

Several women in the room scream. A couple of the military men retch. A few people sob.

Bennett pauses the video to allow them to recover somewhat.

Shaken, Jameson wipes his face with a handkerchief and says, "Dear God in heaven…"

"God had nothing to do with this," Bennett says. "We may have been living in the devil's universe all along."

Jameson says, "So we're just food to them?"

"I'm afraid there's a little more to it than that," Bennett says.

As he restarts the video, the alien undergoes a rapid transformation. The three lidless eyes somehow roll up into its head. The mottled green hue of its skin starts flashing every color of the rainbow. It begins to spasm and convulse in what for all the world looks like intense pleasure. Secretions erupt from a hundred different parts of its body.

The video footage comes to an end as the recon satellite can no longer maintain its trajectory and begins to fall from space.

"To answer your question, Mr. Vice President," says Mr. Bennett, "we appear to be anything but just food to them. We just had a front-row seat to the reason why they've come all this way to harvest us. Unfortunately for us, we seem to be the ultimate in physical pleasure to them. Imagine drinking the finest wine, eating the best caviar and truffles. Mix that with shots of ecstasy, cocaine and heroin. Throw in an erotic, full-body massage, sex, and multiple orgasms. Then roll everything into a single experience. Apparently, we're the ultimate drug to them. We're nirvana itself."

A man's panicky voice calls out. "So is that it? That's how it's all going to end?"

A terrified woman cries, "What do we do? What *can* we do?"

The volume of noise quickly swells as everyone is consumed by rising hysteria.

The president shouts, "Quiet!"

The room goes silent. Everyone looks at her. She glares back. Her voice is sharp. "Everybody calm the hell down. I have a job to do." She turns to Walters. "General, what's the status of our nuclear arsenal?"

"We've had the alien spacecraft targeted from day one, Ma'am. We are locked and loaded for bear."

"Are military communication channels intact?"

"They're stable for now, Ma'am. That will change as soon as the aliens start zapping our bases."

"Major Dawson."

A burly army officer in full military dress uniform moves out of the shadows.

"Yes, Ma'am?"

"Bring me the football."

"Yes, Ma'am."

Major Dawson totes a black leather briefcase over to her and sets it on the conference table. She opens it and removes what looks like an over-sized laptop. She places it in front of the empty chair next to her, then reaches back inside the briefcase and takes out a sealed envelope. She tears it open and removes a single 3x5 card. She glances at it, then peers down the table at General Walters.

"General Walters, will you assist me in authenticating the launch codes?"

"Absolutely, Ma'am." Walters walks over and takes the chair next to her.

Crawford barks to one of her few remaining aides. "Get whatever's left of the EBS network ready to go. I plan to address the American people very shortly."

"Yes, Ma'am." The aide hurries out the door.

Walters pulls the laptop over to him. His fingers hang poised over the keyboard. Crawford clearly and carefully begins reading random letters and numbers one by one off the 3x5 card. Walters just as clearly repeats each character back to her, then carefully enters it into the computer. They've obviously rehearsed this scenario.

Even though her voice is firm and steady, her hand holding the card shakes ever so slightly.

His voice filled with emotion, Jameson speaks. "Claire…"

Crawford says to General Walters, "Pause sequence."

"Authentication sequence paused," Walters responds.

She turns to her second-in-command. "What is it, Vice President Jameson?"

"What are you doing?"

"What am I doing? I'm trying to save the human race."

"But—all those people in that giant sac. They'll die…"

"You think I don't know that?" she says, her voice cracking ever so slightly.

Jameson says with deep and sudden passion. "Claire. Please don't do this."

"Like it or not, Mr. Vice President, we've just learned beyond any doubt that the human species is in an all-out war for of survival. Those who've been gathered up have to be sacrificed so that the rest of us can continue." Her eyes tear up. "Please. Try to understand that I don't have a choice."

"Maybe you don't…" A pause, then "But I do!"

Jameson dives across the conference table and reaches for the laptop. But Walters' man is too quick for him. He shoves the computer down the table out of range, then tackles Jameson. Major Dawson joins the fray. He grabs Jameson by the wrists, pulls him off the table and wrestles him to the floor.

Crawford strides to the door, jerks it open and shouts into the hallway, "Security!"

Two Marine guards rush in. They quickly subdue the vice president, bind his hands behind his back with zip-ties and usher him out the door. Jameson can be heard shouting as he's led away, "Claire! For the love of God, don't do it! Think of all those billions of—!"

The president slams the door.

Everyone in the room is rattled. Crawford and Walters resume their seats. With a shaky voice, Crawford says, "Resume authentication sequence."

Walters says, "Authentication sequence resumed."

They continue the procedure. The others in the room watch with rapt attention. It's as if they're watching a horrible, real-life nightmare, yet are powerless to do anything about it and can't wake up.

A few moments later, Walters says, "Authentication sequence is complete. Verification protocols have been met. All systems are go."

Crawford swallows. Takes a long, slow breath. Closes her eyes. Finally, in a loud whisper, "Launch all missiles."

Walters presses a nondescript black button on the laptop.

He looks up at her. In a quiet voice, he says, "All missiles away, Ma'am."

SOMEWHERE IN THE UPPER MIDWEST

A small farm deep in the countryside. A light breeze stirs the leaves of a weeping willow. A dragonfly hovers over a shallow pond. A pair of vultures performs wide, lazy circles in the sky. The serene setting is suddenly shattered as an explosive bolt blasts a hidden steel hatch sideways, revealing a deep, dark hole in the ground. Three seconds later, the missile's fuel ignites. The rocket hurtles into the sky with a bone-jarring roar. Riding a plume of flame and smoke, it veers west.

JET PROPULSION LABORATORY

A television image sputters to life. President Crawford in the Oval Office.

"My fellow Americans..."

Professor Seifert and a couple of the last remaining technicians turn their attention to the president's broadcast.

"On my last broadcast, I gave you—the American people—my solemn promise that I would report back to you immediately after the flyby to let you know if we learned anything new about the spacecraft, be it good or bad. I'm addressing the nation today to tell you that we've finally discovered the aliens' purpose in coming to our planet. I'm afraid it's not good. In fact, it's as bad as anyone could imagine. I'm going to show you now what was presented to me a few minutes ago. It's footage of inside the spacecraft..."

ALL ACROSS THE UPPER MIDWEST

Dozens more missiles erupt from their silos and streak west in high arcs.

CENTRAL INTELLIGENCE AGENCY

Conroy and Otis take a break from their work. They watch the president's broadcast via a secure video feed from the Situation Room.

"...I must warn you, it's shocking; it's terrifying; it's sickening. But it's real. And we have no choice but to deal with this new reality the best we can. It will run unedited with no commentary..."

The two men share a worried glance.

"Uh oh," Otis says.

50 MILES OFF THE WASHINGTON COAST

A half-dozen ballistic missile submarines hover quietly just under the ocean's surface. They're spread over a square mile.

On cue, the Boomer fleet launches all its weapons. In rapid succession, scores of rockets burst from the water and scream skyward.

SITUATION ROOM

Those who can stomach it watch the footage for a second time as it plays over the EBS. General Walters is one of them. But he's more focused on something at the very beginning of the tape...

ARGENTINIAN BUNKER JOBSITE

Zack and his family are gathered in the meal hall along with many others, watching the footage of the flyby on the large, flat-screen monitor. Kent Hatcher is also present. There's not a sound in the room as the camera pans toward the front of the space ship. When the first alien comes into view, several viewers gasp or cry out in shock.

MINNEAPOLIS

Bill and Cindy Franklin sit in their living room watching the broadcast. Cindy is so large that the only place she can sit with any comfort is the oversized Barcalounger. Bill perches in a chair next to her holding her hand. They both stare at the television with a growing sense of horror.

When the video gets to the part where the unfortunate Chinese man is eaten and the alien creature convulses with pleasure, Cindy loses it.

"Bill?" Her voice shrill. "Oh, God, Bill... Does that mean we're all going to be eaten?! That all we are to them is... is... food that makes them go crazy with pleasure?!" She starts to hyperventilate. "Everything we've worked so hard for... Our jobs. Our house. Our marriage. Our babies." She shrieks, "And that's all we are?!"

Bill speaks in a soothing voice. "Cindy... Cindy, calm down."

She sobs uncontrollably. "Why should I calm down?! It's all for nothing! Nothing!"

Bill has no response to that.

Cindy suddenly sits up, tears streaming from her eyes. "Oh dear god holy Jesus... My water just broke."

ABOARD THE SPACE FREIGHTER

Angie Hardingway sits at the communications console watching the video. As she does so, her face reflects a kaleidoscope of emotions: Horror. Shock. Revulsion. Anger. As the video ends, Angie looks at a small framed photo of her two daughters. Sadie, the college sophomore; and Bonnie, the high school senior. The pretty young women, full of light and life, smile happily into the camera.

Angie reaches out and touches the photograph. Her voice is a pained whisper. "My poor girls..."

A single large tear courses down each cheek.

"My poor babies. I'm so sorry..."

ARGENTINIAN BUNKER JOBSITE

When the flyby video finishes playing, the people in the meal hall sit in stunned, horrified silence. Then the murmurs start, growing rapidly in volume as people react to what they've just seen.

Zack says to his mother, "Mom, that poor man... I sure hope that doesn't happen to us."

Lydia gives him a fierce hug, her eyes moist. "Don't worry. Kent and your dad and everyone here are working as hard as they can so it doesn't."

CENTRAL INTELLIGENCE AGENCY

Otis and Conroy sit in stunned silence.

Suddenly Conroy grabs a glass pitcher full of water off a table and hurls it against a wall where it smashes into a thousand pieces.

"Dammit, Otis! What an idiot I am! How could I have been so blind! Three days ago, I told the president, *They're all smiling. Every person in the cave paintings is smiling, like they know something good is happening.* If I'd kept my mouth shut, she would have blown that thing out of the sky!" Tears suddenly flood his eyes.

"Conroy, take it easy," Otis says. "You're being too hard on yourself. I can go you one better. General Walters wanted to nuke that thing back in the beginning when Beijing was being hoovered up. I, in my infinite wisdom, persuaded President Crawford to not heed his advice. So for what it's worth—"

"Minutes after seeing that video," President Crawford says as she appears back on the secure feed. "I ordered our entire nuclear arsenal launched against the spaceship..."

ARGENTINIAN BUNKER JOBSITE

It's deathly quiet in the meal hall as the president continues her address over the EBS.

"...That attack is now in progress. We don't know what the aliens' defense systems are capable of. But my analysts assure me that all we need is *just one warhead* to get past their defenses and close to within a few miles of the ship, that it would be more than enough to do the job."

Anxious looks are exchanged among the viewers.

"To maximize the chance of that happening," continues Crawford, "the timing of the missile launches was staggered so they would all hit the target at the same time while coming from several different directions. Our strategy is that such an onslaught will distract or confuse the aliens enough for at least one of our warheads to slip through. As it stands now, the enemy ship is fast approaching the northwest corner of the United States."

General Walters appears in the picture. He leans down and whispers in the president's ear, then quickly walks away.

Her words clipped, President Crawford says, "I've just learned that contact is imminent. I have to leave you now. I'll return when I know the outcome of the attack."

Crawford leans toward the camera and speaks with unambiguous sincerity.

"My fellow Americans, please know that in these very trying times, we're doing everything in our power to eliminate this mortal threat to our existance."

Crawford stands and walks away from her desk. The picture turns to snow.

SITUATION ROOM

President Crawford takes her seat at the head of the table. What remains of her cabinet and staff are gathered around it.

"What's happening, General?"

Walters paces the room as he talks. Gesturing at three of the monitors, he says, "We've positioned two reconnaissance satellites over the site of the impending attack. On the third monitor is a live feed from a ground-based telescope. Between the three of them, we should have a front row seat."

OFF THE NORTHWEST COAST

Hundreds of nuclear-tipped missiles roar skyward from all points of the compass, quickly closing the distance to the alien ship.

SITUATION ROOM

The room is completely silent, all eyes on the monitors. The tension is stretched to the breaking point. The Chief of Staff of the Army, a much decorated general, can sit still no longer. He gets to his feet, moves close to the monitors and urges the rockets on in a harsh, passionate whisper.

"Come on, baby... Go get those bastards!"

Others in the room get caught up in this do-or-die moment for humanity. They, too, approach the monitors offering similar cries of encouragement.

"Sic 'em!"

"Take 'em out!"

"Blow those creatures back where they came from!"

OFF THE NORTHWEST COAST

With a thunderous roar, the missiles achieve maximum thrust as they converge on the spaceship. Less than a minute to go before they reach the nuclear blast kill zone.

Suddenly, all the sensors on the underside of the alien vessel come to blinking, whirring life. In one second, the instruments evaluate the threat level of the fast-approaching objects. Another second to determine their trajectories. One more second to analyze the contents of the projectiles. Another to calculate the appropriate response. A final second for dozens of miniature dissolution beams to lock onto multiple targets.

SITUATION ROOM

As the missiles rapidly close with the spaceship, a growing chorus of cheers urge them on.

"They're almost to the kill zone!"

"Go, baby, go!"

"Watch for that big beautiful mushroom cloud in the sky!"

"Go! Go! Go!"

Curiously, General Walters doesn't partake in the cheer-leading. He stands quietly at the back of the room, arms folded over his chest, watching the monitors.

OFF THE NORTHWEST COAST

All of the rockets' fire-belching engines suddenly cut out. The thundering roar abruptly stops like someone tripped a switch. The missiles' forward momentum causes them to continue flying in eerie silence a moment. Then, in rapid succession, they dissolve into smears of black and gray dust and sand, which rains harmlessly back to Earth.

SITUATION ROOM

It's gone quiet in the room. Everyone stares at the monitors in shock.

President Crawford says, "What the hell happened?"

The Chief of Staff of the Army speaks with anger and a touch of awe. "The damned thing just took out our missiles."

"All of them?"

"It appears so."

Crawford's having trouble processing the information. "Did *any* of the warheads make it through? Even one?"

"Not even one," says Walters from the back of the room. They all turn to look at him. "If it had, the nuke would have detonated by now. That obviously hasn't happened."

The exhilaration that had been in those watching the attack has quickly been replaced by fear. To add to their misery, an aide gestures at one of the monitors.

"Madam President. The spacecraft is now passing over Western Washington and fast approaching Seattle. The city had plenty of time to evacuate. What you're seeing is live footage from video-cams placed around the town."

On the monitors, the scenes of a completely-deserted American city are chilling, like something out of a Cold War-era movie. To top it off, air raid sirens reverberate through the barren streets. Because there's hardly any people to harvest, the dissolution beam moves at a rapid clip. In quick succession, the city's iconic structures collapse into dust:

The ferry boats sitting empty at Colman Dock.

Pioneer Square. Pike Place Market. The Space Needle.

Gone.

All the ground cameras dissolve as well, causing the monitors to go dark in the Situation Room.

"So that's it?" cries the Secretary of Defense. "We throw everything we have at it, give it our very best shot, and it's all for nothing?"

His voice flat, General Walters says, "We didn't even slow it down."

"So what do we do? Sit on our hands until they come for us?"

Claire Crawford looks like she's aged five years in the last few minutes. Her voice comes out heavy, defeated. "I don't see that it matters what we do. It's over."

As her words sink in, looks of panic cross the faces of those in the room.

"Maybe not," Walters says. They all look at him. Dare anyone hope the General has a plan to turn things around?

Walters speaks while walking with measured steps down the length of the conference table.

"The Secretary's right. We gave it our very best shot to absolutely no avail. All of our high-tech weaponry is child's play to them."

Walters comes up beside Mr. Bennett and stops.

"That said, while watching the flyby footage, I saw something that gave me an idea. Mr. Bennett, would you mind playing the video again?"

Mr. Bennett shrugs, why not? He hits a couple of buttons on the laptop. The footage begins to play on one of the wall monitors.

President Crawford gives the general a pained look. "Jim, I really don't think watching that gruesome scene again is going to—"

"Please bear with me, Madam President. What I want you to see is at the very beginning of the tape."

Crawford nods.

"As our satellite approaches the spacecraft, you can see the giant sac filled with our fellow human beings. Watch carefully now..."

The camera takes in a broad view of the spacecraft.

"Freeze that."

Mr. Bennett stops on the image.

"Okay, now slowly zoom in on the vessel."

Bennett does so until the craft fills the screen.

"Stop it right there."

As Bennett does so, Walters goes up to the monitor and points to the undercarriage of the craft.

"See all this these whirligigs and gizmos pointed toward Earth? There's hundreds of them. My guess is that many are sensors monitoring the progress of the harvest and helping to keep the vessel on track. And as we just learned from our failed attack, there are obviously powerful defense mechanisms in place as well.

"Now look at the top half of the ship. There's hardly any instrumentation. Think about what that means for a second: What is the primary function of this spaceship? It's certainly not "to seek out new life and civilizations." No. This spacecraft is the interstellar equivalent of a floating fish factory. Its primary function is to harvest us with maximum efficiency. Period. That's why there's hardly any sensors on the upper half of the vessel. The aliens are more concerned about what's going on below them, not above.

"That's why the flyby was able to get so close to the ship without being detected. I'm convinced that if we had launched our nukes from above, the alien craft would never have seen them coming. It would have been vaporized. This may be their Achilles heel."

"Jim," says Crawford, "you know better than anyone that we have no nuclear warheads in space."

"I'm fully aware of that, Madam President. But the weapon wouldn't have to be a nuke. It wouldn't even have to be an explosive. Which brings me to my idea: *We go extremely low-tech.* We sneak up on them from behind and hit them in the back of the head with a blunt instrument. Something big and heavy and traveling at high velocity."

Everyone in the room is looking confused. President Crawford's brow wrinkles in concentration. "But we don't have anything in space that meets the criteria you're—"

Crawford stops in mid-sentence. She suddenly gets what the general is saying.

"Space Freighter One."

"Exactly."

The president thinks about this for a moment, then says, "It just might work. Only..."

"Only what?"

"The guidance computers aboard the Freighter. They'll need to be programmed with a new flight plan."

"So?"

"Any outside changes to the computer's configurations are automatically blocked. The pilot has to consent to allow them to take place." Crawford stares at him. "Jim, we'd be asking her to go on a suicide mission."

General Walters returns the look. "I think she'd prefer that to the alternative."

MINING PIT
FAR SIDE OF THE MOON

Spike sits at his communications console talking with Angie. "Angie, you've got to pull yourself together."

"Why, Spike?" she says, her voice agitated. "Why should I? You saw the flyby, didn't you?"

"Yeah, but that's no reason for you to—"

"It's the best reason in the world!" she shouts. "Did you see what those creatures did?! Eventually, that will happen to every person on the planet! When I think of Bonnie... and Sadie..." She chokes back a sob.

In a soothing voice, Spike says, "Have you talked to them since the president's broadcast?"

With an effort, Angie manages to calm herself. "No. Communications are limited to emergency government channels. I hope they're okay. If I could just speak to them, even for a couple of—"

Angie looks away for a moment, distracted by something. "Spike, I've got a Priority One call coming in. I'll get back to you on my next pass."

"You take care, Angie."

But she's already signed off.

Frowning, Spike turns off his console.

ABOARD THE SPACE FREIGHTER

A woman's voice comes through the speaker at Angie's communication console. "Captain Angela Hardingway on Space Freighter One. Are you there?"

Angie violently rubs the tears out of her eyes. Speaks into the mic.

"This is Hardingway. Who wants to know?"

The image of President Crawford jiggles to life on Angie's screen. "This is President Crawford calling. How are you doing, Angie?"

Angie sits up straight. Smooths back her hair. Clears her throat.

"I've had better days, Ma'am."

"You and me both, sister. Have you got a minute?"

The absurdity of the question under such disastrous circumstances causes Angie to chuckle. Ice successfully broken, Crawford joins in.

"What can I do for you, Madam President?"

ARGENTINIAN BUNKER JOBSITE

The folks in the meal hall sit waiting in anticipation for the president's update. They get more restive with each passing minute.

"It's been an awfully long time."

"Do you think we got the aliens?"

"God, I sure hope so."

"What if we didn't?"

"We keep doing what we're doing. It's our only hope."

The monitor crackles to life. Crawford once again addresses the nation.

"My fellow Americans..."

"Quiet, everybody! The president's back."

The viewers settle down to watch as Crawford fills the country in about the failed nuclear attack.

"...As it turns out, our unsuccessful attack wasn't our last chance to take out the aliens. The nation's top military commander has come up with a plan for another assault—one that we all here agree might just work. General Walters may have found the chink in the aliens' armor. We just crunched the data with JPL's computers and they think so to. So my message to you now is this: All is not lost. Do not lose hope. I'll get back to you when I have more information. I'm signing off for now. Be strong."

The monitor turns to snow. Before the buzzing of the viewers can grow, Hatcher steps to the front of the crowd and speaks loudly.

"Okay, everybody! The government obviously has some things to work out before we hear from them again—whenever that will be. In the meantime, we should all get back to work. I'll keep you posted on any new developments."

No one in the room is in disagreement with him. They all quickly make for the exits to resume their jobs.

LUNAR ORBIT

ABOARD THE SPACE FREIGHTER

Angie stares at the control console, then taps in a series of codes and commands. Words appear on the screen: 'New trajectory coordinates successfully downloaded from Jet Propulsion Laboratory. Press ENTER to activate program.'

Angie takes a resolute breath, then presses ENTER.

The massive Space Freighter glides in perfect silence over the landscape of the moon. Suddenly, its giant engines explode to life. They fire with a sustained roar as the Freighter leaves lunar orbit and turns slowly toward Earth. The engines continue to thunder with maximum thrust.

MINING PIT
FAR SIDE OF THE MOON

Spike sits at his communications console watching the digital clock in the corner of the computer monitor. A small pop-up appears onscreen: 'Freighter One—Horizon Appearance Expected In 5 Seconds... 4... 3... 2...'

Spike keys the mic. "Angie? Are you there? Angie? Come in, Freighter One."

Nothing.

He checks the radar readout. No blip indicating the presence of the Freighter.

Spike slumps back in his chair. "Damn girl... Where the hell'd ya go?"

ABOARD THE SPACE FREIGHTER

Angie perches on the edge of her chair in the ship's control room checking computer readouts. All business now, she speaks into the microphone of her headset.

"Things are looking good, Dr. Seifert. I'm on track for the rendezvous."

Dr. Seifert's voice comes through her headphones. "Good job, Captain Hardingway."

Angie gives a half smile. "Call me Angie."

"Okay, Angie. You are one brave woman."

"Thank you, Doctor," Angie responds. But her voice is tinged with sadness.

CENTRAL INTELLIGENCE AGENCY

Otis and Conroy attempt to absorb the news of the failed attack. Conroy is still upset as Otis continues to try and console him. He paces the room venting his frustrations.

"I still say we should have attacked that thing the second it showed it up."

"Conroy, listen to me. Don't you get what just happened? It doesn't matter that we didn't launch a nuclear attack earlier; it wouldn't have worked anyway. Okay?"

Conroy sighs. Nods. Sits down heavily in a chair as Otis continues. "Which brings me to the question of why are the stick people in the cave drawings smiling like they know something good is happening, when we now know they should have been terrified?"

"That's the question of the day."

"Would you like to hear my theory?"

Conroy shrugs. "Why not."

"We know from the cave drawings that our prehistory brethren were pretty darned advanced. They had cars and roads and buildings and houses. But nothing we saw in the paintings gives us any indication that they had achieved powered flight. Heck, it's very possible—likely even—that the airplane hadn't been invented yet, let alone rockets and satellites. Their world view was wholly ground-based. Keep that in the back of your mind for a second.

"Because the cave paintings exist, someone obviously would have to have been around to draw them, showing what happened after the fact—or at least drawing what they thought happened. What we don't know is how they managed to avoid being collected—but that's irrelevant to my theory.

"I'm thinking that immediately after the last mass collection, with all the trappings of civilization turned to dust, daily life for those left behind must have quickly turned extremely brutal. So brutal, in fact, that to whoever drew those paintings, floating up to the sky in a blue balloon in a blissful state of suspended animation must have looked pretty darned good. Hence, all the smiles.

"Okay, switch to present day. Thanks to man's achievements in space flight, we got a good look at what the aliens are really up to. If anyone's still around to make cave drawings after we all get collected, you can bet the farm that the stick figures won't be smiling. In defense of the cave painters, wishful thinking in times of acute crisis is nothing new. As for us, we don't have that luxury. We know *exactly* what's going to become of us."

Otis pushes his chair back from the table.

"So that's my theory."

Otis watches Conroy as the younger man considers his words. After awhile, Conroy slowly nods his head.

"It sounds logical enough to me."

"Good," says Otis. He stands. "Now, are you ready to get back to work?"

Conroy smiles and nods. He gets up and together they make their way over to their work area.

SITUATION ROOM

President Crawford addresses the nation.

"My fellow Americans: I'm sorry to be so late in getting back to you. A lot has happened. I'll do my best to fill you in..."

MINING PIT

FAR SIDE OF THE MOON

Spike fiddles with his banjo while watching the president's broadcast with less than undivided attention.

"...We learned the hard way that attacking the enemy vessel from Earth is futile. Their sensors are designed to thwart just such an assault. That said, we've launched a new strike, but this one is different. The aliens don't seem to feel threatened by anything from above, so that's exactly where our strike will be coming from.

"A short time ago, I spoke with Captain Angela Harding-way—" Crawford smiles and says, "or Angie, as she prefers to be called."

A photo of Angie appears on the screen. Taken a few years earlier, she's smiling at the camera and looks great.

Spike almost drops his banjo as he gawks at the screen.

The president continues. "Angie is the commander and sole crew member of Space Freighter One. I asked her if she would be willing to perform the ultimate sacrifice for her country. She agreed without hesitation." Crawford's eyes turn moist. "As I speak, Angie's Freighter is on a collision course with the enemy vessel."

Spike gives a half-grin. Awe in his raspy voice, he says, "Shitfire, Angie..."

Crawford continues. "Whatever happens, Angie is a true hero and deserves our love and respect. Please send your most positive thoughts her way."

As unsentimental as he is, Spike's eyes tear up. "You go, girl."

ARGENTINIAN BUNKER JOBSITE

A crowd has gathered in the meal hall to watch the president's latest.

"...The Freighter will be traveling at approximately 24,000 miles an hour when it collides with the spacecraft. My team has confidence this could be the knockout blow we've been looking for. They also agree that—if struck at the right place at the right angle—the giant sac could be severed from the alien vessel. If that happens, those of us still here will do everything in our power to rescue everyone from the giant sac. It'll take time for us to get up to speed on their technology, but be assured that we will not rest until every last person collected is safely back on Earth. That said, I'm afraid there's a downside.

"The thing is, even traveling at maximum velocity, it's going to take Space Freighter One time to reach the Earth. As Dr. Seifert informed us not long ago, the dissolution beam is on track to make three 600-mile-wide passes across the United States."

An animated map of the U.S. mainland showing the three predicted paths appears next to the president.

"Unfortunately, by the time Freighter One is able to intercept the enemy, the dissolution beam will be most of the way through its third pass. As fate would have it, the intercept will occur while the spacecraft is approaching the nation's capital.

Crawford's demeanor shifts into something softer, more compassionate.

"Before I leave you, I wanted to address another...situation that has come to my attention. I've been getting reports that there are large numbers of suicides occurring around the country. After watching the flyby footage, I can understand why that might be a logical reaction to what appears will be our final destiny.

"But please, hear me out: My advisers are in unanimous agreement that this is our best chance at disabling the alien ship. In light of that, I'm urging you in the strongest possible terms... no, I'm *begging* you, don't despair. Somehow, some way, we're going to beat these soulless creatures. I know this in my heart."

Crawford's voice cracks during her last sentence.

The image turns to snow.

Kent Hatcher stands and addresses the group.

"I certainly hope and pray the president is right about putting the alien ship out of commission. But hopes and prayers are no substitute for hard work and a solid plan. Needless to say, our efforts here will continue unabated."

Hatcher turns and walks out of the meal hall. The rest file out behind him, heading back to their assigned tasks.

THE FIRST PASS

The dissolution beam strikes the West Coast. It ranges from just north of Portland, Oregon, to half-way down the length of California. San Francisco is the first major city on this pass to be dissolved.

The Golden Gate Bridge. Alcatraz. Fisherman's Wharf. Cable cars. All collapse in cascades of grit and dust as a wide stream of blue balloons heads skyward.

The beam continues on through Portland, Oregon. Boise, Idaho. Salt Lake City, Utah. Wyoming and Montana. The Dakotas. Minnesota and a chunk of Northern Wisconsin before moving up into Ontario and Quebec, Canada.

CENTRAL INTELLIGENCE AGENCY

Otis and Conroy, their shirtsleeves rolled up, work steadily copying computer files, consulting databases and tinkering with various tools. In a corner of the room lies a pile of empty pizza boxes and soft drink cans. Curiously, the focal point of their attention is what appears to be an oversized briefcase made of solid metal. They keep returning to it with hand-held measuring tapes.

They have a conversation as they continue to work.

Otis ruminates out loud to Conroy. "You know, ever since the aliens first showed up, I've been mystified by two things: Number one, why would a civilization as advanced as they are, go to the trouble to come all this way to Earth, and then once here, not even bother to try to communicate with us? And number two, making things even more mysterious, after the collection process began, they took such great pains to ensure no one was harmed."

Conroy gives a grim smile. Doesn't look up from his work as he says, "Did you figure out the answers?"

Otis gives a grim smile of his own. "For the aliens to try to and communicate with us would make about us much sense as me trying to have a conversation with an oyster I'm about to eat."

"And number two?"

"No human beings are being harmed in the collection process—correction, the *harvesting* process—because we're a valuable commodity to them. The aliens don't want to bruise the fruit."

The only phone in the room rings. The two men look at each without moving, as if waiting for the other to answer it. Otis finally picks up, sounding annoyed.

"Hello." Otis suddenly stands taller. "Yes, Madam President." He listens as the president speaks. After a few moments, Otis says, "Yes, Ma'am. We'll get started on it right away." Otis hangs up and looks at Conroy. "Change in plans. She wants us to pack everything up and relocate to Cape Canaveral, that we can continue our work there. A crew is on its way to help us."

Conroy shrugs. "Fine by me."

Though most means of communications had been knocked out, thanks to the telecommunications satellites that still orbited the Earth some continued to work. If you had a satellite dish on your roof and a source of power, chances were good that you could at least tune in to the EBS network. And if you had access to a satellite phone and

could get past government restrictions,
they tended to work perfectly…

{The Zachary Stone Chronicles}

ABOARD THE SPACE FREIGHTER

Angie sits at the helm of her ship monitoring the controls so that the heavy vessel remains at maximum thrust. It's quiet except for the low rumble of its engines. Resigned to her fate, Angie goes through the motions mechanically. A profound melancholy has settled over her like a lead cape.

Angie hears the ping of an incoming communication. Glances at the screen, sees that it's the president hailing her. She presses a button and Claire Crawford's face stutters to life on the screen.

"Hi, Angie."

"Hello, Madam President."

"Please, call me Claire. I mean, under the circumstances…"

Angie smiles but her eyes are sad. "Okay, Claire."

"I'm calling because there are some people who want to talk to you."

"Uh, Ma'am? Claire? I've heard there's a lot of people who would like to get in touch with me and tell me what a great thing it is I'm doing, but I don't want any part of that. So, no offense if I refuse to take any calls."

Crawford grins. "I think you might make an exception in this case…" She presses a button and the screen splits in two. Claire's image remains on the left side. Jittering to life on the right are Sadie and Bonnie.

"Mom! It's us! Bonnie and Sadie! Can you hear us okay?!"

Angie starts to lose it. "Oh my God! Oh my God! Where are you?! Are you okay?!"

"We're fine! The FBI found us in different parts of the country and brought us down here to Florida. We're calling you from a laptop that's hooked to a satellite phone."

"Oh, girls, it's so good to see you... To hear your voices..." The first of what will be many tears rolls down her cheek. She turns to Crawford. "Thank you, Madam—" She catches herself. Smiles from the heart. "Thank you, Claire, so very much."

"It took a little sleuthing, but it's the least I could do for you."

Bonnie begins to cry. "We miss you, Mom, so much..." Sadie begins to cry as well.

Crawford says, "I'm sure you three have a lot to catch up on. Consider this a toll-free call, so talk as long as you want."

The president signs off, allowing the image of the two girls to fill Angie's screen.

JET PROPULSION LABORATORY

Doctor Seifert and three other dour-face holdouts sit at a long table in the control room watching an animated screen track the progress of the dissolution beam. It's moving at a slight northeast angle across the Pacific Ocean just a couple of hundred miles off the California coast.

All four men are scared to death but do their best to maintain an air of bravado.

Says one, "Looks like we're up next."

"It's about time," says another. "I was starting to get bored."

"I guess now's as good a time as any for this," Seifert says, reaching under the table.

"For what?"

In answer, Seifert sets a plain brown paper bag on the table. Removes a bottle of Scotch and four glasses.

"Thirty-year old single malt Glenmorangie."

The men smile. "Sweet," says one.

"I was saving it for a special occasion," says Seifert as he uncorks the bottle and pours several fingers into each glass. "Thing is, there won't be any more occasions, special or otherwise."

He slides a glass to each of them. "Anyone care to propose a toast?"

They eye each other a moment. Finally, one of them says, "Yeah, I've got a toast for you." He raises his glass in the air. "Here's to hoping the people in Washington know what the hell they're doing."

"Hear hear."

"I'll drink to that."

They all take big swallows of their drinks.

THE SECOND PASS

As the dissolution beam moves through the sprawling cities and towns of Southern California, massive clouds of blue balloons rise from the devastated landscape. They quickly merge into one giant river streaming up to the sky.

The man-made dams at numerous reservoirs across the city give way, sending water cascading down the vast network of storm drains and aqueducts. Near one such breach, the beam strikes an upscale shopping mall that's completely deserted except for the shellfish left behind at a high-end grocery store. As the ceilings, walls, and counters melt away, so does an abandoned glass tank holding dozens of lobsters. As they spill to the floor, the rubber bands binding their claws disappear. Staggering about in a crustacean equivalent of dazed and confused, the lobsters are engulfed in a sudden swell of water that sweeps them outside and down into a storm drain, where they will be washed out to sea.

JET PROPULSION LABORATORY

Seifert pours the last of the whiskey into their glasses. It's done wonders to bolster their courage. They turn their eyes on the approaching dissolution beam on the monitor.

It's just seconds away from Pasadena.

Seifert says, "Bottoms up, gentlemen."

As soon as they down the last of their drinks, they hear the hiss of falling sand and gravel as nearby buildings collapse.

On Seifert's mouth is a sad smile. "Bon voyage," he says.

This pass of the dissolution beam cuts through the very heart of the country. After razing Los Angeles and San Diego, it continues on its relentless path.

Las Vegas. Phoenix. Denver. Kansas City.

MINNEAPOLIS

Cindy Franklin lies sweaty and exhausted in a recovery room after a long and difficult labor. She's given birth to her twins. They lie sleeping in the crooks of each arm. Bill sits attentively in a chair beside her. He looks equally worn out.

"Did you call the nurse?" Cindy says. "I'm really thirsty."

"I've been pressing the call button like, every twenty seconds," says Bill. He gets up from the chair. "I'll go find somebody."

He steps into the corridor. It's quiet. Deserted.

He calls out, "Hello? Nurse? Doctor?"

Silence.

Louder. "Is anybody there?!"

Again silence. But this time, it's replaced by the hiss of crumbling buildings.

Cindy cries out. "Bill!"

Bill dashes back into the recovery room.

Outside the window, the building across the street collapses into a pile of sand.

"Oh, God, Bill! It's here! My babies! My poor babies...!"

Bill instinctively covers his wife and infant sons with his own body. As the hospital dissolves, four balloons—two large and two very small—rise up from the dust and devastation and disappear into the sky.

St. Louis. Chicago. Indianapolis. Cincinnati. Detroit. Cleveland. Pittsburgh.

As the dissolution beam approaches Baltimore, its southern edge just misses the northern outskirts of the nation's capital. It will get hit on the third pass.

Baltimore, then Philadelphia are leveled.

Next in line: The Big Apple.

NEW YORK CITY

A pensive Clifford March wanders the streets of the city he loves. There's a new autumn chill in the air. Orange leaves skitter across the pavement. He pulls the collar of his trench coat up around his neck.

Always-bustling Times Square is an urban ghost town. The chronic cacophony of car horns has been replaced by an eerie silence. The City That Never Sleeps is practically comatose.

The sound of breaking glass. Clifford looks down Broadway and sees a half-dozen disheveled men making their way up the boulevard smashing windows and grabbing merchandise. All are drunk or high or both. These are those misbegotten specimens of humanity that revel in chaos. The breakdown of civilization is another excuse for a moment's fleeting gratification. There's just enough time for a last round of mayhem before the party comes to a permanent end.

The biggest man in the crowd grips a metal baseball bat in one hand, takes a swallow from a bottle of Limited Edition Swarovski Studded Alize Vodka with the other. Despite the cold, he wears only a tank top with his jeans and boots. His arms are thickly muscled. His eyes bloodshot. When he sees Clifford watching him, he drains the rest of the vodka, smashes the bottle on the ground, and begins striding toward him.

"Yo! Whatchu lookin' at, punk?!"

The others pick up the scent of the hunt and fall in behind.

Just as Clifford's going to make a run for it, a yellow cab appears from nowhere like something out of a dream. With a squeal of tires, it pulls to a stop. The driver is a skinny young black man. A fedora is perched at a jaunty angle on his head, but there's nothing jaunty about him. Just the opposite, in fact. His soulful eyes radiate a profound sadness.

The driver rolls down his window and says in heavily-accented English, "Did you call for a taxi?"

Clifford scrambles in and slams the door. "That was me."

"Where to?"

Clifford doesn't even have to think about it.

"Battery Park."

The driver nods as if in approval. The tires squeal again as the cab takes off. The mob gives half-hearted chase for about thirty feet, throwing rocks and bottles, but it's gone. They break off pursuit and go back to systematically smashing windows, grabbing whatever loot they can.

Inside the cab, the driver pulls a flask from his jacket and offers it to Clifford.

"Would you like a drink?"

"Yes, I would." Shaken from the close call, Clifford reaches forward and takes the flask. He uncorks it and takes a long pull of the stinging liquor, whatever it is. "Thank you," he says, handing it back.

The cabbie holds it up briefly as if making a silent toast, then takes a swallow himself. He corks the flask and places it back in his jacket.

"I appreciate the ride," says Clifford. "Getting beaten to death in Times Square wasn't exactly what I had in mind for my last memories of New York."

The cabbie nods. The two men drive in companionable silence through Greenwich Village, Lower Manhattan, Tribeca, then past the One World Trade Center tower. All is empty, deserted.

The driver sighs and gestures at everything around them. "Helluva thing," he says, his words encompassing the entire world.

"Yes," says Clifford quietly. "It is a hell of a thing."

Moments later, the cab arrives at Battery Park. The two men climb out of the car and walk down to the water where they sit on the seawall and gaze silently at the Statue of Liberty. The city of Newark, New Jersey, lies a few miles beyond it.

"Good choice," says the cabbie.

"Thanks," Clifford.

A handful of seagulls wheel and cry around them. After a few moments of silence, the cabbie says, "All my family back in Addis Ababa. Children. Wife. Parents. Brothers. Sisters. I was going to bring them here." He snaps his fingers. "Poof. All gone."

Clifford gives the man a long look. "I'm sorry."

The cab driver continues staring at the statue across the water. He reaches into his jacket and produces the flask. Hands it to Clifford, who takes another long pull. He hands it back to the cabbie, who finishes it. They continue to stare at the statue.

In the near distance across the water, the buildings of Newark begin to crumble. A couple of seconds later, the copper, cast iron and steel structure of the Statue of Liberty twists and turns, writhes and warps as it goes down.

"Good-bye, my friend," says the cab driver.

"Good-bye, my friend," says Clifford.

Providence is next up, then Boston. Portland, Maine is the last major city to go as the dissolution beam completes its second pass across the country.

CAPE CANAVERAL

Otis and Conroy are holed up in a temporary workspace. The area isn't as large or well-equipped as the one at the Central Intelligence Agency, but it's adequate for them to finish the job. The survival kit rests on a metal work bench. Filled to the brim with a diverse selection of items, it's nearly complete.

The strange-looking telephone buzzes. Otis and Conroy glance at each other. Then Otis answers it.

"Yes, Madam President."

"Doctor Larson, the alien ship is about to start its third pass across the country. I've arranged to bring you and Professor Hamilton a live feed of its upcoming rendezvous with Space Freighter One from one of our spy satellites."

"Thank you, Ma'am. Let's hope we get better results this time."

"Let's hope, indeed." Crawford rings off.

BAHIA BLANCA

The modest city teems with folks who were able to flee to the last place in the world that will be dissolved and collected. There is a strange energy in the town: not frantic or panicked, but nervous and anxious as everyone waits to see what's going to happen.

Resigned to the choice he made and whatever fate that will befall him, Nelson wanders the streets with his backpack, taking it all in.

In another section of town, the two dusty soldiers who had accosted Nelson in the desert have organized a makeshift caravan of about 20 vehicles. Most are civilian SUVs plus a couple of commandeered military jeeps. At the head of the column, an old Tanque Argentino Mediano, or Argentine Medium Tank, coughs to life, blowing a black plume of exhaust behind it. Bedraggled young soldiers sit behind the wheels of the jeeps. Just about all of the passengers are civilian friends and families of the soldiers, and range in age from the very young to the very old. Their expressions convey a combination of fear, excitement and *hope*.

The tank rumbles slowly forward, followed by the ragtag line of Jeeps and SUVs.

THE THIRD PASS

After crossing northern Mexico, the dissolution beam begins its next pass over the U.S. Starting from the southeast corner of New Mexico on one end and Brownsville, Texas, on the other, the 600-mile-wide beam moves steadily over the country.

Dallas. Houston. New Orleans.

All are reduced to scattered mounds of grit and dust.

ABOARD THE SPACE FREIGHTER

Angie closely monitors the computer readouts and controls of the ship. Her eyes are alert, her posture straight, her concentration focused.

The ping of an incoming communication. President Crawford's face appears onscreen. "Hello, Angie."

"Madam President." Angie's voice is a little clipped. The ship's captain is a little preoccupied at the moment.

"Less than an hour to intercept," Crawford says.

"Yes, Ma'am."

"I know you're very busy, but I just wanted..." The president's voice catches. "...just wanted to say Godspeed... and to wish you good hunting."

The emotion in Crawford's voice takes Angie off guard. She looks at the image on the monitor and sees that the president's eyes are full of tears. Angie gives her a grateful smile.

"Thank you, Madam President. That means a lot."

"Good-bye, Angie."

"Good-bye, Claire."

Crawford signs off. Angie returns to her final duties.

The dissolution beam continues its work.

Memphis. Tallahassee. Richmond.

All gone.

The next major city in its path—Washington, D.C.

In the Situation Room, General Walters and a half-dozen remaining aides and personnel intently watch a monitor carrying the spy satellite's live feed of the alien ship.

Walters's voice is an urgent whisper. "Come on, Angie... You can do it..."

Elsewhere in the White House, Crawford stands at the window of the Oval Office looking west across the Potomac River where the Pentagon suddenly dissolves in a cascade of sand and dust. An instant later, the proud Marine Corps War Memorial depicting 6 Marines raising the American flag on Iwo Jima is reduced to a shapeless blob of bronze.

The Space Freighter maintains maximum velocity as it streaks straight down toward the alien ship. It's less than a hundred miles from its target. Moving at 7 miles a second, it's just moments from impact.

Crawford swallows in fear as the dissolution beam reaches the foot of the National Mall. The Lincoln Memorial goes down in a spray of pebbles and dust.

The White House is next. Crawford closes her eyes.

The image of the enemy craft fills the screen of Angie's monitor. At the last second, she glances at the framed photo of Bonnie and Sadie. Brings her fingers to her mouth. Kisses them, then reaches over and gently places the kiss on the photo.

On the bridge of the enemy ship, one of the aliens is deep in the blissful throes of eating another human. It then senses a large, quickly growing shadow outside the vessel. Before the creature can react to whatever is there, the Freighter strikes the vessel dead center. The massive collision causes the spaceship to sheer clean away from the giant sac.

Space Freighter One is completely destroyed in the fiery explosion. It falls to Earth in a thousand burning pieces.

As powerful as the impact is, the alien ship is built of very strong material and remains in one piece. Still, the blow is a fatal one. Its propulsion and navigation systems knocked out, the vessel goes into an out-of-control tailspin that sends it careening north over the Canadian border before finally smashing to Earth. There's no way any living thing onboard could have survived.

THE WHITE HOUSE

Mad jubilation in the Situation Room. General Walters and the others shout and laugh and cry and hug.

Walters is nearly unhinged with relief. "We did it! We got the bastards!"

"Correction, General," says Major Dawson, the former keeper of the football. "*You* did it. It was your idea. And a brilliant one, at that."

Walters smiles in humble acknowledgment.

In the Oval Office, Crawford opens her eyes, bewildered that she's still standing at the window. She watches as hunks of moon ore, spewing smoke and flames, thud to Earth around the city. Turning her eyes skyward, she offers a silent prayer of thanks to the brave commander of Space Freighter One.

TEMPORARY WORKSPACE
CAPE CANAVERAL

"We're saved!" shouts Conroy as he dances around the room in unadulterated joy. "The human race is saved!" He notices that Otis remains in his chair, curiously unmoved.

"Otis! What's wrong with you?! It's over! Lighten up, man!"

Otis continues staring at the monitor. "Did you see it?" he says in a serious voice.

"The collision? Of course, I saw it! I was sitting right here next to you."

"I don't mean the collision. Something else, just before impact."

"What are you talking about?"

Otis grabs the remote for the monitor. "I know this is a live feed, but it should have recording capability..." He fiddles with the remote until he gets the footage going in reverse. "Yes, that's it." He rewinds back to just before the collision, then plays it forward in slow motion.

"There. Did you see that?"

"I'm not sure I... What am I supposed to be looking for?"

Otis rewinds again, then replays it in super-slow motion. At the same time, he isolates a small part of the screen and zooms in very close to the edge of the spacecraft. The Space Freighter suddenly looms into view as a large blurry object. Just before it smashes into the vessel, something detaches itself from the alien ship and moves away. Otis freezes on it and zooms in with maximum magnification.

"My God," says Conroy. "The Probe. It got away." He looks at Otis. "Where did it go?"

Otis continues to stare at the monitor. "That, my friend, is the question of the day."

ARGENTINA BUNKER JOBSITE

The meal hall is packed with people watching the president's broadcast.

"...I am so very happy to inform you that the enemy craft has been destroyed," announces Crawford.

Wild cheering and weeping from everyone in the room.

Crawford speaks from the Oval Office. She's flanked by General Walters and the rest of what remains of the White House Staff.

"Our long, horrible, global nightmare is over. The human race has prevailed."

More loud cheers and clapping. Some hush the others so they can hear the president's words.

"The world as we know it is in major disarray. It will remain that way for a long time to come. But at least now, we can breathe a sigh of relief, give thanks for our survival, and begin the process of recovery and rebuilding."

The Stone family is in the crowd. Zack turns to his mother and says, his voice husky with excitement, "Does this mean we can go home?

Lydia smiles at him. "Maybe."

The president continues. "But probably the best news to come of all this is that, due to the anti-gravity properties of the material it's made of, the massive storage sac remains intact. It's hovering in place over Washington. Our first order of business will be to safely return those millions—make that billions—of people trapped in suspended animation back to their homes here on Earth. Our work is cut out for us. We have a lot to learn and a lot to do. Case in point: the graphene barrier on the ground is still in place and remains impenetrable. We need to figure out how the aliens were able to create such a material. But we homo sapiens are pretty darn good at figuring stuff out. Hell, that's what we do!"

The crowd erupts in ever louder cheers, shouts and clapping.

Later that day, Kent Hatcher met with his foremen and forewomen to discuss this great good news and what it would mean for them. The bunker was very close to being finished. Hatcher was all for doing just that, in case something went wrong and the aliens somehow returned. He gave everyone the option of returning home, but no one did. All wanted to keep working to complete the bunker.

Just in case.

In the meantime, in a brief call, Otis told President Crawford about his concerns over the missing probe. Where did it go? He also told her the survival kit was as complete as it was going to get, and that they wanted to send it on its way as soon as possible, if only to act as a kind of insurance for the survival of the legacy of the human race.

The president was swamped with so many other tasks that she quickly agreed. She gave Otis the authorization to launch and then hung up.

That night, a rocket lifted off from Cape Canaveral. It was the last of a generation of ultra-powerful missiles that would propel the tiny payload to the far side of the moon in less than 24 hours.

As it turned out, there wouldn't be a minute to spare...

{The Zachary Stone Chronicles}

The next day, thanks to satellite telephones, the news that the aliens were gone blazed through the towns and cities in the western hemisphere that were still standing. Members of Congress who had managed to avoid being collected trickled back into the nation's capital to try to resume government operations and start the rebuilding process. The state of Delaware, being just east Washington, had not been touched by the dissolution beam. Most of the eastern half of North Carolina was similarly unscathed. The rest of the country remained sealed off by the graphene barrier.

Because of the president's EBS broadcasts, a surprisingly large number of scientists, soldiers, technicians, doctors, and people in many other occupations important to society, had managed to travel to Florida and escape being collected. Now the good citizens began to make their way up to these last untouched places by either boat or plane.

MINING PIT
FAR SIDE OF THE MOON

Spike is at his communications console speaking live with Otis via a satellite orbiting Earth as it transfers the signal to a relay satellite in lunar orbit that is in direct line of sight with both Spike and the Earth satellite.

"...I know you and Angie were friends. It was a great thing she did."

"She was good people," says Spike, his eyes misting a little. "I miss her. But I'm very proud of her."

"We all are. Anyway, the reason for my contacting you is that I wanted to give you a heads-up about a package that's coming your way. In fact, it should be touching down any minute."

Spike scratches his buzz-cut head. "What kinda package?"

"Well," says Otis, "you could say it's kind of like—"

The screen turns to snow.

"Hello?" Spike starts pressing buttons and turning dials. "Larson? Where'd ya go?"

Spike's module begins to vibrate. His banjo propped in a corner falls over. An alarm goes off. A mechanical voice sounds: 'Unknown force. Breach is imminent. Don suit and prepare for depressurization.'

"Holy shit!" yells Spike as he struggles into his suit.

THE WHITE HOUSE

General Walters is on a satellite phone with the Director of Miami International Airport. A 747 packed with high-profile personnel is on final approach for landing at Ronald Reagan Washington National Airport.

"Yes, Director," says Walters. "I understand your concerns. But the airport is fully operational. Dulles is gone, but Reagan Airport was far enough east to remain unscathed. The 395 bridge is open as well. We'll have a full complement of assistants ready and waiting to meet your—"

The phone goes dead. Walters pulls it away from his ear and looks at it. "What the...?"

Thousands of miles above the Earth, the Probe leads the way for another alien ship. Only this one is newer, sleeker, has more instrumentation, and is five times larger than the previous intruder. And it comes in with guns blazing. It shoots a targeted array of powerful dissolution beams that simultaneously take out every satellite in orbit around the Earth. It then takes aim at the moon and turns the abandoned settlements there to dust. Ditto for all relay satellites in lunar orbit.

At 102 miles above the Earth, the angry new harvester picks up where the previous one left off. It quickly reattaches itself to the giant storage sack. Does some recalibrations, then resumes the collection process.

The 747 coming in for a landing dissolves in mid-flight. A couple of hundred blue balloons swoop up into the sky.

At the White House, an aide catches a glimpse of the doomed passenger jet out the window of the Oval Office. Puts a hand to her mouth, whispering "Oh my God..."

She calls out to President Crawford, who is working at her desk. "Ma'am?!"

Claire looks up at her aide just as the Washington Monument outside the window behind her collapses. She closes her eyes. Presses her hand to her forehead. Whispers, "Oh God no..."

The aide has grown more frantic. "Ma'am?! I think we better—"

The White House crumbles to dust.

102 miles overhead, the gleaming new spaceship begins to move, collecting much faster than its predecessor.

The harvest shouldn't take more than a few hours to complete.

ARGENTINA BUNKER JOBSITE

Communications technician Sean walks quickly over the grounds of the compound searching for Kent Hatcher. A foreman directs him toward Hatcher, who is overseeing the loading of supplies into the bunker.

The young ponytailed tech nervously approaches him. "Sir? Mr. Hatcher?"

Hatcher looks up. It's the most relaxed he's been in weeks.

"What is it, Sean?"

"We've lost satellite communications."

"Did you try going to one of our backups?"

"Yes, sir. Those are down, too. They're all down."

Hatcher frowns. "That can't be right. There are literally hundreds of satellites in orbit."

"I know, sir. One second, all the signals are there. The next second, they've just...vanished."

Hatcher's brow furrows in consternation. "How can that be? Unless..." As he considers possible causes for such an event, alarm bells start to go off in his head. He looks up sharply at Sean. "What's the status of our radio telescope?"

"We took it offline a couple of hours ago. With the aliens gone, we didn't think we would—"

"How long will it take to get it back up and running?"

"Thirty minutes?"

"Make it twenty. I want to see what's going on up there."

Sean races off. Hatcher sees Eric Stone driving a forklift with a load of bottled water and waves him over. Eric rolls to a stop. He can see Hatcher is upset. "What is it, Boss?"

"Something's happened. I'm afraid our time frame just got compressed. Start rounding everyone up and get them into the bunker."

"I'm on it."

He dumps the pallet of bottled water and zooms off in the forklift while speaking into a walkie-talkie.

Minutes later, Hatcher sat down next to Sean at the tech's work station watching computerized readouts from the radio telescope.

"Something's definitely out there..." says Sean. "Something big..."

"Can you determine its course?"

Sean taps in commands on his keyboard.

"It's beyond the horizon but the signature is very strong..."

He types in more commands.

"It picked up right where its predecessor left off, only this guy's moving a lot faster..."

"Estimated time of arrival at Bahia Blanca?"

More commands. A light sheen of sweat suddenly appears on Sean's forehead.

"It's on track to arrive there in less than three hours."

Hatcher's mouth becomes a grim line. "Which means it'll hit here a few minutes before that."

The giant new and improved harvester is making short work of South America, the last untouched continent. The fast-moving dissolution beam rolls quickly through cities and countries. As it does so, it draws the graphene barrier ever tighter around what remains of the human race.

A short line of people has formed at the giant elevator, which works quickly and efficiently to lower them down into the bunker. Lydia, Zack and Jeffrey nervously but patiently await their turn near the back of the line. Eric sees them, goes over and tries to be cheerful.

"How's my family holding up?"

"The best we can," says Lydia. "You're coming down with us, aren't you?"

"I'm on the emergency security detail."

"What's that?" says Jeffrey.

"Me and a few others will stay above until everyone else is safely inside. I'll see you down below later." He gives Lydia a quick kiss and heads to a spot near the shaft where Hatcher and some technicians tinker with the three robotic front-end loaders, making sure they're prepared to backfill the shaft once everyone's inside. Hatcher sees him coming.

"Status?" says Hatcher.

"Everyone's present and accounted for. Everything's going pretty smoothly. We should make it under the wire with even a little time to spare."

"Good job, Eric," says Hatcher, looking slightly relieved. "It's a good thing we were so far ahead of schedule. Otherwise, I don't think we—"

Hatcher's walkie-talkie crackles to life. "Mr. Hatcher?"

Hatcher grabs it off his belt. "What is it, Stan?"

"I'm afraid we've got a problem."

Hatcher looks up at the top of the blast wall where Stan is stationed as a lookout. He's staring through binoculars at something in the distance.

Hatcher moves quickly to one of the narrow gaps between the blast walls as Eric follows.

Still in line, Lydia has noticed the sudden worry in the faces of the two men.

Outside the blast wall, Tattoos wordlessly hands Hatcher his pair of binoculars, then points at a plume of dust rising from the desert several hundred yards away.

The ragtag caravan of people from Bahia Blanca has arrived at the outskirts of the jobsite. The tank is in the lead. Women, children, and the elderly are packed into the military jeeps and SUVs behind it.

The column continues to move forward as Tattoos hands Eric a loaded M-16. Eric takes it without enthusiasm as Tattoos distributes more M-16s to a dozen others of the security detail.

At the mineshaft, people are oblivious to this new development. The elevator continues to transport them down to the bunker. Lydia has other ideas. Says to her sons, "Come with me." They follow her through the same gap between the walls. On the other side, she looks around for Eric.

Sees him holding the M-16.

"Eric...?"

Eric turns around and sees his family. They go to him.

"Eric, what are you doing?"

"It was Hatcher's idea," Eric says. "Just a last ditch precaution. I didn't tell you because I didn't want you to worry. But I seriously don't think we'll actually—"

"Halt! That's far enough!" Hatcher shouts in Spanish, holding his hand up in a 'stop' gesture.

The column comes to a stop less than a hundred yards away. Bandanna climbs down from the jeep directly behind the tank. He walks toward Hatcher, his arms spread wide.

"Senor, we mean you no harm," he says in English. "We are only trying to escape the space people—" he points up "—the same as yourselves. There are less than a hundred of us. Surely, you have room to squeeze a few more—"

"I'm sorry," cries Hatcher in English. "But we have no room. And we're almost out of time."

Suddenly, civilians begin pouring out of the SUVs and start walking toward the blast walls.

"Tell your people to go back!" shouts Hatcher. "We have no room!" He switches to Spanish and shouts at the civilians. "There is no room for you here! You have to leave!"

But the civilians keep walking toward the mineshaft. Some hold infants. Others help the elderly over the uneven ground.

"I'm warning you!" shouts Hatcher in English, but the man's heart isn't in it. Besides, he's just not very threatening. He turns to Eric and says, "Is there any way we can take these people in?"

Eric sighs in relief and says, "It'll be a tight fit, but yeah, I think we—"

Suddenly Tattoos lets loose with the rifle on full automatic, firing above the heads of the civilians as warning shots. The women and children scream and fall to the ground for cover.

Thinking they've been shot at, the panicked tank driver fires a shell toward Tattoos. Fortunately for the foreman, his aim is high. The shell explodes harmlessly against the blast wall behind him.

The harvester is now moving over Argentina. As it does so, its 600-mile wide dissolution beam begins to shrink down, causing it to move in a tighter and tighter spiral over the country.

The handful of Argentinian soldiers in the column joins the firefight with automatic weapons of their own.

Eric and his family have taken cover behind a large boulder. Eric cries, "Lydia! Get the boys down into the bunker!"

As terrified as Zack and Jeffrey are, they both shake their heads no.

"Not without you, Dad!" says Zack.

Eric, who has yet to fire his weapon, says, "Lydia! Please!"

Lydia is equally defiant. "You heard the boys."

Tattoos shoves another magazine into his weapon and yells at Hatcher, "You and the rest go on down, Mr. Hatcher! I'll hold'em off as long as I can." He rakes the vehicles in the column.

Hatcher slips back into the compound. He's quickly joined by the rest of the security team.

Eric and his family are about to join them when there's another long loud blast of automatic fire. Tattoos has opened up on the civilians, slaughtering them mercilessly. They shriek and cry out, begging for their lives.

Lydia and the boys scream at the sight of the carnage.

Inside the blast walls, Hatcher and the security team hear this. Panicked beyond all reason, Hatcher shouts at the man operating the elevator, "Go down! Get this thing moving!"

"Yes, sir!

The elevator begins its rapid decent.

Tattoos reloads his weapon and is about to fire on the civilians again when he's suddenly cut down from behind as Eric empties his M-16 into the man. Lydia and the boys sob in shock. Eric's just as devastated. Tears stream from his eyes as he throws his rifle to the ground and says, "Let's go." He leads his family back through the blast wall and into the compound.

The sound of gunfire rapidly dies down. The Argentinian soldiers have witnessed Eric's actions and have ceased fire.

When the Stone family arrives at the mine shaft, they see that the elevator is gone, its cables having been cut after its last decent. The three front-end loaders work like baby mechanical dinosaurs on speed as they move in perfect synchronization with each other, rapidly filling the shaft with different layers of material.

The Stones stand crestfallen, watching the machines work with computerized efficiency.

Lydia says, "He abandoned us."

"Maybe in the confusion, he didn't know we were still out there."

"Maybe..."

Several of the soldiers enter the compound. In addition to automatic rifles, a couple of them carry rocket-propelled grenades. They look warily around. See the Stone family. Head toward them. They stand watching the strange machines work.

Bandana points down into the shaft and says to Eric, "Bunker?"

Eric nods. "Yes."

Bandana quickly considers his options, then says to Eric, "You and your family... Stand away."

Eric is confused as to what the man intends to do until he watches him order the soldiers to fire their RPGs at the machines.

"Wait!" he shouts. "You can't do that!"

Bandana ignores him as the soldiers prepare to fire.

Eric is frantic. Shouts at them, "Do have any idea what—?!"

"Eric!" The sharpness in Lydia's voice gets his attention. He stares into her wise, sad eyes. "Don't you see? It's not worth it. Let it go. Just let it all go..."

She takes his hand. He allows her to lead him and the boys behind a pile of lumber.

The three soldiers fire their RPGs in rapid succession. The powerful explosions are deafening. Smoke and fire rises from the three disabled machines.

Bandana barks orders in Spanish to his fellow soldiers to retrieve ropes and buckets and shovels from the jeeps.

Inside the bunker, it's very quiet except for the gentle hiss of ventilators and fans. A few battery-powered lanterns dimly illuminate the people and things packed into the space.

Kent Hatcher stands close to the massive steel door, studying it for any sign of a breech. Daring to hope, he whispers to himself, "I think we did it."

One of the members of the security detail looks quizzically around, then says loudly, "Hey, where's Eric Stone? He should be in here, along with his wife and two kids."

Silence. Hatcher stares at the ground.

"Why aren't they here?" He turns to Hatcher and says, "Mr. Hatcher, with all due respect, was Eric Stone left behind?"

"They were shooting at us. We had to get out of there."

The man says nothing. Just stares accusingly at him.

"Look," says Hatcher, sweat rolling down his face. "I might have panicked a little, okay?"

The man continues to stare.

At the top of the shaft, the Argentine soldiers work with frantic desperation as they lower empty buckets down by rope and haul up full ones, which they quickly empty, then repeat the process. The muffled huffing and swearing of the men down in the shaft can be heard as they shovel non-stop, intent on digging as fast possible all the way down to the bunker's entrance.

The Stone family stands a short distance away watching them.

Then Eric hears something ever so faintly, just a tickling on the ear... A soft, sandy rustling, fast approaching.

"It's here," he says.

Lydia and his sons watch him with fatalistic calm.

Eric goes down on one knee and gently says, "Come close."

As they gather around him, he spreads his arms and pulls them into a giant hug.

"Hold on tight," says Eric in a fierce whisper. "As tight as you can. Tighter..."

The Stone family holds onto each other with all their strength. Jeffrey quietly whimpers.

"It's okay, Jeffy," says Zack to his little brother. "It's all going to be okay..."

Eric's voice a strangled cry. "... I love you all so very much... So very much..."

A single tear escapes from Lydia's eye. Rolls down her cheek. Falls off her chin. Hits the sere, high-desert ground.

The dissolution beam sweeps over them.

A small cluster of four blue balloons ascends into the sky. They're quickly joined by those of the soldiers and civilians from the caravan.

At the top of the shaft, the three machines crumple into shapeless chunks of metal.

The shaft itself was never completely filled. In addition, the soldiers managed to remove a sizeable pile of material. The dissolution beam lingers a moment at the top of the fill in the shaft. The material begins to gently shake and vibrate, as if it's being liquefied.

Inside the bunker, Hatcher senses something's wrong. He stares at the steel door, afraid to even breathe. He whispers, "Come on, baby, hold..."

It's completely quiet for a long couple of seconds.

Then the giant steel door melts away.

Kent cries, "Nooo!"

He's the first to be sucked from the bunker and up the shaft. The others quickly follow, as if a giant invisible vacuum cleaner is pulling them from their lair.

Immediately after, all the thousands of items and supplies so carefully selected to build a new world, so painstakingly transported and stored, collapse into dust with a swooshing, grainy hiss.

The width of the dissolution beam continues to shrink as it spirals in on Bahia Blanca.

The city is the final destination for those who were most desperate to escape being collected. Those who could make it here did so, causing the normal population of 300,000 to explode to several million. The streets and sidewalks are packed with people standing shoulder to shoulder. Shoving matches and fights break out.

Located in the very center of Bahia Blanca is a small square called Park Plaza Rivadavia. The park's centerpiece is a granite arch erected over a life-sized, bronze stature of Simon Bolivar. Normally, it's a peaceful place. Its lush lawns and large shade trees make it a favorite of young lovers, picnickers, and dog walkers.

But now, because its location will make it the precise spot where the last homo sapiens are gathered up, things are quite different. The modest park teems with human beings.

Nelson stands on the roof of a nearby building packed with hundreds of people. Tempers flare as everyone is jostled and pushed. Nelson manages to remain calm.

Suddenly, the surrounding buildings begin to crumble, causing everyone to panic. Thousands of people run screaming toward Park Plaza Rivadavia, where they climb on top of each other, creating a writhing human pyramid that dwarfs the statue and granite arch. The crying, cursing and shrieking reach ear-splitting levels as those are crushed.

As buildings continue to dissolve, hundreds of thousands of blue balloons jet skyward as if from an erupting volcano.

Nelson is atop one of the last buildings standing. As it disappears beneath his feet, he joins the flow of balloons.

As the dissolution beam closes in around Park Plaza Rivadavia, people pound on and claw at the graphene barrier, desperate to escape.

The spaceship slows to a halt directly above the park at a height of 102 miles.

The last humans to be collected present a searing, heartbreaking spectacle. They crawl on each other's shoulders to avoid the quickly shrinking dissolution beam. They shout, they pull hair, they beg for mercy.

And then, finally, they are gone.

The last blue bubbles soar up to the ship and disappear inside.

The harvest is complete.

The last human being in the world has been collected.

The dissolution beam shrinks to nothing. The last shimmering bit of the graphene barrier retracts up into the ship like a silken blue waterfall running in reverse.

The hatch closes.

On the ground, the grit and dust settle. Bahia Blanca, the world's last city, is no more. It's now just piles of rubble interspersed with patches of greenery. A few stunned animals wander about. Cats. Dogs. Horses.

The world is engulfed by an all-embracing silence.

And then, finally, it was over...
The aliens had collected every single person on the face of the Earth.
Right about now, you're probably thinking—"But if everyone was collected—including you and your family—how can you be here to tell the tale?"
That's a very good question.
Because the thing is, it wasn't over.
It had barely begun...
{The Zachary Stone Chronicles}

PART FOUR

SQUARE ZERO

Instead of heading directly for home with its precious cargo, the spacecraft and gargantuan sac hover in place for several minutes a hundred miles above the planet. It's almost as if the vessel is waiting for something. Sure enough, the Probe suddenly appears in front of the spacecraft. It hangs suspended a moment, as if communicating with the larger vessel. The Probe then takes off, moving at a fast clip over the Earth.

The giant ship follows close behind.

The Probe zigs and zags over the Earth's land masses. Every few hundred miles, it slows to a halt. The ship follows suit. As soon as it stops, the hatch opens and a couple of dozen blue balloons are ejected. They immediately begin plummeting to Earth. Just when they're about to hit the ground, they come to a quick, smooth halt inches from it. The blue material melts away, allowing the bare, unconscious bodies to be gently deposited onto the soil. They all land within a few hundred yards of each other.

Most are preadolescents ranging in age from ten to twelve years. A couple of them appear to be teenagers.

No one is over 15.

The Probe and the spaceship move on, repeating the process at regular intervals around the globe.

It's late in the day when the spaceship appears over the North American continent. It makes several stops, dropping clusters of blue balloons seemingly at random over the land. One of the drops takes place just east of the Rocky Mountains. As soon as the balloons melt away and tenderly spill their human cargo onto the ground, the giant ship, guided by the Probe, moves on.

Zachary Stone opens his eyes. He slowly sits up. It takes him several minutes to come awake. Every stitch of clothing is gone, as are his glasses. The braces on his teeth have disappeared. Instead, there's just a residual grit in his mouth. He uses his finger to wipe it from his gums. Needs to spit several times to get it all out.

Zack staggers to his feet. Shakes his head to clear it, then looks around.

He's on a wide plain of rolling hills covered with tall grass that's turned mostly brown. Unused to being barefoot, he walks carefully to the top of a small knoll. Squinting, he scans his surroundings.

Grassland in every direction, dotted here and there with willow trees. In the blurry distance, he can make out a jagged, purple-hued mountain range. It sits on the horizon like a row of broken teeth. The sun inches toward to it.

"Jesus..." breathes Zack, his voice shaky with fear. "Where the hell am I..."

A warm breeze pushes across the landscape, causing the long grass to ripple in wave-like patterns.

His voice tentative, he calls out, "...Hello? Is anybody there?"

Nothing. Just the billowing of the wind...

Zack is suddenly wracked by a sensation of overwhelming loneliness.

For all he knows, he could very well be the only person in the world.

It feels as though an icy wind is passing through his soul.

In a wild panic, he screams as loud as he can, "Hello?! Can anyone hear me?! Hello!"

Nothing...

Tears abruptly flood his eye and he starts to sob. Just when he feels that he's going to collapse into a trembling heap, he jumps at a sound behind him.

A child's cry.

"Mama!"

Zack spins around. Crouches and moves stealthily back in the direction from which he just came.

He finds several children in the tall grass, some sitting, others standing. None are under 10-years-old. Having just awakened, they look fearfully around. The one who's crying is a Hispanic-looking boy.

"Mama!"

Zack is just about to head over to try and comfort him when movement off to the side catches his eye; a girl of about 13 striding through the grass toward the crying boy. She leads a young girl with a tear-streaked face by the hand.

The older girl is tall and lean and obviously physically strong.

Zack crouches low in the grass to watch as she approaches. She's close enough that he can see her reasonably well without his glasses.

She has high cheekbones, a sharp nose, and lively aquamarine eyes. Darkly burnished blonde hair touches the top of her shoulders. Her body is still mostly that of a child, but shows signs of developing into a young woman.

When she reaches the crying boy, she leans over and speaks to him in a foreign language. Even though he doesn't seem to understand the words, her tones are soothing and he stops crying.

Zack swallows hard. Realizes he's gawking. He's never seen a naked girl before.

As if sensing she's being watched, the girl suddenly stands and shouts something in Zack's direction.

Feeling guilty and embarrassed, Zack rises slowly from the grass. Acutely aware of his own nakedness, he stands with both hands over his genitals.

She speaks sharply to him in the alien language.

He shakes head and says, "I'm sorry. I don't understand. Do you speak English?"

She responds in a heavy Eastern Europe accent. "Yes, I speak some English. The whole world speaks some English. Or it did, until now."

"Are you Polish?"

Sounding a little annoyed, she says, "No, I am not Polish. I am Ukrainian. Why are you hiding in the grass?"

"I'm not hiding. I just, well, I, ah—"

"Oh. I see. You are shy." The girl is grinning.

"Well, yeah… I guess I—"

"I have four brothers. You don't have anything I haven't seen before. Besides, this is no time to be shy. It will be night soon and we don't want to freeze to death. We need to come up with a plan."

Zack finds himself oddly pleased with her directness.

"Sounds good to me."

"My name is Oksana. What is yours?"

"Zachary. But people call me Zack."

"Okay, Zock. Help me gather up the rest of these young people. They are children, but even so, they are going to have to help us build shelter of some kind if we are going to survive the night."

Even as Oksana speaks, the wind is picking up.

Later, as the sun dips behind the mountain range, Zack, Oksana and their young charges burrow deep into the center of a 10-foot shaggy green mound nearly 10-feet tall. Their fingers are raw from pulling up lots of grass, stripping leaves off willow shoots, then using the long, pliant branches to tie everything down. The resulting structure is crude but functional. It gives them protection from the wind while preserving body heat. They all huddle together for warmth.

The younger ones immediately fall fast asleep.

In the darkness of the giant grass cocoon, Oksana speaks in a quiet voice.

"...Zock?"

"Yes, Oksana?"

"I used wrong tense."

"What do you mean?"

"Earlier. I should have said, I *had* four brothers..."

For a long moment, there's only the rustling of the wind outside. Then Zack gently says, "Go to sleep, Oksana."

The exhausted girl is on the verge of nodding off. She stifles a last yawn. "...Yes. You are right. We must gather our strength for tomorrow..."

"...gather our strength for tomorrow..."
And for all the days yet to come...
As tired as I was, I lay awake a few minutes longer, trying to process what had happened. For starters, at least I was alive. And I was pretty sure I was still on Earth. As for where on Earth, I didn't have a clue.

One of the last things I remembered was holding on to my family. Then suddenly I was floating up into the sky. But the weirdest thing was, just before everything went blank, I felt really good.

I mean, like, euphoric.

Why was that? Later, I learned that Oksana and the others experienced the same feeling. Which made me think that, as we were getting wrapped up in the blue balloons, we were also getting dosed by a drug that made everyone feel really happy.

And maybe that was intentional.

So that anyone who got sent back down to Earth would always associate getting transported into the sky with that wonderful feeling; and that those who remained on the spaceship were the fortunate ones...

I'm getting ahead of myself. More about that later.

The next day, out of consideration for my 'shyness', Oksana made us crude 'clothes' from willow branches, grass and leaves. I have to admit, it did make me feel better.

Luckily for me and the others, Oksana had spent the summer on her Uncle's farm in Ukraine, where she learned some skills that would come in handy.

After donning our new attire, the hunt was on for water, food, and shelter.

There was a stream nearby. That took care of our water needs for now. As for food, that turned out to be not so hard to find. There was a simple explanation: wherever there had been towns or farms, all human-built structures had been dissolved. But what was left standing were all the things that occurred naturally, like parks and lawns; like trees and plants ; like crops and gardens. It was late September, so there was still plenty of stuff around that hadn't been harvested, and never would be. It was all there for the taking: Apples. Pears. Corn. Zucchini. None of us knew how to make a fire, so we couldn't cook anything. But we learned pretty fast that if you got hungry enough, you'd eat just about anything raw.

The kids were all from different countries, like we were a cross section of the human race. And all so young.

Why?

At the time, none of it made any sense to me.

Until it did.

Again, more about that later.

Altogether, there were 26 of us. Thirteen females, thirteen males. Except for Oksana—who spoke Russian and some English, and, of course, Ukrainian—we all spoke our native tongues. Communication was difficult.

The first few days were especially hard on the younger ones. They'd been ripped from their families and plunged into conditions that were as terrifying as they were confusing. But I'm happy to tell you that they adapted to their fate surprisingly fast. I think that was because they instinctively knew that something of supreme importance had happened, and was still happening. They sensed that the world had fundamentally changed; that from now on, things were going to be different from anything they had ever known. Just staying alive was going to be a daily challenge. The era of pampered childhoods was over.

Because Oksana and I were the oldest, we became by default the group's leaders.

In time, the kids turned out to be troopers. They did their best to stay in line and do as they were told—as well as we could communicate it, that is. Which was usually in pantomime.

Oksana insisted that we had to get to the foothills. Being from Ukraine, she knew firsthand the danger of blizzards on the plain, how deadly they could be. We were going to have to find better shelter than a grass hut.

After listening to a couple of Oksana's stories, I didn't need any more convincing. We were on the move within days. I could tell from the position of the sun that we were headed basically west.

Not knowing if food would be as easy to find where we were going, Oksana used willow branches to weave crude baskets. We filled them with as much fruit and vegetables as we could carry, tied them to our backs and got on the road.

Traveling on foot wasn't as hard as I expected. The soles of my feet calloused up pretty quick. Plus the remnants of roads were everywhere. The asphalt and concrete had crumbled but the way was clear.

As we walked, we talked to each other as best we could. If anyone had ventured across us, our little caravan would have been quite a sight. Picture a ragged band of over two dozen multi-ethnic youngsters from around the globe dressed in skirts and loincloths made from grass, all jabbering to each other in different tongues.

As it was, no one ventured across us.

On the third day, we came to a pulverized road that was wider than anything we'd seen, over a hundred feet across. It ran in a straight shot from east to west. I remember thinking it was probably an interstate—or had once been one anyway. Whatever it was, it made our journey easier. It occurred to me that, as time went by, grasses and shrubs and even trees would probably overgrow it, and erase any evidence that it was ever there.

Zack comes to an abrupt halt, his eyes fixed on the moun-
tainous vista.

Oksana and the others also stop. They look curiously at
him.

"Zock?" Oksana says. "What is it?"

His voice husky with emotion, Zack says, "Those mountains... Oksana, I know this place."

Perplexed, Oksana says, "How could you know it?"

"Because I've been here. We're very close to a big city
named Denver. Well, what *was* a big city, in Before. My

Mom's sister lived here. We came to visit several times. Our families went camping together up in those mountains. They're called the Rocky Mountains."

"What a foolish name."

"Why do you say that?"

"Because all mountains are rocky."

There's a slight edge to her voice, as if she might be a little envious of his recognition of something familiar to him, when she's so very far away from her own home.

Zack doesn't respond to her snarky comment, but she can see his eyes glisten as he stares at the mountains in the distance, no doubt reliving happy memories. She softens.

"Well, maybe not so foolish. Unimaginative, perhaps."

He looks at her. Gives a tiny smile. "Yeah. Perhaps."

She returns a smile of her own.

The next day, we arrived at Denver's city limits. You'd never know that, up until a few weeks ago, a huge, sprawling city had occupied the space in front of us. But what made it especially eerie was that there was no carnage to speak of, no obvious destruction. I've seen old news footage from World War II that showed cities after a bombing raid. There would be block after block of blasted-out buildings, some still burning and smoking.

Denver was nothing like that. It was just a vast checkerboard grid of empty city blocks covered with mounds of sandy grit. The grid was laced with zones of vegetation, which probably had been parks and gardens—areas that would have been unaffected by the dissolution beam. The resulting landscape was a strange mish-mash of sterility and lush-ness...

{The Zachary Stone Chronicles}

Zack, Oksana, and the rest stand at the city's edge, taking in the bizarre site that's both haunting and peaceful. Just a few birds talking to each other in the distance. No one says anything for several minutes.

Finally, Zack quietly says, "Millions of people lived here... Now, it's just us."

He and Oksana exchange a look that seems to say, What's happened is madness; we're going to have to do our best just to survive.

The little caravan continues on its way.

The young tribe keeps a steady pace through the heart of the dissolved city.

"I don't think we're far from the city center—or what's left of it," Zack says. "Just beyond that is a river. I think it's called the South Platte. We'll have to cross it to get to the foothills. I don't expect any bridges will be standing, but this late in the summer, the river should be running pretty low, so I don't think we'll have any problem getting—"

The air is shattered by an unearthly, high-pitched screech-ing coming from close by. They all freeze and turn toward the unnerving sound, which fades slowly away. Instinc-tively, they draw closer together. A few of the kids begin to tremble.

Oksana grips her tree branch with both hands. Her voice is shaky as she says, "Zock? What was that?"

It's the first time Zack's seen her show any fear. A surge of adrenaline lights up his nervous system. Feeling both scared and protective of Oksana and the others, he grips his own branch tight.

He speaks quietly. "I don't know..." He then looks carefully around, as if trying to get his bearings. "I'm pretty sure the City Zoo is around here somewhere. We went there a couple of times on our visits. The animals are probably running free now. It could have been anything..."

No one says anything for a moment. All remains quiet. Finally Oksana speaks.

"So, no zoo visits this time, okay?"

Zack is happy to see her spirits revived.

"I agree. No zoo visits."

"And I think we keep moving, yes? Maybe faster?"

"Best idea I've heard all day."

Staying close together, the group moves quickly yet cautiously down the middle of the dissolved remnants of Interstate 70.

Shortly after the incident near the zoo, we arrived on the banks of the river. There, the river was low and slow enough that we could wade across.

Moving in single file, we started to cross. Oksana went first to find the best footing. I brought up the rear so that I could keep an eye on everyone, in case somebody slipped and fell.

As we were crossing, I noticed a lot of different-sized mounds in the water that looked like piles of shiny wet sand or

Having immersed itself in the river to cool off from the heat of the day, the hippopotamus is not happy at being disturbed by the group of kids. The 3,000 pound animal surfaces. Glares in their direction and snorts. Trudges menacingly toward them. Zack is the only one to see it.

He quickly scans the bank on the other side of the river. It's steep but rocky, which would make good hand- and footholds.

"Oksana!" Zack shouts. She and the others turn, hearing the fear in his voice.

Zack points at the river bank. "Move the kids as fast as you can!"

The others now see the hippo coming at them. The younger ones erupt in shrieks and cries.

Which annoys the moody beast even more. He moves faster now, lumbering steadily, powerfully through the shallow water. He's less than a hundred yards away.

Oksana grabs up the youngest of the group and sprints for the river bank.

Zack shouts, "Run!" Even for those who don't speak English, his meaning is clear. They break into a mad dash through the water.

The hippo charges.

A girl stumbles. Disappears beneath the water. Zack throws down his club. Thrusts his arms into the murky river in a frantic search. Feels something. Grabs hold. Yanks the choking, sobbing child out of the water. Cradling her in his arms, he runs as fast as he can for the bank. The others have reached it and are scrambling up the incline.

The charging hippo steadily closes the gap between it and Zack. He can feel the ground tremble from the pounding of massive, tree-trunk feet.

Zack makes it to the bank just ahead of the hippo. Scrambles frantically up the incline but it's nearly impossible to climb while holding onto the terrified girl. If he lets her go, he'll survive, but she'll be crushed.

Suddenly is Oksana there. She reaches down. Grabs the girl from him just as the hippo nears the bank. Zack desperately claws his way up the slope. The beast lunges forward. Its momentum carries it up the incline so that its mouth is inches from Zack's legs. In a final, extreme effort, Zack heaves his body over the top of the bank just as the hippo's crushing jaws and giant teeth slam shut with the force of a bear trap, biting air where Zack had been an instant before.

The hippo slides harmlessly on its stomach back down into the river. Trembling and exhausted, Zack lies on his back on top of the riverbank, taking deep gulping breaths, waiting for his heart to stop ricocheting around in his chest.

After the encounter with the hippo, we were feeling pretty vulnerable. I started looking for anything that could be made into a weapon. I managed to find several long sturdy sticks, which I then sharpened by rubbing them against rocks. It was slow going. But when the others saw what I was doing, they joined in to help. We also collected a decent pile of rocks for throwing at whatever threat came our way. It wasn't much, but it was better than nothing.

That night, we took shelter in what I'm pretty sure had been the vault of a small bank. Much of the bank itself had crumbled, but enough of the vault was left standing to give us four walls and a roof. Technically, the material was no longer steel. The dissolution beam had broken it down into its basic components, which is mainly iron. Even though it was brittle, the structure was still pretty solid, and we felt reasonably safe there.

The former vault would make decent shelter for the night, but it was still too close to what had been the Denver Zoo. Who knew what animals were roaming about? As soon as it was light, we would need to move on.

From now on, someone was going to have to stand guard at night. I took the first watch. Oksana would take the second. As the others were too young to be relied on to stay awake, she and I would alternate through the night. As I tried to make myself comfortable just inside the vault opening, I realized that the nights were turning cool.

I wasn't the only one who sensed that Indian summer was coming to an end...

{The Zachary Stone Chronicles}

As Zack peers out into the darkness lit by a half moon, a chorus of howling starts up in the distance. Coyotes? Wild dogs? Hyenas? He grips his sharpened stick a little more tightly.

Oksana pads silently up behind him.

"Zock?"

"Yes, Oksana?"

She sits down by his side.

"Do you know how to make fire?"

"You mean, like, build a fire?"

"Yes."

"I can't say that I do. I was never in the Boy Scouts."

"What is Boy Scouts?"

Zack smiles. Shakes his head. "That's not important. Why do you ask about fire?"

"Because without it, we will all soon die."

A simple statement, spoken with unnerving assurance.

He doesn't respond. It's just light enough that they can make out the shape of each other's face and a silvery glint of eyes. The two stare at each other a long moment. She then stands and pads silently back to where the others are fast asleep and curls up with them.

Oksana was totally right.

We needed fire. Period.

And if we couldn't get it, we were all going to die.

While standing watch that night, I wracked my brains, trying to remember something, anything, about starting a fire. A few half-baked thoughts came to mind: Something about rubbing two pieces of wood together but I didn't have a clue how to go about that... I knew that certain chemical reactions could start a fire, but I didn't know what the chemicals were, and even if I did, where would I find them?

Then a memory came booming into my brain from out of nowhere. Why the heck didn't I think of this earlier?! My Uncle Jay—my Mom's sister's husband—was quite the outdoorsman. These were the same folks we would go camping with in these mountains. One day he showed us how to make a fire without using a match. I remember him striking a piece of metal against a rock. It made sparks, which he directed at a small pile of dried grass. He kept striking the rock until the grass started to smolder, then smoke. He blew gently on it until a flame appeared. He kept adding tiny twigs and kindling and then logs until he had a roaring fire.

I remember thinking at the time that it was sure a heck of a lot of work to go through when all you had to do was strike a match.

Except now, matches didn't exist.

The rock Uncle Jay used was quartz, or flint—something like that. I was pretty sure the metal was either iron or steel. With that in mind, I held on to a small piece of iron that I found on the floor of the vault.

I decided that each day, I would keep my eye out for rocks that might work and strike them with the iron. Hopefully, I would come across one that threw off sparks.

The next morning, I told Oksana my idea. She said she thought it was a good plan—even if she did look doubtful.

Still, it was better than doing nothing.

Oksana didn't say anything more about it, but I knew she was counting on me. I didn't want to let her down.

Over the next several days, as we searched for a place to call home, I tested dozens of rocks. Out of those, I found a handful that—after some hard scraping and grinding—produced a few sparks. It wasn't exactly the Fourth of July, but it was a start.

Yet try as I might, I couldn't make sparks that were hot enough or large enough to cause dried grass to smolder.

Meanwhile, the days got steadily colder; the nights more so. Our once-thick grass clothing had become threadbare. We stuffed whatever leaves we could find between our skin and the grass to help protect us against the cold. It didn't do much. Plus it was scratchy as heck.

Our chances of survival weren't looking very good. In fact, they were looking pretty bad.

I banged rocks and iron together until my hands were raw and bleeding.

During that time, one good thing that happened was we found a home. It was located a few miles west of Denver in the low foothills of the Rockies.

As far as I could tell, the house had been built by someone who was very rich. The crumbled concrete of the foundation area was enormous. But what clinched it for us was a large living space that had been carved deep into the granite—probably some billionaire's idea of the ultimate man cave.

Even the aliens' dissolution beam couldn't 'undig' a cave cut into solid rock.

The only entrance was a single narrow doorway leading off from the foundation, making it very defendable. The massive solid oak door that had fallen from its crumbled hinges was still intact. At night, we were able to muscle it back into the rock frame of the doorway. That made it completely dark inside, but it least we were safe from any nighttime animals making the rounds. It also gave us protection from the wind and cold.

Another big plus was that the cave had a source of water. Springwater coursed down through interconnected granite pools that ranged in size from a sink to a hot tub. This part of the cave had an exotic, grotto-like feel to it.

Best of all, taking up one whole wall was a fireplace. There, we kept dried grass and kindling positioned under a giant pile of firewood. All we needed was a decent spark.

Which I kept working at, hour after hour after hour. Try as I would, my meager sparks wouldn't light the fire. That's where things stood when the storm hit.

Not just any storm.

It was as big and bad as they come.

Wind. Hail. Rain. Snow. Thunder.

And lightning. Lots and lots of lightning.

We all crouched trembling just inside the cave's entrance, watching the storm blast across the land, lightning strikes hitting ever closer to us.

Growing up in Southern California, I'd only seen lightning a couple of times. It was always far off in the distance.

But here, it was right in our faces. It scared the crap out of me.

I stole a glance at Oksana. She wasn't a bit scared. Just the opposite, in fact. She was watching the advancing storm with a strange intensity. Out of the corner of my eye, I saw a blinding white flash. Half a second later, the thunderclap rang my body like a bell.

The bolt had smashed into a nearby copse of trees. It was the closest strike yet, about 500 feet away.

I noticed Oksana's body suddenly tense up. Her breathing became shallow. Her eyes narrowed.

I peered out the entrance, trying to see what she was looking at with such interest.

There. Rising from the broken trees.

A tendril of smoke...

And there. Flickering at its base.

A flame...

{The Zachary Stone Chronicles}

Oksana grabs a flagstone next to her the size of a frying pan, shoves it into Zack's hands, and shouts, "Follow me! Hurry!"

She bolts from the cave like a shot. Zack stares after her, dumbfounded that anyone would go charging out into such a dangerous storm.

Without slowing down, she turns her head and shouts at him. "Zock! Come on!"

Then it hits him. He knows exactly what she's doing. Gripping the flagstone, he takes off after her.

The instant he leaves the cave, he's hammered by hailstones the size of ping pong balls. A dozen red welts bloom on his skin. He pumps his legs as fast as he can.

Seconds later, he's at the copse of trees where he finds Oksana struggling to break a burning branch from a dead tree. Zack drops the flagstone to help. The branch is about half the size of a baseball bat. Together, trying not to burn their hands, they manage to yank the limb free. As soon as they do, the cascading hail changes into a cold, driving rain. The burning branch hisses and sputters.

"Zock! Get the stone!"

With Oksana carrying the branch and Zack holding the flagstone over it to protect it from the rain, they moving steadily but awkwardly back toward the cave. They're just about to the entrance when another lightning bolt blasts the ground a hundred feet away, knocking them off their feet.

Stunned, ears ringing, Zack looks over to where Oksana has fallen. She's hit her head on a rock. Blood pours from a gash near her temple.

"Oksana—!" Zack staggers to his feet. Starts to go to her.

She quickly becomes alert. Sees the burning branch next to her getting pelted by rain.

The flame has gone out.

But it's still smoking.

She picks up the branch and tries to rise but collapses. Zack reaches her side. Kneels down to help her to her feet but she resists. Thrusts the smoking branch at him.

"Zock! Get it into the cave!"

He takes it from her. Limps to the cave's entrance. Once inside, he makes a beeline for the fireplace. His hands trembling with cold and shock, Zack turns the wood over and over until he finds the spot that's still smoldering. He blows as gently as he can on the hot spot but his breath is too jagged. The ember appears to go out completely. Then a single wispy tendril of smoke curls into the air.

Oksana's voice behind him. "Let me try."

Zack holds the branch out to her. She wipes the blood from her eyes and takes it, handling it like it's a piece of the finest china. She finds the smoking spot and ever so gently blows on it.

The ember glows the slightest bit brighter.

Oksana whispers something to it in Ukrainian: A plea? A prayer? A wish?

She gently blows again. The ember glows brighter still. Oksana continues to nurse the ember until, like magic, a flame the size of a small fingernail appears.

Both she and Zack gasp, afraid to breathe lest that might somehow extinguish it.

But the tiny flame holds steady. Grows larger centimeter by centimeter. Oksana, cradling the flame against any stray breeze, walks slowly to the fireplace. Zack follows close behind.

Once there, she carefully lowers the flame to the tinder nestled at the bottom of the stack of kindling and firewood.

After a long, tense moment, the tinder catches. Flames climb slowly, steadily into the kindling. Before long, the massive fireplace is blazing with heat and light.

Zack and Oksana, their skin covered with welts and bruises, hair singed and matted, hands blistered and blackened with soot, step back from the roaring fire, their eyes filled with happy tears.

The rest of the young tribe gathers around them, smiling at the beautiful flames.

We were warm—I mean really warm—for the first time since BEFORE. It felt so good to take off our scratchy grass clothing. We no longer had to all pile together for body warmth just to survive the night. Having fire was a miracle...

{The Zachary Stone Chronicles}

That night, everyone sleeps close to the fire. Only Zack and Oksana are still awake.

Oksana lies on her side with her head propped up on her palm watching Zack, who lies on his back beside her. His head rests on a pile of grass clothing, using it as a pillow. He gazes into the glowing red coals. Listens to the sounds of the children sleeping around him. He speaks quietly so as not to wake the others.

"Oksana?"

"Yes, Zock?"

"...Today? When you ran out of the cave into the storm to get the fire?"

"Yes. What about it?"

"That was the bravest thing I ever saw."

Oksana's quiet a moment. Then, "Thank you, Zock." Another moment goes by. "You know, you were very brave yourself."

"You think so?"

"I know so."

They look into each other's' eyes. Then Oksana very deliberately kisses him hard on the lips. This flusters and confuses Zack. He's probably blushing in the dim firelight.

Oksana watches him, a little confused herself. "Zock? Are you all right?"

"Yes. Yeah. It's just..."

"Just what?"

"That's the first time I ever kissed a girl."

Oksana smiles. Snuggles closer to him.

"For everything, there is a first time..."

She kisses him again, very gently this time. He responds in kind...

Zack and the others stare at Oksana in horror. She stands calmly on the edge of the cliff looking down at the dead calf.

"Oksana," Zack manages to say. "Why in the world did you—?"

"Meat," she says, turning on her heel and striding away.

One by one, they all turn and hesitantly follow her down to the base of the cliff.

butchered it using nothing but a sharpened rock. I had never seen so much
blood. It was totally sickening.

But let me tell you something:

The chunks of roasted veal we had for
dinner that night was hands down the
best thing anyone had eaten since BE-
FORE.

It wasn't so sickening after that.

It turned out there was a fair amount
of food animals around. Cattle. Sheep.
Pigs. Goats. They were pretty easy to
catch. We just had to kill them and
butcher them and cook them and eat
them.

One day, we came across chickens.
Which meant eggs! We didn't have a way
to fry or scramble them, but by heating
up one of the granite pools of water with
rocks from the fireplace, we could boil
them. Boiled eggs never tasted so good.

Another big plus was that, under Oksana's guidance, we were able to turn the
skins of the animals into clothing—another reason to be grateful for the time
she had spent on her Uncle's farm. The
clothes were crude and smelly, but at
least they were warm—especially the
sheepskin.

It was slowly beginning to dawn on
me that humanity—meaning our little
tribe—had a chance of surviving into the
future. That maybe we weren't going to

become extinct. But, man, was it going
to be a long, hard slog.

One day when we were out gathering
firewood, Oksana and me had a conversation. Turns out she had some questions and concerns of her own that she'd
been bottling up. They were some of the
same things that had been bothering me.

It was the first time we really talked
about what had happened. We were both
still trying to process it. To try and
make sense out of it—if that was even
possible. If it would ever be possible...

{The Zachary Stone Chronicles}

Zack, Oksana, and some of the others make their way through a forest of scraggly pines. Zack has a large basket made of willow branches on his back. It's half-filled with the firewood that Oksana is collecting. They work steadily and in silence. She picks up another piece of wood. Is about to drop it into the basket but suddenly smashes it against a nearby tree, startling Zack. He turns to face her.

"Oksana? Are you okay?"

"No! I'm not okay!" Her aquamarine eyes flash as she speaks with heartrending passion. "Why didn't they take us, too, Zock? Why are we here and everyone else is gone!"

Zack peels the basket off his back and sets it on the ground. Rubs his shoulder where one of the branches was chafing.

"It's a good question."

Oksana continues. "I mean, what's so special about us that we didn't become food for the aliens?!"

"I've been thinking about that myself."

"Well? Did you come up with an answer?"

"Here's what I think: the fact that we're *not* special is exactly why we're here."

Oksana gives a slow shake of her head. "I don't follow you."

"What I'm saying is, I believe we—our little tribe, a cross section of humanity—were randomly selected."

"Randomly selected for what?"

"We're the seed crop for the next harvest."

Her voice drops a notch. "What are you saying?"

"Do you want to hear my theory?"

"Yes."

"You promise not to laugh?"

Oksana smiles. "I make no promises about anything. But there is so little to laugh about these days, I reserve the right to do so."

Zack gives her a wistful smile. "I can't argue with that."

They sit down beside each other on a fallen log. Zack's smile fades. "I think the aliens have harvested us more than once. Maybe a lot more than once. There's no way of knowing how many times."

Oksana doesn't say anything. Watches him speak, her expression sober.

"I think their probes pass through on a regular basis, probably every couple of thousand years or so. To track our population growth. And when there's enough of us to make it worth their while, say a few billion, we're ripe for harvest. The probe then signals one of their interstellar processing factories and the harvest begins. They collect every last one of us. But. They don't want to fish us to extinction, right? They don't want to deplete the stock. They want to keep the harvests going indefinitely, so they've set up a system that will generate a sustained yield of human beings. They do that by sending a random selection of boys and girls back down to Earth. To begin the cycle all over again."

Oksana is looking sad. "I don't think I'm going to be doing much laughing today."

Zack nods. "At first I thought that we—the members of our little tribe—were specifically chosen to start the next incarnation of the human species; and because of that, I really thought the aliens would watch over us and shield us from danger, if only to protect their investment. But it's become pretty obvious that no one's protecting us from anything; that we're totally on our own. We're in a sink or swim, survival of the fittest situation. We can be wiped out at any time by weather, starvation, fire, disease—any number of ways. And that leads me to believe that we're not the only people on Earth, because the aliens would never put all their eggs in one basket. We're too valuable a commodity to them. So, that being said, there must be dozens—maybe even hundreds—of other tribes similar to our own, spread across the globe. And I'm sure the aliens expect all of these tribes to eventually discover each other, which will lead to another population explosion, which will make us ripe for another harvest. And maybe they'll hope that we have fewer wars this time around, so that there will more of us faster and the harvest will come a little sooner.

"So we need to find these other tribes. And not just for breeding or intermarriage or whatever, but so that we can band together, pool our resources and knowledge and claw back civilization. So that we can accelerate our technological progress and be ready for them the next time."

Zack stops speaking so Oksana to allow her to digest his theory. After a moment, she says, "But, let me ask you something... 50,000 years between harvests? That's an awfully long wait."

"It depends on how fast the population grows. It could be ten thousand years or a hundred thousand."

"Still. A very long time."

"I think how they perceive the passage of time is completely different from the way we do. That's why 50,000 years between harvests wouldn't be a problem for them."

"But—time is time. How could it be different?"

"In Mr. Thatcher's science class last year, we learned about mayflies. Have you heard of them?"

Oksana shakes her head no.

"They're flies that live around lakes. They're pretty common. Their entire lifespan is less than a day. Sometimes it's just a few minutes. We could be like mayflies to them. 50,000 years for us could be fifty or a hundred years to them. And who knows what their lifespan is? Maybe it's a thousand years. Or even more."

"Still..." Oksana's brows furrow in concentration. "...The aliens are so advanced. It seems they can do anything. Wouldn't it be easier for them if they raised human beings on a planet close to their home, where they could totally control the breeding?"

"You mean like a fish farm."

"I guess so. Yes. Then they would have access to as much...human meat as they wanted, whenever they wanted it, without having to depend on the harvest."

"I'm sure they already do."

Oksana looks puzzled. "But, if that's the case, why come after us?"

Zack smiles wryly. "For the same reason a lot of people prefer to eat wild salmon instead of farmed."

Oksana shakes her head. "I don't understand."

"Think about it. Farmed human beings are probably pumped full of growth hormones, antibiotics, steroids, fertility drugs—God knows what—to artificially enhance their size, to increase the population, to alter the taste..."

Oksana winces at the thought. Zack keeps going.

"Us Earthlings, on the other hand, have been running around wild for thousands of generations, living natural lives. Basically, we're free-range. We're like line-caught salmon, fresh off the boat. It makes us a much more valuable commodity than if we were farmed. Which would explain why the aliens go to the trouble of harvesting us, even risking their lives to do it, as we saw."

Zack is quiet for a moment. When he resumes talking, his voice takes on a bitter edge. "If there really are people being raised on farms for food, what really bothers me is this: How are they being treated? What kind of lives do they lead? What are they given to eat? Are they raised in cages? In pens? In a concentration camp environment? Just to be hauled away when an order comes in from a restaurant down the street?"

Oksana shudders at his words. "Zock, these are such crazy ideas. Enough talk about human beings as food. Let me change the subject and ask you your thoughts about something else."

"Sorry I got carried away. This stuff's been rattling around in my brain it seems like forever."

Oksana says, "Why did they have to destroy everything in the world made by human hands?"

Zack ponders the question a moment before answering. "I think the aliens have always sensed that we're a pretty clever species. I don't think they want us getting too clever. So come harvest time, they dissolve everything so that we have to start over from scratch. So that survivors like us don't have any infrastructure and can't build on any previous knowledge. It's also probably why there aren't any adults around to guide us back to civilization."

"But if the aliens are so far advanced, why would they even be concerned about that?"

"Because I think there's a possibility, a small one, that they're afraid we might figure out a way to fight them the next time they come. We definitely surprised them this time. They weren't expecting that we'd started to explore space. That we had rockets and satellites and orbiting freighters. If the probe had passed through just a hundred years earlier, that first harvester would have easily completed its job and not been knocked out of the sky. Instead, we caught 'em with their pants down. So they're not invincible. They do make mistakes."

Oksana looks a little confused. "What do you mean by this 'pants down'?"

Zack grins. "Sorry. It's just an expression. Anyway, I think that because of what happened this time, they're going to increase the frequency of their probes, so they can keep a closer eye on us."

"...God, Zock. It all makes me want to lie down and curl up in a ball."

"You and me both. But that's something we can't do. We have to count on each other, Oksana. We need to be strong."

A long silence as Oksana absorbs Zack's words. Finally, she nods in agreement.

Tears suddenly appear in Zack's eyes. His voice is quiet as he says, "You know, at times...I wish they had taken me. I miss my family. A lot. I think about them all the time. I'm actually glad it's a daily struggle to survive, because it helps take my mind off them."

Oksana's eyes also fill with tears. "I know, Zock... I feel the same." She gently caresses his cheek with the palm of her hand. "*We* are family now..."

Hunting quickly became our favorite pastime.

We got pretty good at it.

It was no longer shocking or horrible. No longer brutal and sickening.

It was exciting. It was fun. And it re-sulted in the tastiest food!

As the days went by, we ventured out on regular hunting parties. We dried excess meat in the sun so that we would have plenty of jerky on hand for the coming winter months. The kids want-ed to hunt more than anything else. I enjoyed it as much as they did. Maybe more.

That's when I started thinking about the conversation that I'd had with Oksana.

That's when I began to worry about what was happening to us...

{The Zachary Stone Chronicles}

All the young tribe members are sprawled about the cave, sleeping where they fell after feasting on the roasted flesh of a pig. Some of them still clutch greasy hunks of meat.

Oksana and Zack lie on a wooly sheepskin next to the fire.

"Oksana?"

"Yes, Zock?"

"Can we talk? I mean seriously? About something im-portant?"

His earnest tone gets her attention. "Of course. What do you want to talk about?"

Zack hesitates a moment before going on. "...This isn't right."

"What isn't right?"

Zack sweeps his hand, indicating all that's in the cave. "This. Everything."

Oksana shakes her head. "I don't understand."

"Don't you see what's happening to us? We're evolving backwards, *fast*. We're living like savages."

There's a flash of anger in Oksana's aquamarine eyes. "You are correct, Zock. Emphasis on *living*. I don't know about you, but I'm pretty happy we didn't freeze to death without the fire."

"Yeah, but there's got to be a better way. We need to do more."

"Right now, our only priority is to stay alive."

"I don't agree. That is our main priority. But it shouldn't be our *only* one."

"What, exactly, are you proposing?"

"We should be trying to educate ourselves."

"What does that mean, educate ourselves?"

"We need to try and preserve as much knowledge as we can from BEFORE. Anything and everything that we can remember. Math. Science. History. How to add and subtract. That the world isn't flat; it revolves around the sun and not the other way around. That there are other continents to be discovered out there. There's lots of stuff we need to pass down to the generations that follow us."

"You can't go to school if you're dead of starvation."

"True. But if our whole lives are going to be about survival just for the sake of survival, then we're no better than cattle. Or chickens. Or salmon."

"Why is this so important to you?"

"If we don't do this, it's just going to happen again."

"What's going to happen again?"

"They'll be back. We've got to try and jumpstart civilization so that next time, we'll be ready for them."

Oksana frowns. "Do you really think they'll be back?"

"They're addicted to us."

Oksana goes silent. She stares at Zack. Finally she speaks. "Okay, Zock, I understand your concerns. And I think perhaps you are right. I will make you a deal. First, we need to get through the winter. That must be our first and only priority. It will not be easy. We're going to need lots and lots of firewood. That task alone will require much effort, because all we have to chop with are sharpened stones. And we'll need to stockpile a lot of food. We need to keep hunting meat and gathering vegetables from gardens and orchards until it's too cold to do so. And we'll need to keep scraping and drying animal skins for clothing. Only then, next summer, when it is warm again and if we are still alive and things are going okay, maybe a couple of times a week we can have this *education*. I will help with it as best I can. So. What do you think? Do we have a deal?"

Zack smiles. "Yes. We have a deal."

She puts her hand out. He does the same and they shake on it.

Oksana was right, as usual. It was hard getting through the winter. But we made it without losing anyone. And when summer finally came, twice a week for about an hour a day (we had no way of keeping accurate time), we gathered in a nearby grassy meadow for 'class'. We cleared a spot down to the sand-like dirt to use as our blackboard. For chalk, we used a stick to draw on the ground. The kids sat on boulders and logs arranged in a double semi-circle around Oksana and myself.

The kids had various levels of comprehension. We did our best to pass on what we knew to them, all of it pretty basic: world geography, arithmetic, how to read and write simple English words and phrases. Because all of the world's cultures and civilization had completely vanished, we didn't teach any history. It seemed kind of pointless and weird. Maybe down the road we would tell some stories about them, but right now we needed to concentrate on nuts and bolts stuff that would help get civilization back up and running.

The kids hated going to class at first. They would much rather have been out hunting and exploring. But after a few sessions, they grudgingly came around to accepting 'school' as an annoying yet unavoidable chore.

As summer progressed, the days grew warmer, the hunting got better, fruits and vegetables became more plentiful.

But the most surprising development was that the kids now seemed to be enjoying class. The grass in the meadow had grown long and lush. Some of the kids had taken to sitting or lying on the soft greenery, watching with earnest expressions as me and Oksana tried our best to convey what little useful knowledge we possessed from BEFORE.

Thinking back, those were unexpectedly pleasant days. For the first time since the last day of BEFORE, I felt like I could relax a little bit; that everything was going to be okay. That, even if it took thousands of years, the world we knew would come back. Except this time, people would be better. Stronger. Wiser. Prepared to meet the challenge of another harvest.

And then, something happened.

Something horrible.

It would change everything.

I remember it was a warm sunny day. We were all in the meadow, where Oksana and I were teaching the multiplication table. There was a girl about 11 who was very smart. She grasped what we were teaching quicker than most of the other kids. We called her Prissy because once she 'got it', she quickly become bored. She would roll her eyes and sigh. We'd let her wander off a short distance to play with imaginary friends, so long as she remained in sight.

The thing was, the grass had grown very tall...

{The Zachary Stone Chronicles}

Oksana stands near the edge of the clearing while Zack leads the kids in reciting the multiplication table.

"...nine times eight is seventy-two; nine times nine is eighty-one; nine times ten is ninety; nine times eleven is—"

A low, loud growl fills the air, followed by the high-pitched shriek of a child.

Prissy.

All heads turn toward the sound. A flash of brown fur moving quickly away through the grass.

Zack squints his nearsighted eyes. "What the hell was—?"

"Come on!" Oksana grabs her spear. "It's got Prissy!"

She charges after the animal as Prissy's cries continue. Zack is right behind her, followed by the rest of the kids.

Oksana and Zack run as fast as they can through the tall grass. Just as they seem to be gaining on whatever it is that's got Prissy, three female lions the size of small horses emerge snarling from the grass in front of them, ears pinned back, massive teeth bared.

Oksana and Zack pull up short. The three lionesses creep forward, muscles twitching, readying to pounce.

Zack and Oksana slowly back up, spears at the ready. Oksana shoots Zack a terrified look. Whispers, "...Zock? What do we do?"

Just then, the rest of the young tribe materializes beside them. The lions freeze at the sight of 25 spears pointed their way.

The tribe starts shouting and howling at the beasts, shaking their spears, trying to run them off. But the lions don't scare easily. They remain in their menacing crouches.

Meanwhile, Prissy's screams fade as she's hauled farther away.

The tribe members jab and feint with their spears, doing everything they can to get past the giant cats. Finally, growling and roaring, the lions start to creep slowly backwards, moving in their own good time.

Zack charges the one on the right and jabs at her with his spear, but the lion bats it away quick as a striking snake.

"Zock!" yells Oksana. "Be careful!"

There's one last shriek from Prissy, then her screams stop altogether. As if on cue, the lionesses melt back into the grass.

Zack is trembling as he slowly lowers his spear. His breath comes in shaky gulps of air. He looks at Oksana.

"She's gone," she says, her voice flat.

The tribe stands silently, helplessly, as a light breeze rustles the grass.

Early the next morning, the tribe heads back to the meadow bristling with spears, clubs and rocks. There's no talking as they move quickly, determined to find Prissy.

Or what's left of her.

At the meadow, it's not difficult to follow the flattened grass and the blood trail. Zack and Oksana lead the way.

After about half a mile, they come across Prissy's remains, which consist of nothing more than scattered bones dark with dried blood. The buzz of flies fills the air.

As the tribe gathers round, Zack moves to shield the youngest of them from the grisly sight. But Oksana pulls him aside. "No. Let everyone look. This is our lives now."

Zack sighs. Watches as his tribe presses forward for a better look. Speaking quietly to himself, he says, "I guess school is out for good."

Things would be different from then on. The world had suddenly become a menacing and deadly place. The overriding lesson we learned that day was that there's safety in numbers.

The rest of that summer and fall, we did everything as a group. Hunting, gathering fruits and vegetables, collecting firewood—all of it. The lions, having had a taste of human flesh, apparently liked it. Sensing that we were not very threatening with our little spears and rocks, they became bolder. Anyone who straggled behind the tribe was in danger.

And it wasn't just lions we had to worry about. More animals from the zoo were turning up. It was crazy. We saw giraffes. Leopards. Elephants. Tigers. Gorillas. In addition to those were the natives, like bears, mountain lions, coyotes and packs of wild dogs.

Only in our shelter did we feel safe.

Needless to say, hunting with the whole tribe was difficult and inefficient. A lot of game was spooked by such a large group. We hoped we had enough meat to get us through the winter.

And wouldn't you know it—the following winter was particularly harsh...

{The Zachary Stone Chronicles}

Zack stands at the entrance to the cave staring out at the snow blowing sideways.

Oksana comes up beside him. Touches his arm. "Zock," she says gently. "You're letting cold air in. Worrying about weather won't change anything. Close the door and come next to the fire." Oksana helps him move the big wooden door into place.

As they head toward the fire, they pass others trying to keep busy while trapped indoors. Some sharpen rocks and sticks. Others are scraping and tanning hides.

Something catches Zack's eye.

Someone sitting cross-legged on the ground, drawing on a wall.

Zack moves closer. Looks down at the young artist. Having grown up in Southern California, Zack can speak some Spanish. He addresses the boy.

"I didn't know you could draw, Manuel."

The 11-year-old looks up with dark, shining eyes. "Yes," he says, his voice weak, his breathing raspy. "I like to draw." His body is suddenly wracked by a coughing spell that goes on for several moments.

Zack kneels down and watches him with concern. Pats the boy gently on the back until he recovers.

"How are you feeling?"

"I'm all right," Manuel lies.

"I wish I had some aspirin or cough syrup to give you."

"Thank you, Zack. But I'll be okay."

Manuel turns his attention back to his drawing. Zack takes a closer look at it.

A half-finished drawing of buildings dissolving and stick-figure people running away in terror, mouths open in mid-scream, tears spraying from their eyes. In the distance, blue bubbles float up to the sky where a child's rendition of an alien is biting a stick-figure boy in half.

Next to Manuel are a half dozen piles of different-colored pastes. Each pile has a small soft twig sticking from it—paintbrushes.

Curious, Zack asks, "Where did you get the paint?"

The boy answers without looking away from his work. "I made it."

"How?"

"In the summer. I collected all kinds of plants and flowers. Squashed them up. Added a little water. Some of them made colors."

"Aren't you clever."

Zack stares some more at the drawing. He pats Manuel on the shoulder and stands up. Exchanges a sober look with Oksana. They move toward the fire.

That night, Oksana and Zack lie next to each other under thick fur skins. The rest of the clan sleeps nearby. The fire crackles low and steady. There's a troubled look in Zack's eyes. Speaking quietly, he says, "Oksana, I don't think we're going to make it here. Between the growing population of wild animals and these winters..."

"I am with child."

Zack's mouth stops working. Eventually, he manages to eke out a response.

"What did you say?"

"I'm pregnant."

Zack sits up. "Are you sure?"

Oksana also sits up. Pulls a fur skin around her shoulders. "I think I know my own body."

"How in the world did that happen?"

She gives him a look as if to say, "Are you really asking me that?"

"Oh."

Oksana lays back down. Turns on her side. Snuggles her back up to Zack, who lays down and gently places an arm over her, his mind racing.

I never got around to having the talk with my dad.

So that's how I learned about the birds and the bees.

...A baby.

We were still babies ourselves.

Then again, maybe not. After all we'd been through. And in such a short time.

As Oksana slept beside me, I felt a renewed sense of urgency for our tribe. We had to survive at all costs.

I stayed awake that whole night, my brain on fire with all kinds of crazy thoughts.

It was getting close to sunrise when I had the craziest thought of all...

{The Zachary Stone Chronicles}

Oksana stirs in the half-light of dawn. She awakens to find Zack lying on his side, his head propped up by a hand, staring at her.

Oksana offers a sleepy smile. "Good morning."

"I've been thinking."

She's instantly aware of his fevered look. Alarmed by his intensity, she says, "Zock, are you all right?"

"We're going to California."

It's Oksana's turn to be rendered speechless. Finally, she speaks. "You are a crazy boy."

Zack's voice is filled with passion. "*Think* about it, Oksana. The climate is so much milder in Southern California. No snow, no freezing temperatures. There's tons of stuff that grows year round. Oranges. Avocadoes. Grapes. And the ocean is warm. We should be able to catch lots of fish.

We could even live on the beach. Oksana, I'm from there. I know the area."

Some of the kids have come awake and are listening to his words. They don't understand all of them.

But California is a word everyone knows.

Oksana coats her ire with sarcasm. "And how would we get to California, Zock? Do you suggest a nonstop flight? Maybe a passenger train? How about a bus? Or maybe we hire a fancy limousine?"

"We walk, of course."

"Oh, yes. Of course. We walk. What is it, like, ten thousand miles?"

"Nowhere near that. Only about a thousand."

"Ah. Only a thousand miles. Zock, have you lost your mind?! We would probably die out there."

"True. But we're definitely going to die here."

Standoff. They stare stubbornly into each other's eyes. Zack is the first to blink.

"Oksana, hear me out: *I know* that route. I've driven it with my family more than once. It's impossible to get lost. We stay close to the Interstate—or what's left of it. We walk every day and we walk fast. If it gets too hot, we'll walk at night and sleep in the day."

"What about water? What about food? How would we carry enough to... to..."

Zack offers helpfully. "Sustain?"

"Yes. To sustain us?"

"I've thought of that. We'll build a cart. Pile our supplies on it."

"And we are supposed to push this cart halfway across the country?"

"Have you seen all the mules running around here? We catch the biggest one and use him to pull our cart. We'll need some sturdy rope. We can start on that today. Right now, even while it's snowing. We put the kids to work cutting strips of leather off the hides, then braid them together.

"As for water, right now we have a surplus of animal skins. We boil them, which will sanitize them and soften the leather. Then we lace them up and fill them with water.

"Having enough food for the journey shouldn't be a problem. As soon as it warms up, we'll hunt down a couple of cows and make a big pile of jerky. In addition to that, we'll gather fruits and vegetables and dry them in the sun so they'll keep. We'll have enough food and water to get us to California.

"If we start preparing now, we can get on the road as soon as the snow melts."

Oksana has to admit that his enthusiasm is contagious; his plan well thought out. Still...

"We can do this, Oksana. You have to believe me..."

A child's scream pierces the air from the back of the shelter. Startled, Zack and Oksana grab their spears and run toward it.

Another scream.

They charge through the collection of frightened kids. Arrive at the stone wall on which Manuel had been painting the previous day. Manuel lies before it, wrapped in a thick fur skin. This is the spot where he usually sleeps.

Only he doesn't appear to be sleeping.

The girl who screamed stands shivering with her hands over her mouth, staring down at Manuel.

He's not breathing. His eyes are open.

"I tried to wake up him up, but he wouldn't..." She can't go on.

Zack and Oksana kneel down next to him.

"Manuel...?" Zack reaches out to stroke his face.

It's cold to the touch.

Zack pulls his hand back as if it's been scalded. He looks at Manuel's unfinished drawing. Then looks at Oksana kneeling on the other side of Manuel.

She stares back at him. Her eyes are calm, her lips set.

SIX MONTHS LATER
SOMEWHERE IN THE SOUTHWEST

A mule pulls a cart across a flat, dry landscape. Barren, brown mountains loom in the distance.

The cart is made of rough-hewn wood. Its four wheels look like they've been hacked from a solid log, then holes painstakingly chipped out of the center of each for the two axles to pass through. The platform is made of wooden poles stripped of their bark, then lashed together with ropes of braided leather. It's the crudest of designs but it works.

Piled high on the cart are animal-hide blankets; woven baskets containing dried meat, fruit and vegetables; other bladder-like skins bulging with water; chickens in simple wooden cages; spare firewood.

The time Oksana spent on her uncle's farm continues to benefit the tribe. Leading the mule by a leather rope, she keeps the animal moving parallel to the remnants of an interstate that extends into the distance as far as the eye can see. Oksana is well into her pregnancy but her muscles are toned, she looks strong. Her skin is deeply bronzed by the sun, causing her aquamarine eyes to stand out in startling contrast.

Some of the young tribe walk alongside the cart. Others shepherd a small herd of sheep and goats behind it. Bringing up the rear is a pair of fire-tenders. One carries a flat rock the size of a large serving platter. Its center has been ground down to a hollowed-out depression, filled now with glowing embers. The other fire-tender carries a basket from which he regularly feeds bits of kindling to the smoldering flame. The rock is heavy, so the fire-tenders must trade places a couple of times an hour. Tendrils of smoke trail behind them.

The hard work required for survival combined with a lean diet of unprocessed foods has rendered childhood obesity obsolete. All of the tribe members have developed sinewy muscles and look healthy and hearty. The exception is Zack. Although he's grown several inches taller, he remains very much on the skinny side. The early makings of a beard sprout from his face. He walks with a gangly stride next to the cart.

The hair of all the tribe members has grown long and wild. Their animal-skin garb is weathered from continuous use. Looking like a ragtag band of Stone Age gypsies, the motley little caravan moves across the land at a steady pace.

The hardest part of getting ready for the journey to California was reinventing the wheel. And I mean literally. It took the whole tribe working in shifts with sharpened stones to bring down a tree and then carve four wheels out of it. But it was worth the effort because there was no way we could have carried everything we needed on our backs.

It helped that once we got on the road, we were able to forage off the land. Thanks to the sprawl of people and towns in BEFORE, there were wells and irrigation ditches and overgrown gardens and crops. Not having enough food and water was never a problem.

Each night, we built a big fire, which we kept burning hot and bright until morning. We did this for two reasons: The first was warmth, even though it never got very cold. The second and more important reason was keeping wild animals at bay. We heard lots of coyotes at night and I think even some wolves. Who knew what else was out there roaming the land? We slept with our spears and clubs within easy reach.

Even so, everyone remained in surprisingly good spirits. I think that was because we were relieved to actually be doing something. To be working toward a definite goal, instead of spending all our time and energy on just trying to stay alive from day to day, from hour to hour.

Our little one-wagon wagon train made decent time. I'd figured that, once we set out, if we traveled at least ten miles a day, it would take us about a hundred days to get to the California border—or what had been the border. There weren't any road or mileage signs to mark our progress, but my gut feeling told me we were ahead of schedule.

Our journey was going surprisingly smoothly. I'd be the first to admit that, at the beginning, I was really afraid we'd lose people to an accident, or starvation, or sickness, or snakebite, something. Now we were coming up on the homestretch. Thankfully, none of those things had happened.

So far.

I figured we had to be somewhere in southern Nevada, not far from the border.

The thing is, I wasn't seeing anything recognizable. In the desert, landscapes blend into one another. One direction looks much like another.

In addition to that, the last several days had been strangely misty and overcast, rare for the desert. It limited our vision to just a few miles.

I was starting to get anxious as doubts invaded my mind. At what had been major freeway interchanges, the remains of the roads were often so scrambled together that it was hard to be a hundred percent sure about which road was ours. Were we following the right interstate? Was it possible we'd taken a wrong turn? Were we hopelessly lost?

I kept my concerns to myself for as long as I could. Finally, I resolved to tell Oksana first thing in the morning that my sense of direction might not have been as clear as I'd let on, that we could be in serious trouble.

The morning dawned with bright sunlight and clear blue skies. The tribe was beginning to stir as they made their daily preparations to get back on the road. I sat up in the bed of furry animal skins. Saw that Oksana was helping to tend the fire.

I totally dreaded Oksana's reaction to what I was about to tell her. I got up, pulled a thick pelt over my shoulders and made my way toward her.

And then...I saw it. Even with my crappy eyesight, there was no mistaking what it was.

Looming up in the distance were the snow-covered peaks of the Sierra Nevada Mountains.

{The Zachary Stone Chronicles}

Zack shouts at the top of his lungs, "Whoooo-hoooo!!! Yeeeaaah!!! Hallelujah!!!"

This startles every member of the groggy tribe. They all look at Zack, wondering if he's gone crazy. He smiles and points at the mountain range. "California!"

Everyone turns to see. They all gasp as one, then begin chattering away with an excitement Zack had never seen before.

Oksana approaches him. Hesitantly asks, "Is it possible, Zock? Are you sure?"

Zack's excitement is contagious. "As sure as I've ever been about anything!"

Oksana looks at the sparkling mountains, then back at Zack before breaking Sag into happy laughter.

Overcome with emotion at the thought of being so close to home, or at least what used to be home, tears appear in Zack's eyes. His voice drops to a husky whisper as he looks into her eyes. "We're almost there, Oksana. Another week or so should do it. Trust me, you're going to love it."

Oksana places her hand on his cheek and returns his look. "I do trust you, Zock..."

Zack gives her a radiant smile before turning away. There's a spring in his step as he heads over to help others load the cart. Unable to contain his exuberance, he suddenly bursts into song, once again startling the young tribe.

"California, here I come!

Right back where I started from!"

Zack doesn't know the rest of the lyrics but he doesn't care. He keeps humming the tune.

I couldn't believe it! We were almost there. After all we'd been through, this final stretch was going to be a walk in the park.

Or so I thought.

That night, we built up the fire like we had done every night.

Except this time, instead of keeping wild animals at bay, the fire did just the opposite.

It attracted the wildest animals you could ever imagine...

{The Zachary Stone Chronicles}

The sound of Oksana's voice pulls Zack out of a deep slumber.

"Zock? Zock! Wake up!"

He sits up, groggy from sleep. "What is it? What's the matter?"

"Something's happening!"

Zack hears the fear in her voice and quickly rouses himself. Cries and screams can be heard over the crackling of the fire.

Zack grabs his spear and jumps to his feet. Oksana does the same.

Even if Zack had perfect eyesight, it would still be hard to make sense out of the commotion surrounding him in the half-light of the fire.

Shadowy figures dart among the tribe, whose members are still not yet fully awake. The sound of blows struck is followed by cries of pain.

Zack squints at the chaos surrounding him. "What the hell is going on?!"

As if in answer, one of the shadowy figures comes to a halt in front him. Zack crouches, his spear at the ready. Oksana does the same. As the figure comes into focus, Zack's mouth drops open in surprise. Standing before him is a strapping giant of a boy about the same age as himself. His blonde hair and beard and blue eyes are striking even in the murky light. His hand grips a large wooden club.

It's been almost two years since Zack has seen another human being other than those in his tribe. He stares at him in wonder. "You're human..."

The very pregnant Oksana remains in a crouch. "Zock, be careful..." The blonde boy's eyes flit to her, then back at Zack.

"I *knew* there were more of us." Zack slowly lowers his spear. "We come in peace. We mean you no harm."

Alarmed, Oksana hisses, "Zock! What are you doing?!"

Zack lets his spear drop to the ground. He then slowly extends his arm to shake hands. "Friends?" Zack is so relieved to finally see another human being that he's actually smiling. "Okay? Friends?"

The blonde boy returns the smile. But there's something off about it. It's not exactly friendly. More of a smirk. Zack realizes that dropping his spear may not have been such a good idea.

Quick as lightning, the blonde boy lashes out with the club. Zack sees it coming and tries to move out of the way but isn't fast enough. A loud thock as the wood cracks against the side of his head. As Zack goes down, Oksana cries out in rage and lunges at the blonde boy with her spear. He easily sidesteps it. Before she can lunge again, she's tackled from behind by two other strangers not of her tribe.

MORNING

Zack's eyes flicker open. It takes a moment for the events of the night to register. As soon as they do, he tries to jump to his feet but falls heavily onto his side. Only then does he realize his wrists are tied behind his back and his ankles hobbled. Dried blood mats his hair. He manages to sit up and look around.

All the males of his tribe are gathered around him, their hands and feet also tied. Most are battered and bloodied like him. Unfortunately, a tribe member named Dessu is hurt worse than anybody. His foot is bent at an unnatural angle. His ankle appears to be broken. From Ethiopia, he's the youngest and smallest member of the clan. He also happens to be one of the toughest, and probably fought like hell, which no doubt led to his injury. He sits quietly with his eyes closed, trying to will the pain to stop. Sitting near him, Zack sees the two fire-tenders. They are also tied up. Zack notices with alarm that the fire has gone out.

About a hundred feet away, Oksana sits in the cart. She, too, is tied up, but soft animal skins have been placed around her as if to make her comfortable. The rest of the females of the tribe are tied up and sit in a cluster behind the cart. The mule is tethered to the front of the cart as if they are about to get on the road.

Oksana spies Zack. They exchange a helpless look.

Zack hears the whinny of a horse. He looks over to where several members of the new tribe sit astride horses. The blonde boy is mounted on the largest steed. These new people have managed to capture horses and then learn to ride them bareback. The blonde boy shouts in a language Zack's never heard. The consonants are abrupt and sharp, the vowels drawn out and lilting. It appears he's giving orders as other members of this new tribe gather around Zack and the other prisoners. They carry short thick leather whips and wooden truncheons.

There's no question that the blonde boy is the leader of this group.

The new tribe members surrounding Zack and the others are apparently soldiers or guards. They begin shouting and beating them, urging the prisoners to their feet. Once standing, they're pushed into a ragged line. A long thin rope of woven leather is tied around the massive chest of the large horse, then played out back to the line of prisoners, where a loop is placed around the neck of each captive, then tied off in a neat knot, allowing a couple of fingers of space between rope and skin. Dessu, standing on his good leg, is last in line.

Behind the cart, the women aren't strung together but will be closely watched as they are herded along by several guards.

They are about to begin a forced march. Zack glances back at Dessu with concern. It's clear the boy won't be able to walk. He stares calmly back at Zack.

From his horse at the head of the column, the blonde boy shouts, "Framat marsch!"

As the procession starts to move, Dessu takes one step, yelps in pain, and collapses. Two guards descend on him immediately, shouting and beating.

Dessu cries out "No can walk! No can walk!" but it does nothing to stop the beating. He curls into a fetal position and covers up as best he can.

Blonde Boy notices the commotion in the rear, halts the column, dismounts and strides back to see what the holdup is.

The guards continue beating Dessu. Zack can stand his friend's torment no longer. He shouts, "Leave him alone, you sons of bitches!"

The two guards ignore Zack's outburst and continue the beating. Zack screams, "Can't you see he's hurt and can't walk?! Why don't you put him in the cart with the woman, or at least let us carry him!"

Just then Blonde Boy walks past Zack, giving him a curious look as he does so. As he nears Dessu and the guards, he says in a loud voice, "Vad ar problemet?"

The two guards step back and point at Dessu, who looks up defiantly at Blonde Boy. He shouts through his bloody mouth, "No can walk!"

Blonde Boy steps close to Dessu, then kneels beside him. "Du kan inte ga, ja?" he says in a soothing voice. Taken off guard by the gentle tone, Dessu doesn't reply but stares warily at Blonde Boy, who smiles back at him. More soothing words. "Kanske jag kan hjalpa till..."

His large hands moving quickly, Blonde Boy reaches out and grabs a length of the slack leather twine in two places, wraps it around Dessu's neck, doubles it up in each fist and pulls the garrote tight. His smiling face is inches from Dessu's, as if savoring every second of this exquisitely up close and personal murder.

It's only then Dessu realizes this young sadist is going to kill him. He manages to spit in Blonde Boy's face. This just causes him to grin even more broadly as he pulls the garrote tighter. Dessu's eyes go very wide. Choking sounds come from his throat.

"What are you doing?!" Zack screams. "Stop it, you're killing him!

Dessu's eyes look as if they're about to pop out of their sockets. They roll up into his head as his body spasms and twitches. Finally, he goes completely still. Only then does Blonde Boy release his iron grip on the cord. He stands up, breathing heavily. He licks his lips. There's a light sheen of sweat on his face, which glows with twisted pleasure. He gives an order, his voice a hoarse whisper.

"Skara honom los."

One of the guards kneels. Uses a large sharpened stone to cut the rope from Dessu's neck.

Blonde Boy turns and starts walking back to the front of the column. As he moves past the line of prisoners, tears of frustration and rage burn in Zack's eyes.

Zack speaks loudly and clearly.

"Hey! Blondie!"

Blondie gazes curiously at Zack as he continues walking.

"I hope you burn in hell!"

Blonde Boy doesn't react. He turns his gaze ahead and keeps walking.

Zack shouts after him. "I know you don't understand my words, but I think you have a pretty good idea what I'm saying!"

The forced march resumes. Blond Boy rides his horse at the front of the procession, jerking the young male prisoners along by the neck.

To Zack's pleased surprise, they don't go west in the direction of California, but instead head north, deeper into Nevada. It occurs to Zack that it's possible no one in this new and aggressive tribe has any idea how close they are to the relative paradise of Southern California. They were no doubt randomly collected from around the world like his own tribe, which means that none of them has any idea where on Earth they are.

Zack decides it's a good idea to keep it that way.

We walked for three days, stopping at night to eat and sleep. Each time we stopped, I was surprised to watch the big blonde kid make a fire from scratch in just a couple of minutes. That was a skill I'd have given anything to have in Colorado. But the weird thing was, he got the fire going by himself out of sight, like he wanted to keep the procedure secret. Maybe he figured it was a way to control the members of his tribe.

On the fourth day, we arrived at their permanent campsite; a spring-fed oasis in the middle of the Nevada desert. From our time on the road, I'd seen enough sites that had once been villages or cities in BEFORE. This one had mature trees and several small orchards and gardens, which made me think it had once been a prosperous town.

Unfortunately, the ambience of the setting was pretty much wrecked by the dozens of human skulls mounted on stakes lining the approach to the campsite.

This new tribe numbered about 300 members. They lived in crude adobe huts scattered about the oasis. About a third of them were infants or small children. Most of the females were in various stages of pregnancy.

A collection of nearby enclosures made of densely-packed sticks and brambles each held about a half-dozen horses, cows, sheep, pigs and chickens. Except for the horses, when it came to food, it looked like my tribe's survival instincts were similar to their own. Other than that, I soon learned that our way of life was very different from theirs.

The biggest difference was that they preyed on other tribes. I know. You're probably wondering how that was even possible, given how few people there apparently were in the world.

Emphasis on 'apparently'. Turns out there were more than we thought. No doubt the aliens had their formulas and processes for determining how many tribes needed to be scattered about the Earth in order to seed a new crop of humans and be assured of a good harvest.

Because of the random distribution of tribes around the world, many of them ended up in harsh environments where they had to struggle to survive, like us. And also like us, many of them decided to pull up stakes and try to move to milder climes.

With the Sierra Nevada mountain range acting as a natural barrier, migrating tribes had little choice but to skirt around it down to its southern slopes where it became crossable.

Which was where this predator tribe happened to have had landed.

A nearby mountain peak served as a lookout. Here, tribal members with the keenest vision stood watch for telltale signs of people on the move.

The two most obvious indications were fire and smoke. Once spotted, ambushes were set up and raids launched on unsuspecting tribes like ours.

Another big difference was that Blondie ruled his tribe with an iron fist. He was its uncontested leader. He made the rules by which the rest lived:

Male tribe members were both warriors and workers, and were permitted to move freely about.

New male captives automatically became slaves. Over time, if a slave earned the trust of Blondie, he could eventually become a full-fledged member of the tribe. Unless or until that happened, slaves lived miserable lives filled with hard labor and bad food. If they became injured or ill and were unable to work, they were put to death.

Female tribe members were forbidden to become warriors. Blondie had decreed that their main purpose was to bear children. (As it turned out Blondie was the father of most of the clan's children.) Women were also required to cook, clean, harvest crops, skin food animals, scrape hides, and so on, basically performing all the tasks that slaves did not.

Even with its rigid organization and ready access to food and shelter, daily life at the oasis was squalid and brutal. I guess what I'm saying is there was zero forward progress. If anything, what was left of the human race appeared to be on a fast-track heading backward in time to an era of savagery and barbarity.

I got a glimpse of things to come on my very first night at my new home...

{The Zachary Stone Chronicles}

Exhausted and famished after the three-day forced march on little food and inadequate rest, Zack and his fellow captives are herded into a pen whose walls bristle with sharpened sticks. Guards untie their hands but their feet remain hobbled and the snares left in place around their necks. They collapse in a line onto the dirt. Moments later, a slave from a previous capture enters the pen and wordlessly tosses chunks of charred, gristly meat in front of them. They fall upon the food, grabbing it with dirty hands and tearing into it with their teeth. Grease runs down their chins and arms.

Out of nowhere, Blondie appears. He squats down onto his haunches directly in front of Zack, who stops mid-chew. Blondie studies him with blue, calculating eyes. Warily, Zack sets the meat on the ground and watches him, not knowing what to expect.

After a moment, Blondie begins speaking perfect English with a lilting accent.

"When I was in school—back when schools still existed—we were required to take a class on World History."

Alarmed to see that Blondie is fluent in his language, Zack blurts out, "You speak English."

Blondie continues in a matter-of-fact tone.

"I hated that class. I thought it was incredibly boring. I mean, who cares about stuff that happened hundreds or thousands of years ago, yes?"

"Sure," Zack says, unsure where this is going. He can't quite place the accent. Scandinavian? German?

"Then we read a book about Genghis Khan. Do you know of him?"

"I've...heard the name. I think he was a conqueror or something..."

"I didn't think I would like the book. But I did. Very much. Did you know that Genghis Khan killed more enemies and conquered more territory than anyone else in history?"

"I didn't know that."

"He killed more than Alexander the Great. More than Adolph Hitler. He was the most powerful man the world has ever known..."

Blondie stops talking. He stares off into the distance for a moment. Licks his lips. His gaze focuses back on Zack as he resumes his discourse.

"I started...*fantasizing* I think is the word, yes? Fantasizing about him. To have lived the life he lived. Then the spaceship arrived. I thought we were all going to die. But we didn't. And so now..."

A small, strange smile appears on his face.

"...here we are."

A sudden chill surges through Zack's body.

The smile quickly fades. "You are American?"

"Yes."

"The whole world has become what you Americans call the Wild West, yes? Everything is up for grabs."

"How did you know I was American?"

"A couple of years ago, I went to the Jamboree in the United States. I met a lot of Americans."

"'Jamboree?' What's that?"

"The annual gathering of Boy Scouts. I was part of the Swedish contingent."

A Boy Scout, thought Zack. Which would explain the survival skills; the ability to build a fire; the fancy knot in the snare around his neck.

"So you are Swedish."

"I *was* Swedish. But Sweden no longer exists. Countries no longer exist. We're all on our own now."

"Why did you kill Dessu?"

"Who is Dessu?"

"The boy who couldn't walk."

A smile appears on Blondie's face, as if he's reliving a pleasant memory. "Ah, yes. Him."

"You could have put him in the cart with Oks—with the pregnant girl. Or we could have carried him."

"This is true. I could have ordered it."

"You didn't have to kill him."

"No."

"Then why?"

"Why did I kill him?" Blondie says, his tone suggesting the answer is obvious. "Because I could."

Zack can't believe what he's hearing. "Because you could? Is that the only reason?"

"No."

"Then what else?"

The smile returns to Blondie's face. "Because it was fun."

Another chill passes through Zack. He's too shocked to say anything.

"While we're on the subject..." Blondie says, still smiling. "This is what I came to tell you: My name is Odin..." A happy gleam appears in his eyes. He lunges forward. His large, powerful hands are suddenly around Zack's neck, his bearded face inches from him. "If you ever call me Blondie again, I'll kill you the same way. Only with my bare hands..."

Odin squeezes. Zack tries to claw his hands away but he's no match for the much larger, stronger boy.

The other captives try to move away as best they can, but they are all still tethered to each other at the neck.

Animal sounds come from Zack's throat. His face turns purple. Just as he starts to go limp, Odin releases his grip. Zack sags to the ground gagging and coughing.

Odin rises to his feet. Looks down at Zack and says, "I'm going back to my house now to get acquainted with the newest female additions to the tribe. In the meantime, try to get some rest. You are going to need it. Have a nice day."

He strides calmly away.

Thus began my life as a slave. We were worked to exhaustion every day, sunup to sundown, seven days a week, digging latrines, cutting and hauling firewood, tanning animal hides, all hard labor.

Fortunately for my fellow tribe members, they were quickly absorbed into the new clan. As for myself, the months dragged by with no sign that my status as a slave was ever going to change. I got the feeling I would remain one indefinitely. In hindsight, that probably seemed like a good idea to my captors. In their eyes, I wasn't much good for anything else. I had bad eyesight. I wasn't very strong. I wasn't very coordinated. I guess you could also say I had an attitude. I wasn't inclined to grovel.

I will say this: Most of the members of the new tribe were decent to me. Many smuggled me food. It was just Blondie and his guards and warriors who tormented me every chance they got.

I thought about trying to escape, but the odds of success were terrible. Of the handful who did try, all were hunted down by Blondie and his warriors, dragged back to camp, then tortured to death in the most horrible ways. Of course, Blondie always insisted on doing the honors. All the other slaves were made to watch. No need to go into details.

It turned out that was a very effective way to discourage escapes. Slaves didn't need to be closely guarded. It was only in the daytime that they stayed on us to keep us working. At night, we were 'locked' in a mud hut. The door was made out of wooden poles lashed together with strips of leather. It was tied shut each night with one guard posted outside—not exactly Fort Knox. If we really wanted to, it would be easy to break through the gate, overpower the guard, and make a run for it. But we'd seen firsthand what happened to escapees, so why bother?

In the end, all I could do was struggle to make it through the day.

And the day after that...

And the day after that...

And the day after that...

This was by far the worst time of my life.

I say that because after about a year of living like this with no end in sight, I began to lose it. If this was how I was going to spend the rest of my days, it was time to start seriously thinking about checking out. Even though we were all still quite young, suicide wasn't unheard of. A number of kids simply couldn't adjust to this new way of life and did themselves in.

I had pretty much made the decision to do the same. The only thing holding me back was the thought of leaving Oksana at the total mercy of Blondie.

The whole time I'd been a slave, I'd only seen Oksana on a handful of occasions, and then only from a distance. Which was really frustrating, because with my crappy eyesight, I couldn't make her out well enough to see how she was doing, or to read her facial expressions.

Then, one night, my questions were answered. While in a deep sleep after a particularly grueling stint of digging

ditches on a very hot day, I was awakened by a familiar voice.
    Just when I thought things couldn't get
any worse...

{The Zachary Stone Chronicles}

"Zock..."

Zack stirs. He's positioned himself close to the entrance to catch any stray breeze. But the hatch gate stands wide open. There's no guard to be seen. The light from a nearly full moon floods through the entranceway.

"Zock, wake up..."

Zack jerks awake. Sits up, ready for anything.

"Who's there?"

He feels a soft touch on his forearm. "It's me... Oksana."

"Oksana?" He sees her sitting on the ground next to him in the moonlight. Reaches out to her. "Is it really you? Am I dreaming?"

"You're not dreaming, Zock. It's me."

"But—how did you...?"

"There's just the one guard. He wasn't particularly hard to bribe. Just a chunk of goat cheese."

Instinctively, he reaches out to embrace her but she push-es him gently away.

"Careful. I'm not alone."

This confuses Zack. "What do you mean you're not..."

He's interrupted by the soft cry of an infant.

Oksana says, "There's someone I want you to meet." She shifts her body so that he can see the baby she's cradling.

"This is Vera," Oksana says. "Our daughter."

Zack stares at her in shock. Tears suddenly fill his eyes. His voice a whisper, he says, "Our daughter...?"

"Would you like to hold her?"

Zack reaches for the infant. Oksana leans forward to place her in his arms. As she does so, Zack notices discoloration on her arms. Cradling the baby in one arm, he reaches out with his other hand and takes her gently by the wrist. Looks at the marks.

"Oksana? Are you okay?"

She pulls her arm away. "I'm fine."

He looks carefully at her face in the moonlight.

Bruises.

"No. You're not."

Oksana doesn't reply. Just stares at the ground.

"Who did this to you?"

"I said I'm all right."

Then Zack notices something else.

"You're pregnant."

Oksana looks into his eyes. "I'm so sorry, Zock."

"Who's the father?"

But he knows the answer as soon as he asks.

Oksana's voice breaks as she says, "I tried so hard to fight him off. He was just too strong..." She begins to sob. "I'm sorry... I'm sorry..."

Zack has never seen her like this. She's always been so strong. Her words come out in an agonized rush. "He's crazy, Zock! He's trying to get as many girls pregnant as he can. He says he's going to create a generation of boy warriors as powerful as himself. That it will be the beginning of a new dynasty."

Zack says nothing. Strangely, a deep calmness settles over him. Yet even though on the outside he's sitting very still, deep within him violent emotions roil and surge like the magma in a volcano about to erupt.

In a voice both tearful and savage, Oksana says, "I think I'm going to kill it as soon as it's born. Then I'm going to kill myself."

Zack says nothing for a moment. Slowly nods his head as if he can't blame her for such thoughts. Then says, "But who will take care of Vera? She'll be totally at his mercy."

The thought shakes up Oksana so badly, she can't reply. She starts to cry. He gently holds her. "It's all right, Oksana... Everything's going to be all right..."

I held her a long time and just let her cry.

As she wept, it became clear as day to me what I had to do.

I was going to kill Odin.

And the sooner the better.

The next day was the same as all my other days as a slave. Except now I had a purpose and a plan. Such a simple plan.

And it was going to happen that night.

The past few days had been so hot that pretty much the entire tribe had taken to sleeping outside. And because it was a relatively small community, everyone knew where other people worked. Where they ate. Where they lived.

Even we slaves had a pretty good idea of the lay of the land.

As soon as it was dark, using the sharpened stone I'd swiped from the tanning station earlier that day, I went to work on the leather ropes that kept the gate to the slave garrison tied in place. The only hang-up was timing my cutting as the lone guard made his rounds of the slave pen, so that he was out of earshot as I was doing it. The other slaves, exhausted as always, slept soundly around me.

It didn't take long.

As soon as I was free, I began making my way toward Blondie's hut. The moon was pretty full, so I kept to the shadows. I'd heard that Blondie didn't have bodyguards standing watch over him. The word was that because he was the biggest and strongest boy in the tribe, he figured he could take on any and all comers. Another obvious deterrent was that if anyone were to attack him, whether the assailant survived the encounter or not, he would be sure to be captured and meet with an unpleasant end.

Unfortunately for Blondie, I was so angry, I didn't care about what might happen to me.

I wasn't far from his hut. I began scanning the ground, looking for a rock or boulder that would do the trick. The desert is filled with every rock imaginable, so my search didn't take long. I picked one that wasn't so heavy I couldn't lift it, yet had enough heft to strike a fatal blow.

Carrying the boulder in my arms, I walked as steadily and quietly as I could toward Blondie's hut. In the moonlight just outside the doorway, I could see three figures sleeping side by side.

The giant boy was lying on his back between two girls. Light from the moon was just bright enough that I could make out the blondeness of his hair and beard.

These poor girls were about to have the rudest awakening of their young lives in the form of getting splashed with Blondie's blood and brains.

I stepped carefully over to where they slept. There, I positioned myself so I was standing directly over Blondie, his head at my feet.

My heart was pounding as I struggled to raise the boulder high over my head. Just as I was about to slam it down on his skull, a bright orange light suddenly flashed in the sky, causing me to look up. As I did, a giant fireball streaked overhead, followed by a deafening boom, which quickly subsided into a loud whooshing sound, as the fireball continued toward the horizon.

One of the girls screamed. Before I could look back down and finish the task, my feet were kicked out from under me. The boulder tumbled from my hands as I fell to the ground. The last

Sunrise. Oksana stands on the outskirts of the village. Holding Vera by the hand, she watches a small caravan moving off in the distance. Tears roll silently down her face.

Zack wakes up in a small wooden cage about three feet on a side. His hands are bound so tightly behind him that his wrists are bleeding. His face is bruised and caked with dried blood. He looks groggily around. Realizes he's moving. The cage he's in is lashed on to the wooden cart, along with containers of food and water. Instead of the mule, it's being pulled by a draft horse. Surrounding the cart are a half-dozen of Odin's mounted boy warriors. They don't pay him any mind but stare ahead. The pace is quick.

Zack glances up at the sun high in the sky. He's been out for a good twelve hours. It's another very hot day. He struggles to sit up. Grimaces in pain at his leather bindings.

Zack catches movement out of the corner of his eye. Odin, riding atop his giant steed, appears beside him. He calls out cheerfully to Zack in his lilting Swedish accent.

"I see that my would-be assassin is awake and alert. That is very good news. I was afraid I had fatally injured you. Which would have been unfortunate."

Zack manages to speak through his dry, cracked lips. "Why is that such good news?

Odin is in the best of spirits.

"I've brought you along with us as this evening's entertainment. For fun and games, yes?"

Zack's heart fills with dread.

"You brought me along where?"

Odin grins brightly. Ignores the question. "Fun and games tonight, yes?"

With a laugh, Odin kicks his horse into a gallop and resumes his place at the head of the small party of boy warriors.

I found out after the fact that a couple of tribe members who hadn't been able to sleep because of the heat had watched the object pass over the camp from start to finish. They told Blondie that they thought it had hit the Earth near the horizon, about 20 miles away.

Blondie immediately gathered his best boy warriors and some supplies to go check it out. He was concerned that another tribe had developed gunpowder or rocket fuel of some kind, and that what we had seen was a crude rocket or a cannonball. If that turned out to be the case, he would launch an immediate search for this other clan and make such a powerful new weapon his own.

After a full day of hard traveling, it was starting to grow dark. Blondie was looking for a place to make camp for the night and continue the search in the morning, when one of his warriors scouting ahead returned with information. He had spotted smoke and fire from the top of a nearby ridge.

The news excited Blondie. The fire and smoke could be only one thing: the result of the projectile smashing to Earth. He insisted on going to investigate right

away while there was still light in the
sky.

Being jostled all day on the cart had
caused the leather to cut deeply into my
wrists. The pain was incredible. I just
wanted it all to end.

When we reached the top of the ridge,
we could see a small fire burning at the
edge of a broad flat plain that stretched
far into the distance. Odin immediately
had us head directly for the flickering
orange light.

As the cart and horses trundled closer
to the site, a strange noise floated on
the air toward us.

Blondie brought the caravan to a halt
and put his finger to his lips, calling for
silence. He and his boy warriors sat very
still, straining to hear the odd sound,
which had stopped. As everyone quieted
their horses, it started up again.

A banjo.

Playing a tune that I recognized.

Back in BEFORE, I had watched a doc-
umentary on the early days of television.
What we were hearing was the theme music of a show from that time.

The Beverly Hillbillies.

The source of the sound wasn't more
than a hundred yards away.

{The Zachary Stone Chronicles}

Spike Penovitch leans with his back against a boulder playing his banjo. His hands are blurs of motion as he plays the tune perfectly, effortlessly, and wickedly fast. In addition, he throws in all kinds of musical flourishes and embellishments.

The pre-programmed escape pod performed as expected, depositing Spike back to Earth three years to the day from when he started his second moon mining stint. The vessel lies on the ground nearby, scorched from its reentry into the atmosphere.

It's been a long three years for Spike. He looks like a wrung-out version of himself. Skinny and pale. Lots of new lines in his face. Dark circles around his eyes. His khaki jumpsuit is stained and frayed. Yet for all that, he still looks as tough and crusty as ever. He plays his instrument with fierce passion. As if this is what sustained him for over a thousand days.

The pod's hatch is open. Various items lie strewn about. Depleted oxygen tanks. Empty water canisters. Several wadded up wrappers from energy bars. Plus something else that seems oddly out of place. Lying next to Spike is what appears to be a large metal suitcase. The lid is open. It's packed full of various items, which are hard to make out it in the dimming light.

Odin and his boy warriors quickly dismount, tie their horses to the cart and arm themselves with thick wooden clubs and crude obsidian knives. Odin shoots Zack a glance, his eyes alight with the thrill of the impending encounter. On a wordless gesture from their leader, they move off in the direction of the music with Odin leading the way. They melt into the gathering darkness.

Zack stares after them, his eyes filling with emotion at the thought of what they're about to do.

"No..." he says, his voice a choked whisper. "You can't do this!"

Odin and his crew crouch low and creep stealthily forward.

Spike plays on, oblivious to the approaching danger.

From his cage in the dim light, Odin can just make out the top of Spike's head above the boulder as they approach him from behind. Odin signals his boy warriors to hang back, that he'll handle this himself. It will be another notch on his belt of glory.

Spike wails away, a kind of desperation in his movements. The banjo is loud, pinging and tinging what sounds like twenty notes a second. Suddenly he frowns. Stops playing. Plucks one of the strings a couple of times. Is not happy with what he hears.

He reaches up to tighten the string with one of the tuning pegs. When he's satisfied, he's about to resume playing but then stops. He looks at the desolation around him: the remnants of what was once the giant space center. Now it's just a flat empty expanse stretching out into the gathering darkness. No buildings. No takeoffs and landings of spacecraft. No nothing.

An all-encompassing sigh escapes from Spike, followed by a single word that drips with disparagement, hopelessness, and loss.

"Shit..."

He takes a pull of water, emptying the flask. Tosses it to the ground. Takes up his banjo. Is about to resume playing when he hears something in the distance. It's very faint. He can't quite make out what it is. It's just a tickling on his eardrums. It seems to be coming from behind him.

He sets the banjo down. Turns his head. Cups his ear. Listens carefully.

"Look out!"

Someone shouting. The voice is ragged, hoarse, as it struggles to be heard.

Very distant and hard to hear but very real, it's the first human voice Spike has heard in three years.

Odin has heard the shout, too. He bares his teeth in anger. Would happily slit Zack's throat right now for spoiling his surprise attack. Nevertheless, he keeps moving forward in a half-crouch.

Spike shouts an answer in his gravelly voice.

"Hello! Who's out there?!"

"Look out! They're coming for you! You're in danger!"

Spike senses movement in front of him. He freezes as a giant, shaggy-haired, bearded man materializes out of the gloom. Suddenly the man breaks into a run, heading straight for him, a club raised high over his head.

"Jesus...!"

Spike scuttles away, looking frantically for the metal suitcase. He finds it. His hands scramble desperately over the items. Find what he's looking for—a 10 gauge Browning pump-action shotgun with both barrel and stock sawed off.

He looks up.

The man is almost upon him.

Spike grabs the shotgun and in a single, fluid motion, gets to his feet, swings the gun around, pumps a round into the chamber, and levels it at his attacker.

"Stop right there!"

The figure never breaks stride. Keeps charging at a dead run for Spike, now just a few feet away.

"I swear to Christ, I mean it! Don't make me—!"

BLAM!

The powerful blast hits Odin square in the chest, knocking him backwards off his feet. The recoil from the shotgun nearly drops Spike as well.

Again he reaches into the metal briefcase. Grabs something—a large flashlight.

Holding the shotgun in one hand and the flashlight in the other, he walks the few steps over to Odin's body and trains the beam on his face. Sees that what seemed a large, shaggy man is a boy not even out of his teens.

"Oh, crap..."

Spike Penovitch was as tough as they came. He'd been in more than his share of scrapes. A few of them had left his opponents with life-threatening injuries.

But Spike had never actually killed anyone.

Until now.

And one so young...

Staring down at the body, he felt a great sadness well up in his chest.

Spike had no way of knowing it at the time, but with that one shotgun blast, he had radically altered the course of human history...

{The Zachary Stone Chronicles}

Spike is jarred from his reverie by the snap of a twig in front of him. He jerks the flashlight beam up and shouts, "Who's out there?!"

The light illuminates the half–dozen boy warriors crouching in the growing darkness. Spike pumps another round into the chamber.

"All of you—drop your weapons!"

The sight of the shotgun and Odin's bloody body has sent a huge scare into them. They all remember enough from television and movies from BEFORE to know that guns can be extremely hazardous to one's health. They drop their clubs and knives.

"On the ground! Now!"

Most of them understand the command. Drop face down onto the dirt. The others quickly follow suit.

Keeping the shotgun trained on them, Spike delves back into the metal case. Removes a roll of nylon twine. Heads over to where the boy warriors lie. One by one, he begins tying their hands behind their backs.

Zack lies in his cage on the cart in the dark. He heard the blast of the shotgun. Nothing after that. Even though his arms and hands feel like they're on fire from having been tied up so long, he's managed to fall into an exhausted and delirious sleep. He's awakened by a light shining in his eyes and a gravelly voice.

"Jees... What the hell did they do to you, kid?"

Spike stares at Zack's bruised and bloodied face. At his emaciated, deeply sunburned body. At his hands covered with blisters, cuts and callouses.

"You're the one who yelled the warning."

Zack tries to respond but nothing comes out of his parched throat. He manages to nod.

"You poor kid. Let's get you out of this damned crate and get you some water."

Spike pulls out a pocketknife. Cuts through the leather ropes of the cage. He eases Zack out and gently turns him over. As he does so, he sees the filthy leather cord biting into his wrists.

"Jesus Christ…"

He cuts through and removes the bindings, then helps Zack to the ground.

Spike grabs one of the leather bladders off the cart, sits down next to Zack and watches him guzzle much of the water. As soon as Zack's thirst is slaked, a deep exhaustion catches up with him. He lies down and promptly falls into a deep sleep. Spike grabs an animal skin blanket off the cart and covers him.

A couple of hours later, the pain in Zack's wrists and ankles causes him to wake up. He looks blearily around.

Spike has built a small fire nearby. By its light, Zack sees the six young warriors sitting back-to-back in three pairs, hands tied together. Spike notices the apprehension in his face.

"Don't worry about them," Spike says, grinning. "Believe it or not, I was a Boy Scout once. It was a long time ago, but I can still tie the hell out of a knot."

Spike has the metal case with him. He opens it. Using the flashlight, he rummages around in it. While he's doing so, he says tenderly, "What's your name, son?"

"Zack."

"Zack what?"

It's been so long since he's used it, Zack has to think a moment to remember his full name.

"Zachary Stone."

"Spike Penovitch. I'd shake hands with you but that may not be a good idea at the moment."

Spike finds what he's looking for in the metal case—a first aid kit. He removes a plastic bottle.

"Hold out your arms."

Zack does as he's told.

"This is disinfectant. I'm gonna put some on your wrists and then your ankles. It's gonna sting some."

Zack flinches at the pain as Spike swabs it on with a cotton ball but doesn't cry out, much to Spike's amazement. Spike then wraps sterile gauze bandages around his wrists and ankles. After treating Zack's wounds, he says, "I'm gonna go look after these horses, make sure they're watered. You rest easy, kid. I'll be back soon." Zack nods dully.

When Spike returns later, he finds Zack has again dropped into a deep sleep.

Spike smiles in sympathy down at the battered boy, then sits down next to him. Cradling the shotgun, he leans against the wheel of the cart. He glances over at the six 'warriors'. Now they just look like tired boys. Still tied back to back, they're lying on their sides and have managed to fall asleep.

Spike turns off the flashlight. Watches the fire slowly die down. Allows himself to doze off.

The next morning, Zack is roused from sleep by Spike gently shaking him.

"You awake, kid?"

Zack sits up and looks woozily around. The cart is loaded and ready to go. The horses are tethered to the cart. The six boy warriors are tied in a line behind it—similar to how Zack and the male members of his tribe were transported as slaves after being captured by Odin. He notices that they're surprisingly subdued. Docile, even. Which makes sense because these young ruffians aren't stupid. They can see the handwriting on the wall: The King is dead. Long live the King.

Spike says, "We're running out of water. We need to be gettin' on the road. How are you feelin', Zack?"

Zack sits up. "Pretty bad." He tries to stand and nearly falls over. Spike steadies him, then helps him back down to a sitting position. He removes the bandages from Zack's wrists and inspects the wounds. They're red and swollen and oozing a yellowish pus.

"I was afraid of this," Spike says.

"Of what?" Zack says, his voice weak.

"Infection." He reaches out and feels Zack's forehead. "You're burnin' up."

Spike stands, grabs the metal case off the cart and drops it to the ground next to Zack. He kneels, takes out the first aid kit, removes a plastic bottle filled with pills. He quickly reads the directions, twists the top open and shakes four of them into his hand.

"I shoulda given you this last night."

"What is it?"

"Antibiotic." He grabs a bladder of water off the cart and hands the pills to Zack. "Drink these down."

With Spike's help, he does so.

Even feeling as bad as he does, Zack's curiosity is piqued. He nods at the metal case. "What else you got in there?"

"You mean my survival kit? A little bit of everything." Spike raps his knuckles on the metal. "Titanium alloy. This thing is indestructible. I was in the middle of talking to one of the guys on Earth who put it together when the second spaceship showed up and blew everything to hell. I was afraid my module was going to dissolve around me but it held. The survival kit landed a couple minutes later near my worksite on the moon. It was the only item in the payload bay of the rocket. It had a handwritten note taped to it telling me to take it back to Earth with me in the escape pod. The note said don't bother trying to open it before then, that it would open automatically when it returned to Earth. Which it did as soon as I landed. The note said 'All will become clear at that time'."

While Spike talks, Zack's eyes hungrily scan the contents of the case. There's a wide variety of items, a lot of them tools which would be extremely useful.

"I spent most of yesterday doing inventory," Spike continues, "The two guys who put this together did a pretty good job. But there's some stuff here I don't get. Like, why all this blank paper? There must be a couple of hundred pages in here. And some things, I don't even know what they are. Like this." Spike picks something from the case. Holds it out for Zack to see.

"I think that's a miniature printer."

Spike's sighs in frustration. "A printer? Really?"

Something at the bottom of the case gets Zack's attention as Spike continues to vent. "What a waste. Why in heck would they include something as useless as a—"

"Is that a laptop?"

Spike grimaces in embarrassment. "Ahh... yeah. It is. See, that's gonna be a problem, kid. I'm not exactly the computer type—to put it mildly. But I guess they knew that because they included a copy of Computers for Dummies. Still, it's gonna take me awhile to get up to speed on that thing. I haven't even turned it on yet."

Zack swallows. His voice nervous with excitement, he says, "Can I see it?"

"Be my guest." A glimmer of hope appears in Spike's eyes. "You know anything about computers?"

"A little."

Spike removes the laptop from the case and hands it to him. "Have at it. But just for a minute. We need to get on the road."

Zack gently takes the laptop from him, handling it like it's the Holy Grail. His hands tremble as he opens it. He looks closely at the keyboard and screen. It's a higher-end model than what he was used to working on back in BEFORE, but there isn't anything too unusual about it.

Zack closes his eyes. Whispers a silent prayer: *Please. Let this be what I hope it is...*

Zack opens his eyes. His scarred, dirt-encrusted finger begins moving toward the computer. He stops it an inch above the power button and glances at Spike, as if afraid to proceed; as if he doesn't want to take the chance of having to deal with the soul-crushing disappointment that will surely come if the computer is damaged, or its hard drive somehow wiped clean, or its power source dead—any of a number of things that could have gone wrong.

Spike nods. Says quietly, "Go ahead."

Please...

Zack swallows. Takes a deep, shuddering breath. Presses the power button.

The screen comes to life.

The desktop is filled with scores of icons, each of them containing hundreds of gigabytes of data.

In the very middle of the screen is an outsized icon with the title 'Open Me First'. Zack ignores that for moment but quickly scans some of the many other titles:

The History of Mankind. Museums of the World. The Library of Congress. Languages of the World. Carpentry. Mathematics. Chemistry. Physics. Electrical Engineering. Metallurgy. Mechanical Engineering. Medicine. Mining. Manufacturing.

On and on the titles go.

One file in particular gets his attention. It's entitled:

The Record—A Detailed Timeline from First Sighting to Launch of Survival Kit to Moon.

Zack realizes he's smiling.

"So," Spike says. "What's on the computer, kid?"

Zack looks up at Spike. Tears of happiness flow unchecked down his face, cutting trails through his grime-encrusted cheeks. His eyes are on fire with excitement at the thought of the great tasks that lie ahead.

His voice a husky whisper, Zack replies:

"Everything."

As much as I wanted to dive into that computer, I was just too darn sick, so that would have to wait. It took us two days to travel back to camp. Spike rode Blondie's steed. It turned out he was comfortable on a horse, having ridden them as a boy in West Virginia.

Spike wanted me to get as much rest as I could while the antibiotics did their work, so I rode in the wagon and made sure we stayed headed in the right direction. The former boy warriors were tethered in a row behind the wagon. They walked the whole distance without giving us any problems.

Late in the afternoon of the second day, we were less than a mile from camp. We could see trails of smoke rising from cooking fires. I could tell Spike was excited at the prospect of meeting more people. It was all he could do to not spur his horse into a gallop.

But as we got closer, something protruding from the ground made him frown. When he was a few feet from it, Spike stopped his horse and stared ...

{The Zachary Stone Chronicles}

"What the...?"

Spike stares at the head mounted on a stake. It's been here awhile. The skin has dried and pulled tight against the skull, contorting the mouth into a nightmarish grin. Hollow sockets for eyes. Black dusty hair hanging limply.

Twenty feet farther on is another head on a stake. Then another. And another. And another.

Dozens of them, leading all the way into camp.

Spike shakes his head in disgust. Spits on the ground. His lips curl into a scowl as he says, "It sure as shit didn't take long for the human race to go to hell."

"No," says Zack sadly. "It didn't."

He turns and looks at Zack. "Was this that big blonde fellah's doing?"

Zack nods.

Spike glares back at the former boy warriors and yells, "I don't suppose you boys know anything about this?!"

The boy warriors say nothing. They stand very still, their heads bowed, possibly in shame, their eyes on the ground.

Spike turns back to the head, then looks at the camp in the distance. He grabs the shotgun cradled in his lap. Pumps a round into the chamber and says, "This shit stops today."

He fires into the sky.

"There's a new sheriff in town."

He nudges his horse toward the camp. He's followed by Zack and the wagon, the tethered horses and the former boy warriors.

In camp, the powerful shotgun blast has shocked everyone. They've stopped what they're doing and look fearfully around.

A few of the braver inhabitants move tentatively toward the source of the sound. One of them is Oksana. Still very pregnant, she leads Vera into their adobe clay hut and tells her to remain there until she comes back. Vera nods solemnly. Oksana heads back out, but not before grabbing her spear by the entrance.

As she makes her way across a short stretch of desert toward the approaching party, she's confused by what she sees. A strange man—actually a very old strange man—rides the lead horse. He's the one with the shotgun. The six former boy warriors tied to the cart, as are their horses. And on the cart—Zack. He's not tied up.

"Zock!" Oksana drops her spear and runs clumsily toward him.

Nearsighted Zack can see the blurry shape of someone heading his way.

"Oksana?" Moving unsteadily, Zack manages to climb down from the cart. When Oksana gets to him, they hold each other in a tight embrace. Tears fill her eyes.

"You're alive! Oh, Zock, I was so sure Odin was going to kill you."

"I'm sure he thought he was, too."

She glances nervously at the captives tied to the cart. "So where is Odin?"

"Let's just say, thanks to Spike here, things didn't go his way."

In a voice coated with wet gravel, Spike says, "I like to think of it more as a team effort."

Oksana looks up at Spike on his horse, then back at Zack. Her eyes search his. "What are you saying?"

Zack says, "Blondie's dead."

Oksana tries to suppress a spontaneous sob of relief but isn't very successful at it. She looks up at Spike. Whispers a heartfelt "Thank you."

Spike gives her a half-grin that's more sad than victorious. Tips an imaginary cowboy hat.

"My pleasure, ma'am."

While Blondie was alive, everyone in the colony was very much aware that they could become the target of his wrath at any time for any reason. Even the boy warriors feared him. As word spread that Blondie was dead, it felt like a black shadow was lifted from the camp. Spike and me soon found ourselves on the receiving end of bottomless gratitude.

After a couple of days of rest, fresh food and medicine, my infection was nearly gone. In the meantime, Spike had been regaling the young tribe members with his banjo. No one had heard anything resembling music in years. He quickly won them over with his nimble-fingered performances.

Then it was time for me and Spike to see what was in the Open Me First file.

We used Blondie's former hut for the viewing. Even on the hottest days, it stayed relatively cool and dark inside. I set the laptop on a flat stone, flipped it open, and pressed the power button. The crowded desktop once again appeared onscreen. I checked the battery level. It had plenty of power even after sitting dormant for nearly three years. I moved the cursor over the Open Me First icon.

I glanced at Spike, who was sitting a couple of feet away...

{The Zachary Stone Chronicles}

"Ready?"

Spike gives a fatalistic shrug. "As I'll ever be."

Zack clicks on the icon. The screen goes dark for a moment, then a video begins to play.

A close-up of President Claire Crawford in the Oval Office. She looks very pale and tired. She manages a smile, which emphasizes the new lines on her face.

"Hello, Spike. I hope you don't mind if I call you by your first name. God knows the time for formalities is past."

Spike and Zack's mouths drop open. They shoot each other a WTF look, then turn back to the video.

The president's smile fades. Her face becomes serious.

"Spike, if you're watching this, it means two very important things are true. Number one: You're still alive. And Number two: You're back on Earth. I hope and pray these are both the case."

She leans toward the camera.

"Spike, I was asked by my science advisor to make the introduction to this video specifically for you. In fact, he insisted on it. He thought this message coming from me would be the best way to get your attention."

Spike says, "I'd say mission accomplished."

"I'm talking to you from three years in your past. As you no doubt know, all the people of the world are being gathered up and all manmade objects dissolved, with no exceptions. Barring a miracle, every human being will be transported to that ship—except for you, Spike. That's because Otis and Conroy are betting that having the entire mass of the moon between you and the dissolution beam will protect you. I pray that's true."

Zack listens closely to her words, but also finds himself staring at her surroundings: the curtains on the window in the background, the mahogany desk, the leather chair, her blouse, pretty and clean. Strange to see things that were once so mundane and taken for granted now looking like unimaginable luxury. Zack feels a sudden pang in his gut, a wistful yearning for how life was in BEFORE. He sighs, thinking about how much things have changed in so short a time.

"So, Spike," continues the president, "if you are watching this, I have a request to make of you. If you like, think of it as a mission, a very important one, assigned to you by your president—America's last president—in one of her last official acts. As you well know, I'm in no position to order anybody to do anything, especially from three years in the past. But at least give it some thought, and do as you see fit."

The video starts breaking up. After a couple of moments, it settles down.

Crawford stops talking as someone off-camera says something to her. A worried look crosses her face. She nods and continues.

"Communications are getting dicey, so we need to transmit this to Doctor Larson and his colleague while we still can. They're putting the rest of this video together. They'll fill you in on what we would like you to do. I've got to sign off now."

Tears suddenly appear in her eyes. Her voice becomes an emotional whisper.

"Good luck to you, Spike. And may God bless you."

The screen goes dark.

Spike and Zack glance again at each other, eyes wide.

"Wow," Zack says.

"You got that right, kid," Spike says.

A couple of seconds later, the screen jitters back to life. The image of two bearded, sweating men sitting at a table appears. On the table between them is Spike's metal case. The older, more distinguished-looking of the two starts to talk into the camera. He speaks briskly and concisely, as if there's no time to lose.

"Hello, Spike. I'm Doctor Otis Larson, and this is Professor Conroy Hamilton."

The younger, wild-looking man with tattoos on his neck nods at the camera.

Otis continues. "It's our fervent hope that you've survived and are watching this. What you're seeing right now is being recorded at Cape Canaveral, Florida. Conroy and I are convinced that time here is growing short, so I'll try to make this is as brief as I can."

Otis shifts in his chair, folds his hands on the table, and continues speaking.

"You're no doubt aware that the aliens came here to harvest us, and they were doing it with 100 percent efficiency until we knocked them out of the sky. The thing is, the Probe has disappeared. We think it may have sent for help. We're worried that this may be just a temporary reprieve; that the aliens could return at any time. If they do, the human race as we know it will soon cease to exist. All except for you, Spike.

"Because of Conroy's detailed analysis of a couple of recent archaeological discoveries in Kenya and California, evidence suggests that a race of human beings very similar to ours lived on Earth around 60,000 years ago. I'll let him fill you in on the rest."

Conroy speaks to the camera. "They disappeared suddenly and without a trace. We think they were harvested by these very same aliens. We also think there's a possibility that the aliens have done this many times before, and will continue to do so indefinitely.

"I don't know about you, Spike, but Otis and I like to think that man's destiny in the universe is more than just being a drug-like food crop." Sudden passion fills Conroy's voice as he slams his fist on the table. "It has to be!"

It takes him a moment to calm down. "Anyway, as Otis and I brainstormed what this all meant, we became convinced that if human beings are indeed nothing more than a crop to be harvested—and sustainably so—the aliens would absolutely have to leave behind a seed crop to start the next round of breeding.

"So with President Crawford's blessing, our mission here at Cape Canaveral changed. It's become more than just preserving man's legacy. We think that we might, *just might*, be able to give mankind a fighting chance to break free of this horrific cycle. That's where you come in. Otis?"

Otis takes over the presentation. He stares intensely into the camera.

"Spike, find the people left behind. Find them and do everything in your power to make them understand what's at stake."

Spike quips to Zack, "I'd say the people left behind did a pretty good job of finding me."

Zack grins as Otis continues. "You're all going to have to work together to bring these harvests to a stop."

He puts his hand on the metal case.

"To help you, we've put together a survival kit of sorts. Keep in mind it's not just for you; it's for the human race. We designed it so it would fit inside the escape pod with you. That probably made for an uncomfortable ride back to Earth, but I think you'll find it was worth it.

"Unfortunately, we no longer have the capability of reprograming the flight program of your escape pod, which means you'll be landing at the spaceport in Nevada—whatever's left of it. Obviously, there won't be any facilities there, so we've included water plus some power bars, enough to hold you until you can get out of the desert."

He opens the metal case and turns it around so Spike can see its contents. Lying on top is the shotgun.

"We've tried to imagine the Earth you'll return to. One of the first things we realized is that, because all the animals that were formerly in zoos will be running free, mating and multiplying, you're going to need a means of defending yourself from the bigger, more aggressive ones."

Sadness in his voice, Spike says, "If they only knew..."

Otis continues. "It won't do the human race any good if you're gored to death by a rhinoceros. The shotgun will also come in handy for hunting food. As you can see, we've also included a selection of tools, plus necessities like matches, dinnerware for one, a flashlight, a knife, a first aid kit, et cetera. We've also included this video-cam."

He points to an item the size of a small wallet with a three-inch screen. "It requires very little power. You can recharge it with just a few minutes of sunlight. It has the capacity to film and store thousands of hours of video. We thought it might be a good idea if you—or someone—documented the inception of this next cycle of the human race."

Otis points to something else—a laptop computer.

"And here, by far, is the most important item. It's small but powerful. We've loaded it with as much useful data as possible.

"In researching your background, we learned you're not exactly the most computer-savvy person in the world. Being able to access the trove of information on the laptop is crucial. Which is why we included this to help you find your way." Otis holds up a copy of Computers for Dummies.

"We've included three separate power sources for the computer: Rechargeable batteries, a small solar panel, and a hand-crank generator. That should keep it up and running until you're able to manufacture your own power sources. We've also included a small printer and as much paper as could fit into the case. Your people are going to want to have their own manuals, instructions, blueprints, schematics— whatever—in front of them as they figure stuff out.

"We've also included as much information on the aliens as we could find. Hopefully, you'll find a way to use it against them. As advanced as their technology is, the biggest takeaway from our encounter with them is that they're not perfect. The aliens do make mistakes. Not many. In fact, they made only one, but it was a doozy. We knocked their damned ship out of the sky." Otis allows himself a brief, victorious grin.

"Okay, Spike, I guess that's it. We're going to sign off now. We want to get your survival kit off the ground and on its way to you ASAP. I'll also try to contact you by satellite relay in the next day or so. Before we go, I just want to say—we're counting on you, Spike. The entire human race is counting on you. But, hey, no pressure."

Otis gives a small ironic grin as the screen goes dark.

Spike and Zack sit in silence, staring at the blank screen. After a moment, Spike turns to Zack and says, "What do you say, kid? You up for saving the human race?"

Assuming the demeanor of a supremely bored teenager, Zack says, "I guess so. There's nothin' else to do."

They grin at each other, eager to begin.

With Blondie gone, Spike was the natural, if reluctant, choice for leader of the tribe. By unspoken decree, I became his second-in-command. With Blondie's iron-fisted rule a thing of the past, the members of the tribe now had the freedom to go their separate ways. I was concerned that my new clan would soon start breaking up.

Boy, was I wrong.

Everyone was super curious about what was on the laptop, so Spike and I decided to show them. In small groups at a time, we let them view clips from a variety of movies, television shows, and documentaries.

All members of the tribe were old enough to have some memories of what daily life had been like in BEFORE. Looking at the footage made it all come roaring back. Some of the reactions were heart-rending. Images of women in make-up with styled hair and wearing soft, clean, beautiful clothes brought many girls to tears. Mirrors no longer existed, so they didn't know what they looked like.

As for the boys, it was the food that got to them. Some openly salivated at the sight of people eating cheeseburgers and pizza; cake and ice cream; chocolate bars and cherry pies.

To see people enjoying the comforts of civilized society was a game-changer. Anything was better than fighting for survival every minute of every day. It was a powerful reminder of what life was like then, and could be again. Virtually overnight, me and Spike found ourselves overwhelmed by young people excited to join in the task of rebuilding civilization.

But before embarking on this grand new adventure, I made my case to Spike that we should relocate to the coast of what was formerly known as Southern California. He thought it was a good idea. So did everyone else.

It took us several weeks to make the move. It went as smoothly as could be expected. Arriving at our destination, we encountered a couple of small tribes already settled in the area. They were suspicious of us at first, but when we showed them some clips from the laptop, they acted like we were bearers of the Holy Grail and readily joined our clan.

It was time to get to work.

It was time to jumpstart civilization.

Thanks to Larson and Hamilton and the laptop, we had access to most of the accumulated knowledge of the human race. Now we were going to put that knowledge to work rebuilding civilization from scratch.

One of the first major tasks before was the making of metal. That meant finding the right ore, then mining it, smelting and extracting it. Even though we had detailed instructions on how to do it, actually doing it was going to be extremely hard, to say the least.

Luckily, we had a powerful secret weapon: Spike. A lifelong miner, he was key in getting the operation up and running.

There was so much to learn. So much to do. So many skills needed. Every day was a crash course in something.

Our only limitation was a shortage of workers. Despite the fact that everyone was eager to work, there just weren't a whole lot of human beings in the world. We tried to fix this in two ways: Number one, we sent out search parties on horseback far and wide to find other tribes. They took with them metal objects and tasty food to entice them back to our group, where we showed them video clips from BEFORE. That never failed to bring them into the fold.

Number two, most of the females were now between 13 and 17 years old—their most fertile years. In many cases, the combination of raging hormones and no parental supervision had compelled nature to take its course. Oksana and me were accidental members of that club.

Knowing that repopulating the planet would be a top priority, Larson and Hamilton had included whole sections on fertility, pregnancy, child-raising, etc. on the laptop.

As our population grew, it would soon be time for us to start thinking about the future; things like marriage, fidelity, crime, punishment, justice, equality—all that. Except for Spike, there were no adults around to guide us. We scoured the laptop for information, and struggled to create morals and codes of conduct for our new society.

We didn't feel that any of us were wise enough to draw up something like the Constitution. When we asked Spike to give it a try, he just laughed and said he wasn't about to tell anyone how to live their lives.

In the end, we decided it would be a work in progress, that we'd figure it out as we went along. In the meantime, we put together some basic ground rules, like no killing and no stealing. On the whole, people were pretty well-behaved. Just about everyone had been permanently traumatized at seeing their homes dissolved and their family and friends gathered up to be eaten. In addition, living like wild animals for the last three years proved to be a huge motivator for people to work together to make a better world.

Thanks to what was on the laptop, we realized we had a golden opportunity to bypass thousands of years of untold human savagery, struggle and hardship; to leapfrog past all the wars, inquisitions and slaughter. As for scientific discoveries, we wouldn't have to go through centuries of experimentation by trial and error: we already had the work of Newton, Einstein, and all the other great scientists literally at our fingertips.

Still, our hopes for the future notwithstanding, most of us would get hammered by a deep, debilitating sadness on a regular basis. I'm talking about our fellow human beings who had been taken away. How the hell long does it take to eat eight billion people, anyway? Probably a long time. Thousands of years, even. Which meant that, right this very minute, they were being held in the alien equivalent of a deep freezer. The thought of them waiting in hibernation until one of the bastards wanted a snack and to get buzzed was agonizing to us. The sadness and pain kept recurring like an open wound that was never going to heal.

It was during one of the worst of these episodes that an insane idea came to me. It was sparked by a piece of information I'd come across in The Record. It was a long shot, but my whole life had turned into a long shot. I'm going to keep that idea to myself for now. Otherwise, you might think I'm crazy.

And I'm not crazy.

At least I hope not.

Anyway.

In the early days, Spike and I took turns filming the tribe's progress with the video camera. Otis had been right. Many years down the road—if we made it that far—this could be amazing footage of the rebirth of the human race. The only annoying thing about that was Spike kept bugging me to tell my particular story on video. That it would be important documentation of the horrors that some of the tribes had experienced.

This morning, I decided to give in to him, just to get him off my case.

So now I've come to the end of my story.

It's been a long day.

I should be getting back.

There's so much to be done...

{The Zachary Stone Chronicles}

Zack sits very still for a moment, staring at us. He then reaches forward and flicks a switch on the side of the camera. The screen goes blank.

EARLIER THAT SAME DAY

Walking in silence, Zack and Spike emerge together from the village. It's early morning with clear blue skies. They hike across several large sand dunes. In the distance, the Pacific Ocean greets the first rays of the sun. Its waters are calm, the sound of the surf a gentle rustle.

The two enter a small grove of pine trees where a rough-hewn wooden chair and table have been placed. The outdoor furnishings aren't exactly Adirondack quality, but are a far cry better than what they had been using just a few months earlier.

Zack's hair has been washed and roughly trimmed. His scruffy beard remains intact. Even though his cuts and bruises have mostly healed, they've left many permanent marks and scars.

Zack takes a seat in the chair. Spike sets the tiny video camera on the table. He fiddles with it some, then aims it at Zack.

"What am I supposed to say?"

"Just tell your story, kid. Start from the last day of BEFORE and go on up to the present."

"You mean, like, today?"

Spike rolls his eyes. "Yeah. Like today." He walks away.

Zack stares at the camera for a long time as emotions play across his face. He's aged far beyond his years. The pupils of his eyes burn black with pain and remembrance. Finally, he leans forward and presses the button to begin recording.

No one saw it coming.

No one was prepared for the day the world changed forever.

September 7th, 2026.

The day when all of human history was rewritten...

PART FIVE

A TASTE OF RECKONING

50 YEARS LATER

SOMEWHERE IN WHAT WAS KNOWN AS
CANADA

A clear cold day. Snow and ice cover a rugged plain that extends as far as the eye can see.

A stripped-down, ultralight aircraft cruises at an altitude of five hundred feet over the desolate landscape. There's no enclosed cockpit, just a seat with a steering lever. For protection from the icy breeze, the pilot of the one-person craft is wrapped from head to toe in thick leather and fur. Just his eyes are visible behind a pair of large, crude-looking goggles. The noise from the battery-powered propeller is barely a whisper.

He scans the ground below. Every so often a glint of sunlight reflecting off the ice catches his eye. He pulls a walkie-talkie the size of a shoebox out of his wrappings and speaks into it. His youthful voice is slightly muffled by the fur.

"I'm not seeing anything. Are you sure these are the right coordinates?"

"All I'm sure of, is this is what was posted in The Record," responds Zachary Stone into his own giant walkie-talkie.

Zack looks good for 67. Tall and trim. Clean-shaven. Silvered hair cut short. Despite a few wrinkles, his face retains its boyishness. Many of his scars have faded from sight. He wears glasses of which the frames look like they were cast in a foundry—which they probably were. The glass lenses magnify his eyes.

As cold and quiet as it is up in the ultra-light, it's just the opposite where Zack is: a hot and noisy control room in a giant machine making its way across the snow and ice.

"Global Positioning System satellites were everywhere back then," continues Zack. "You'd think the information would be accurate."

The young pilot glances down at the giant machine, a steam-powered snow-cat as big as a mansion. Its massive metal treads plow steadily over the ice and snow. It tows a gargantuan sled made of wood and metal a hundred yards wide and two hundred yards long. Trailing behind is a smaller sled holding a couple of enormous cranes and a solid metal container about the size and shape of a boxcar. It's all quite a sight.

"You've told me stories about what a chaotic time that was," says the pilot. "Maybe the information got screwed up somehow."

Zack sighs into the walkie-talkie, then says, "That's a possibility. But we're here now and we're going to make the best of it."

Zack watches through the thick, scratched windshield while steering the snow-cat with a giant wooden wheel. He wears simple, loose-fitting pants and shirt made of coarse but comfortable cotton. The other workers in the control room are similarly dressed. They monitor pressure gauges while tweaking levers and knobs. A light sheen of sweat covers their skin. The steady pounding of steam-driven pistons rocks the air. The three women working in the room are in different stages of pregnancy.

High above the snow-cat, the pilot checks the ultra-light's battery-level indicator, then speaks into the walkie-talkie. "I've only got a couple minutes of power left. I need to come down."

"Okay," Zack says. "Come on down and we'll get you a fresh battery."

Just as the ultra-light starts to make a banking turn to begin its descent, another glint of reflected sunlight light from the ground gets the pilot's attention.

Only this one is different. Brighter. Sharper. Larger.

"Wait. I think I see something..."

He pulls the craft out of the turn. "I'm going in for a closer look."

"Be careful, Tyler," says Zack, worry in his voice.

Tyler guides his craft closer to the spot where he saw the reflection. As he nears it, there's another flash of light, even brighter than before.

But it's not from ice.

It's from metal.

That's when Tyler realizes what he's looking at. "Hol-ey shit..."

In the control room, Tyler's voice comes screaming in over the walkie-talkie. "Grandpa! I see it! I see it! It's the spacecraft!"

Zack and the others exchange a look that's both victorious and grim. It's a look that says 'Be careful what you wish for...'

A few minutes later, the snow-cat crests a snow-covered rise and halts. There below it lies the spacecraft. It suffered some damage when it fell from the sky but nothing too serious. There are cracks and fissures but it's still in one piece.

The ultra-light glides in for a silent touchdown on its sledded landing gear.

A couple of days later, the enormous steam-powered cranes work in unison to lift the spacecraft onto the gargantuan sled that has been custom-built to hold the vessel. The craft is surprisingly light for its size, probably because it's made of material similar derivative of the extremely strong but light-weight graphene barrier.

On the smaller sled, white vapor pumps from a vent in the boxcar-like container. A giant steam-powered refrigerator, it's designed to keep the bodies of the aliens in deep freeze until they can be dissected and studied.

After a couple more days of work, it's time for the long trek home. In the control room of the snow-cat, Zack begins pushing buttons and pulling levers. Gears kick in with a guttural roar. Giant metal treads begin to churn.

Weeks later, the massive snow-cat arrives back at the village towing its alien cargo. Over the last five decades, the 'village' has grown into a small yet bustling city. Buildings three and four stories tall dot the landscape. A fishing fleet can be seen out on the calm waters of the Pacific Ocean. A giant dirigible floats in the distance.

Townspeople line the street, cheering the crew of the snow-cat. Zack, Tyler and the rest wave from the cat's windows. There are many thousands of children and many hundreds of adults—though none between the ages of 53 and 63 because no one younger than 10 years old had been sent back to Earth as breeding stock 53 years earlier.

The crowd falls eerily silent as the spacecraft and then the refrigerated container pass by.

As the snow-cat enters the town, Zack sees Oksana in the throng and brings the vehicle to a halt. He emerges from the hatch and beckons to her. She runs to the idling vessel and climbs the rough metal stairs. They embrace very tightly. She then steps back, gently takes his face into her hands and looks at him with those amazing aquamarine eyes.

"Zack... Are you all right?"

Zack smiles confidently. "Yes. I am definitely all right."

Tyler suddenly appears at Zack's side. "Grandma! We did it!"

Oksana gives him a strong hug. "Yes, you did, Tyler. Yes you did..."

The snow-cat passes through a town square in the middle of which rises a memorial—a larger-than-life granite statue of Spike Penovitch. It nicely captures the crusty features of the Moon Miner-turned-civilization-builder, whose death from natural causes occurred a couple of decades earlier.

As he passes by, Zack gives the statue a grateful smile and a nod.

Days later, the spacecraft has been towed into a warehouse built specifically for the analysis of the alien vessel. The brightly-lit structure is easily the largest building thus far constructed in the young world.

Zack and a team of young scientists crawl in, on, around and under the craft, picking and prodding at it as they try to learn its secrets. The ship's interior is in surprisingly good shape. Many of the controls and consoles on the bridge seem to be intact.

But as the days, and then weeks tick by, they have little to show for their efforts. Try as they might, Zack and his crew are unable to make any sense out of what they're examining. Zack keeps hoping that one of them will make an intuitive leap to an *aha* moment, but it's just not happening.

The only thing they've managed to agree on is that much of the ship seems to have been powered by electricity. There are what appear to be electrical conduits running from an indecipherable power source to the bridge. Other than that, they're stumped.

After another long fruitless, frustrating day, Zack decides that drastic action is needed. He tells his team to meet in the conference room first thing in the morning.

That night, Zack and Oksana lie next to each other in a large, wood-frame bed. The animal fur blankets from 50 years ago have evolved to rough-woven cotton and linen. A single candle illuminates the room.

A table and two chairs occupy a corner of the room. On the table sits a large tube radio that looks like it was built in 1956. A thick electric cord runs to it from an outlet in the wall. Classical music plays quietly—music gleaned from the archives of the laptop.

The Spartan furnishings are an odd hybrid of very old and very new. Most things have an unfinished look to them. Wood hasn't been sanded completely smooth. Nothing has been painted or varnished. Metal edges are sharp and exposed. Everything is slightly outsized and not exactly attractive to look at, but they are simple and functional.

These are strange times for the human race. It's not that the quickly growing population doesn't have the knowledge or technology for miniaturization and slick finishes. It's just that such refinements are not needed at this time and therefore are not important. For now and the foreseeable future, it's function over form.

"You and me have been through a lot together, Oksana."

Oksana gives him a world-weary smile. "Understatement of century, Zock."

"I guess what I'm saying is, we've been incredibly lucky."

Oksana sits up and says, "Excuse me? Luck had nothing to do with anything. We worked hard every single day to be where we are."

"You misunderstand me. By lucky, I mean being with *you*. We were thrown back into this world with no friends. No family. Not even the shirts on our backs. I'm just so happy we ended up together."

"Ah, yes, I remember that first day." She lies back down. "You looked pretty good without your shirt. And your pants."

Zack can hear the lascivious smile around her last three words. He blushes in the candlelight. "Oksana, please, I was only 14. Still such a virgin."

"And still so shy after all this time."

They lie quietly for a moment wrapped in each other's arms. Then Zack says, "Do you ever think about them? Your family, I mean?"

Oksana give a long sad sigh. "Yes. A lot. I'm sure you do, too."

"I miss them so much. Jeffrey was the sweetest kid... I feel bad that I teased him a lot."

"That's what you're supposed to do to brothers. I was merciless with mine."

"And my parents. They were amazing. They did everything they could to protect us." Zack suddenly sits up. "Listen to me, talking about them in the past tense, like they're already..."

Zack takes his face in his hands. "It just kills me, Oksana. Every time I think about them... Not knowing if they're still alive—if you could even call it that—still waiting in suspended animation to be revived, and then eaten alive. Even though it'll just be a moment, I can't stop thinking about the sheer terror they'll experience."

Oksana sits up as well. Drapes her arm around him. Whispers, "I know, Zock, I know... Try not to think about it. They are beyond our help."

"If only I could..."

"If only you could what, Zock?"

But Zack just shakes his head and says nothing. They hold on tightly to each other.

Early the next morning, Zack and his crew gather in a corner of the giant warehouse. This area serves as the control center for the analysis of the spacecraft. It is also a conference room/data clearing house/computer headquarters. In the background is an actual computer. It looks like an IBM mainframe circa 1970. Its motors whirr, its lights blink. Even though it's the size of a two-bedroom apartment, that's still pretty good progress for just fifty years.

Zack takes a seat at one of a dozen mismatched stools around a large wooden table. The others do the same. Most of them clutch steaming ceramic mugs of coffee and tea.

Zack dives right in.

"Okay, here's the deal. We've been at this for two solid months now and we're not getting anywhere. We still don't have a clue about how their anti-gravity propulsion system works; Or their dissolution beam; Or their impermeable barrier. We don't even know what their main source of power was."

Zack stops to let that sink in. He takes a sip of hot black coffee before continuing.

"The only thing we *do* know—or are pretty sure of anyway—is that at least part of the ship's bridge ran on electrical power. With that scrap of knowledge in mind, I've decided to stir the pot up a bit. To try and make something, *anything*, happen. We need a starting point. Something we can sink our teeth into. Something we can learn from."

A young scientist named Grady who has hair to his shoulders and a thick goatee says, "What did you have in mind, Boss?"

"We're going to run an electric current through their conduits and into the bridge."

All the scientists at the table exchange looks of surprise and worry.

Grady says, "Do you think that's a good idea?"

"No. I don't. In fact, I think it's a terrible idea. It could even be disastrous. That said, does anyone have a better idea?"

More looks circulate. A few shake their heads no. Others shrug their shoulders.

Zack rises from his seat. "Okay, then. Let's get started."

The rest get up and follow him to the spacecraft.

It turned out that splicing a power cord from the settlement's main generator into the alien electrical conduit was a surprisingly straightforward procedure. It took Zack and his team just over half a day. He now stands on the deck of the bridge of the spaceship, walkie-talkie in hand, peering out the windshield at Grady, who is at a cluster of controls about a hundred feet from the ship with his own walkie-talkie. About half the team has chosen to watch the results from there. The other half is inside the vessel with Zack.

Grady speaks into his walkie-talkie, "So, Boss. Are you ready?"

"As I'll ever be," he Zack replies nervously into his own device. "We're going to do this nice and easy."

For at least the hundredth time in two months, his eyes scan the massive console in front of him packed with strange-looking controls.

"Okay, Grady. Go ahead and close the connecting breaker. At the least, we'll find out if we have electrical compatibility."

A hundred feet away, Grady uses one hand to hold the walkie-talkie to the side of his head. His other hand pulls a breaker switch. "Breaker closed."

There's silence as Grady studies various electrical gauges and meters. Finally he says into the walkie-talkie, "No alarms. No ringing bells. All's quiet. It looks like these two just might play well together."

"Okay," Zack says. "Time to turn on the juice. Start with five volts."

Grady turns a large knob a tiny fraction of a turn. "Done."

Zack and his team study the ship's console for any changes.

Nothing.

"Add another five volts."

Still nothing.

"There's got to be some kind of a power threshold that will bring this thing to life. We're going to keep going until we hit it. I want you to increase the juice by five volts every ten seconds until I tell you to stop."

"Roger that," says Grady. "Here we go."

Several minutes later, Zack speaks into his walkie-talkie. "How we doing, Grady?"

Grady replies, "We're at T-minus five minutes and counting. Current voltage is 150."

"Steady as she goes..." says Zack.

Grady continues to give progress reports to Zack. After an hour has passed, Grady again contacts him.

"We're at 1800 volts, Zack."

"Steady on."

"How long do you want to do this?"

Zack replies, "As long as it takes."

"Okay. But I should tell you right now that we can't go much over 7000 volts or we'll overload our own cables. They'll burn up."

"Understood."

Three more hours go by. It's now full dark. Grady's control station is brightly lit by artificial lighting. He looks at the bridge of the spaceship, which remains in darkness as Zack and his crew watch for anything out of the ordinary. Grady again contacts him, his voice anxious as it comes over the walkie-talkie.

"Zack, we're at 7000 volts and counting."

"What's the maximum we can go?"

"7200 volts is the absolute max. We're going to hit that in about 6 minutes."

There's an uncharacteristic silence from Zack.

"Zack? Are you there? Did you hear what I just said?"

A big disappointed sigh. "I heard you all right… Okay. You win, Grady. Go ahead and shut it down before—hold on."

Zack's voice is muffled as he speaks to his other crew members.

"Did any of you see that?"

Sounding shaken, a couple of them answer.

"Hell, yeah."

"What was it?"

Zack speaks excitedly into walkie-talkie. "Something's happening, Grady. We're getting activity from the console."

"What kind of activity?"

"It was real quick. Flashes of light… Now there's a kind of electrical humming, or vibrations, coming from all around us…"

"Zack, we have less than three minutes."

Zack's voice is impassioned. "Grady, listen to me: We're this close to lighting this thing up. I can feel it. Keep increasing the voltage until I tell you to stop."

"Zack, I can't in good conscience do something that could put lives at—"

"There! Freeze the power level right there!"

Grady pulls a switch, halting the voltage at 7150. As he's giving a sigh of relief, Zack's voice blasts over the walkie-talkie.

"Holy shit! Grady, are you watching this?!"

Grady glances at the alien ship and gasps. He can see through the vessel's windshields into the bridge, which appears to be on fire, except that the flames are every color of the rainbow. A deep throbbing concusses the air.

Grady finally manages to speak. "...What in the world is going on in there?"

"There's nothing in the world going on in here. At least nothing in *our* world..."

"Are you guys okay?"

Inside the control room, Zack and his crew are awash in the intense, pulsating light. He finally replies, "I'm not sure if I know how to answer that..."

They stand in awe, watching bizarre images and holograms materialize and dissolve before them; orbs of all sizes and colors that might be planets; otherworldly vistas and landscapes; clusters of structures with architecture just this side of sanity that could be alien cities; dozens of strange items spasm into view and just as quickly disappear, leaving Zack and the others with no clue what they are or what their purpose might be.

The ever-changing, phantasmagoric display swirls nonstop around the dumbstruck humans. Zack is the first to recover from the sensory onslaught.

"Listen up, people. This spaceship has been incommunicado for more than half a century. I think it's safe to say that we're looking at passive imagery. I don't think it poses a danger. If something bad was going to happen, it would have happened as soon as we lit this thing up. I want you all to settle down, spread out and investigate. Look for patterns and repetitions. Focus on any sequences that appear half-way logical or mathematical. Don't be afraid. Trust your instincts. Let's try to make some sort of sense out of this. We'll work through the night and meet back here exactly six hours from now and compare notes. Good luck."

Zack and his crew fan out into the maelstrom of light and noise...

The hours of the night creep steadily by. Grady stays close to his control station, keeping the incoming voltage at a steady 7150.

Word about the breakthrough has spread quickly through the community. Curious citizens start to trickle over. They gather at a respectful 20 feet behind Grady and his team members, where they can watch the mesmerizing light show taking place inside the spacecraft. They wait patiently through the night for the return of the crew.

Zack is the last to show up at the rendezvous point. When he finally does appear, his young crew can't help but notice the strange light in his eyes. It burns with a giddy, manic energy.

"Zack...?" one of them asks, concern in her voice. "Are you okay?"

"Do you see it?" he answers, breathless with excitement. "Can you see what this is?"

They've never seen Zack in such a state. Worried that he may have gone off his rocker, the crew members exchange looks of alarm.

"See what, Zack?"

"Do any of you remember the Internet? The World Wide Web?"

One of the crew members speaks up. "I...sort of remember it. And we learned about it in school from the history files."

"What if I told you that what we're looking at right now, is the alien equivalent of the Internet—but instead of World Wide, *it's Galaxy-Wide*."

"What?!"

"How is that possible?"

Zack says, "I think this is the default setting of their main console computer for when they power up their ship. Kind of like a home page. I think we're tapped into a live feed from a network of interconnected wormholes. What we're seeing before us is happening right now in real time at various places around the galaxy."

"But—won't this alert them to our presence? That we're messing with one of their ships? And they'll come for us?"

Zack shakes his head no. "I believe this display is passive, meaning we're strictly receiving and not transmitting. We can study this all we want and they'll never know." Zack gives them a cryptic smile. "At least not right away."

"It all looks so complicated."

With barely-suppressed elation, Zack says, "Trust me— we've struck the Mother Lode of information. We're going to have access to the equivalent of tutorials, how-to videos, and instruction manuals on everything from anti-gravity propulsion to the dissolution beam to the blue balloons, and so much more. It's going to take time and it's going to take a lot of hard work, but we will figure it out. Because that's what we homo sapiens are pretty darn good at—*figuring stuff out*. It's what we do!"

By dawn, most of the colony's population has made its way to the site of the biggest event to happen in 50 years. They talk quietly yet nervously amongst themselves, speculating about what Zack and his team are finding in the dreaded alien vessel.

It's well after sunrise when Zack's voice crackles over Grady's walkie-talkie.

"Okay, Grady, we're coming out. You can shut it down."

"Will do."

Grady pulls a series of levers that rapidly dials back the power going into the spacecraft until it registers zero volts.

Zack and his crew emerge from the spacecraft looking fatigued, having been up all night working. The crowd of people breaks into spontaneous applause. Zack gives them an appreciative wave. There a few anxious shouts.

"Zack, tell us what you found!"

"Did you learn anything about the aliens?"

"Are they coming back?"

Zack and the others make their way to Grady's control station. Tired as he is, Zack knows he needs to speak to these folks who are so rightfully hungry for information. And right now, he couldn't be happier to tell them of their findings.

At Grady's station, he climbs up onto the thick wooden table. The buzzing of the crowd quickly dies down. The throng of people moves forward until the closest are only feet from him.

Even though he's worn-out, Zack's eyes burn with fresh purpose. A mysterious smile plays at his lips.

He waits until the crowd is completely silent, then begins speaking in a loud, clear voice, carefully choosing his words.

"Fifty years ago, when I was 17 and combing through The Record, I came across the story of the freighter that smashed into the alien spacecraft. At the time, we still had satellites orbiting the Earth. They watched the encounter.

"The force of the impact caused the freighter to break into pieces, which burned up in the atmosphere as they fell from the sky. Because the spaceship behind me—" Zack jerks his thumb back at the alien vessel—"had been made with superior materials and technology, it survived the collision in one piece. For the same reasons, it didn't burn up as it plunged to Earth. Satellites tracked its fall, logging the coordinates where it came down, which was in an area that had already been dissolved.

"As sad as the story is about what happened to that brave woman pilot, the important thing to remember is that we caught the aliens with their pants down. In his video introduction to Spike Penovitch 50 years ago, Otis Larson said that, as advanced as the aliens were, they weren't perfect, that they do slip up. He said getting their ship knocked out of the sky was a 'doozy' of a mistake.

"Unfortunately, we haven't come across any other mistakes made by them."

That mysterious smile.

"Until today. And trust me—this one's an even bigger 'doozy'."

An excited buzz courses through the crowd.

"I hope you won't think I'm crazy when you hear what I'm about to tell you—or not *too* crazy anyway."

There are a couple of impatient laughs from the crowd. Zack continues.

"When I was going through The Record 50 years ago, I didn't see any evidence that the aliens had retrieved their downed ship, so I figured it was probably still sitting up there in Canada.

"Then it hit me—the wildest, most insane idea anyone's ever had. Something I've never told anyone—until now. The idea was this: *If* the spacecraft was still there—which it was; and *if* we could find it—which we did; and *if* it was still in good condition—which it is; and *if*—this was the biggest if—

if we could find a way to unlock its secrets, which we have just discovered how to do; then I say…let's go after the bastards."

A stunned silence. No one can believe what Zack has just said.

Zack shouts, "Did you hear me?! I said, *let's go get the bastards, and bring home our people!*"

The sheer audacity of the idea electrifies the crowd. There are scattered cries of agreement.

Zack continues shouting. "We can do this! We have the means at our fingertips! It'll take years of hard work, but I know we can do this! Let's go get the bastards! Are you with me?!"

The crowd answers as one with a resounding roar. It's as if a dam has burst, sending a tidal wave of pent-up emotions that have been building for decades surging across the land.

Spellbound by Zack's passionate words, the crowd quickly quiets down. Tears appear in his eyes as he continues, his voice cracking at times.

"I say let's go after the bastards who stole our loved ones; who took away our families and our friends; who destroyed everything we ever built; and who will come for us again one day! *Let's go get the bastards!*"

The crowd answers with another bellow of support. Cries of *"Yeah! Let's go get the bastards!"* roll through the throng, coming from the throats of men, women and children alike. The very air seems charged with a dark and growing energy.

Zack again waits for the crowd to calm itself. With his eyes clear and his voice stronger than ever, his words ring out over the mass of people.

"So now, I pledge to you, on my life, *on my very soul*, that from this day forward, nothing else will matter except going after the bastards, and we won't stop until we've destroyed every last one of them!"

Zack's words trigger something deep within the psychic core of all who hear them. Something raw. Primeval. Deadly. He has touched on humankind's all-consuming determination to survive whatever the cost, period. Nothing else matters. It is a thing that is totally unyielding and utterly without mercy.

Instead of erupting in spontaneous cheers, the crowd takes its time responding to Zack's rallying cry. It starts as a few shouts and screams, then intensifies into a guttural, animal-like growl coming from the throats of these thousands of people lucky enough to still be alive on this Earth. It's not a happy sound. Building steadily, becoming ever louder, the shouting and yelling morph into something else. Something ominous. Something deeply menacing.

Thousands of fists thrust into the air. Teeth are bared. Tears stream from half-crazed eyes. The sound finally reaches a fever pitch, becoming one long hellish crescendo; a sustained, howling roar of anguish; of pain; of remembrance; of black hatred; of murderous rage; of thirst for vengeance; of a bloodlust that knows no bounds. It's a sound the likes of which has never been heard on this Earth.

The human race has been pushed to the very edge of extinction.

But now it is coming back.

Bigger.

Badder.

Stronger than ever.

And this howling throng of people is putting the very universe itself on notice:

It will never happen again!

That night in the colony, a strange and powerful euphoria fills the air. Dozens of bonfires burn brightly in and around the city. People feast and drink. They shout and laugh.

They sing and dance as musicians ply their instruments with manic energy. In the colony's 50 plus years of existence, there has never been anything like this. Everyone is fired with the same burning purpose.

At the Stone compound, most of the clan is gathered in a torch-lit open field, where the largest bonfire of all crackles and roars. The extended family mingles cheerfully together. They dance, play games, run races, join in friendly wrestling matches.

At the edge of the field, Zack happily tends to the barbecue, which consists of a large steel grill suspended on rocks over a pile of burning coals. With his left hand, he clutches the handle of a giant ceramic mug filled with ale. With his other hand, he uses long metal tongs to flip a generous collection of cuts of beef, pork, chicken, and shellfish. Even though physically exhausted, Zack is still energized by the events of the day and has found his second wind.

Grady spies Zack and joins him at the barbecue. Normally low-key and serious, he's working on his fourth ale. He slaps Zack on the back.

"Zack, that was such an amazing speech you gave today!" He takes a big pull of ale.

Zack smiles. "Thanks, Grady. I honestly don't know where that came from. I was so jazzed about what we found on the spaceship, the last thing on my mind was giving a speech. It just sort of happened."

"In fact," Grady says, "that's what they're calling it." He makes air quotation marks. "'The Speech.'"

"What do you mean 'they'?"

"Everyone! I predict your little oration will go down through the ages." He drains his mug. "As it deserves to. I'm going to get some more grog. Save me a steak."

Grady wanders unsteadily away. After he's gone, Oksana appears by Zack's side, an earthen-ware cup of wine in hand. He looks into her glowing aquamarine eyes. Even by torchlight, they're as beautiful as they were when he first gazed into them 53 years ago.

"It's been a long haul, Oksana."

"Yes, my love. And we will never stop the hauling."

With her free hand, she puts her arm around his neck and pulls him down to her height so she can kiss him. He hangs awkwardly on to the mug and tongs. A tentative voice comes from behind him.

"...Grandpa?"

Zack breaks away from the kiss and turns around. "Hey, Tyler."

"I don't mean to disturb you and grandmother."

"That's okay. Isn't it, Oksana?"

"Of course," she says. "We'll always have time for you, Tyler."

"What's up?" asks Zack.

"I just wanted to say..." Tyler swallows. Gets his courage up. "I don't want to sound all mushy, Grandpa. But I just wanted to say that I was so proud of you today!"

Zack is genuinely touched, "Why, thank you, Tyler. What a nice thing to say."

There's a touch of awe in Tyler's voice as he continues. "I mean it. The things you said...it sent chills up my spine."

"Coming from you, that means a lot."

"Zock...?" Oksana is leaning over peering at something on the barbecue. "What is it that you are cooking on the grill?"

"The usual suspects. Pork chops. Steaks. Chicken."

"Yes, I see that. I know food as well as anyone. But this?" She points at a piece of sizzling meat that is unlike anything else on the grill. The flesh is pale blue in color. The juice dripping off it crackles loudly on the coals. "What is it?"

Zack takes a long pull of his ale. Sets the mug down on a nearby table. The mysterious grin reappears, accompanied by a mirthful gleam in his eye.

"I was going to tell you."

"Tell me what?"

"Earlier today, on my way home from the spaceship, I made a quick stop at the Deep Freezer."

Oksana frowns. "...The Deep Freezer. Isn't that where they keep the..." Her mouth springs open in shock. "Oh, Zock! You didn't!"

"Actually, I did."

"But...why?"

"I kind of figured what goes around, comes around."

It dawns on Tyler what they're referring to. "Grandpa, are you saying what I think you're saying?"

Zack doesn't answer, just gives him a quick wink. He leans over and sniffs the cooking meat. Gives it a couple of prods with the tongs.

"I think it's done." Zack looks up at them with an amused expression. "Who am I kidding? No one's ever cooked any before."

Oksana and Tyler watch in horrified fascination as Zack uses the tongs to transfer the charred, sizzling meat to a cutting board. Holding the strange meat steady with the tongs, he uses a large carving knife to slice cut off a morsel about the size of the tip of his little finger. He spears it on the point of the knife. Sniffs it. Turns it this way and that, studying it.

"Okay. Down the hatch..."

Zack slips it into his mouth directly from the knife.

Oksana shudders. "I can't believe you actually..." Her voice trails off.

Tyler says, "Grandpa, that is epically harsh." He's grinning as he says it.

Zack chews slowly. Deliberately. Thoughtfully. Eventually he swallows. He stands there a moment, considering the taste. Finally, he nods in approval. He turns back to the cutting board, slices off a much bigger piece and slides it into his mouth. He chews with gusto, genuinely enjoying it.

"So, Grandpa," says Tyler. "What's it taste like?"

Zack looks at him.

At that moment, a fat laying hen wanders by, clucking and pecking at the ground.

Zack looks down at it, then back up at Tyler.

Swallows.

And smiles.

THE END